IN ITALY FOR LOVE

LEONIE MACK

Boldwood

First published in Great Britain in 2024 by Boldwood Books Ltd.

Copyright © Leonie Mack, 2024

Cover Design by Alexandra Allden

Cover Images: Shutterstock

The moral right of Leonie Mack to be identified as the author of this work has been asserted in accordance with the Copyright, Designs and Patents Act 1988.

Every effort has been made to obtain the necessary permissions with reference to copyright material, both illustrative and quoted. We apologise for any omissions in this respect and will be pleased to make the appropriate acknowledgements in any future edition.

A CIP catalogue record for this book is available from the British Library.

Paperback ISBN 978-1-83603-346-2

Large Print ISBN 978-1-83603-345-5

Hardback ISBN 978-1-83603-344-8

Ebook ISBN 978-1-83603-347-9

Kindle ISBN 978-1-83603-348-6

Audio CD ISBN 978-1-83603-339-4

MP3 CD ISBN 978-1-83603-340-0

Digital audio download ISBN 978-1-83603-343-1

This book is printed on certified sustainable paper. Boldwood Books is dedicated to putting sustainability at the heart of our business. For more information please visit https://www.boldwoodbooks.com/about-us/sustainability/

Boldwood Books Ltd, 23 Bowerdean Street, London, SW6 3TN

www.boldwoodbooks.com

*For the wonderful readers who have read all my books
and for those who are just trying out this one.
It's a privilege to write stories for you to enjoy.*

1

'Be reasonable, Jules! You can't just *leave*. We haven't sold the building yet.'

Jules felt anything but reasonable. If she didn't get away from Luca in the next ten minutes, she was going to break something – and it wouldn't be her heart. It was too late for that. 'You have my number. You can call me when we need to talk about offers.' *Generous* offers, she bloody well hoped, after the sinkhole of debt their B & B had become.

Her Italian dream was well and truly over, destroyed by renovation hell, persistent low occupancy and a partner who'd performed a giant relationship U-turn at the first sign of trouble.

She grabbed another handful of clothing out of her wardrobe and stuffed it into her overflowing backpack with too much force. She'd brought that backpack to Europe from Australia four years ago full of curiosity, courage and hope for the future, and now it was fraying at the seams like a bad metaphor for her life.

'How are you even going to pay your phone bill? I don't understand,' Luca added too calmly. 'You can stay at my mother's as long as you need. If you're planning to go back to Australia...

You remember your passport expired, right? And you haven't applied for an Italian one yet.'

She wasn't likely to forget the fact that she currently held no valid passport. 'I'll sort it out while we wait for offers.'

'Why not wait here then? You need an address to apply for passports. You need *help*.'

After the bureaucratic nightmare of applying for Italian citizenship, she knew he was right, but Jules was done accepting help from Luca – the kind of help that came with strings and side effects.

'I'll manage. You can have all the time you want with Claudia without your awkward ex hanging around like a bad smell. I thought you'd be relieved you won't have to babysit me any more.'

'Babysit you? Jules, we...'

She straightened and looked him square in the face. 'We what? That is exactly the problem, Luca. I should never have thought I could stay here after we broke up. I shouldn't have moved to Italy in the first place when we barely knew each other.'

'You regret our entire relationship?'

Arco whined from where he sat in the doorway, cocking his head in confusion so one curly ear hung low. The dog could probably feel the dread shooting through her veins. Jules wanted to rub his belly, reassure him that she loved him and she'd never regret adopting him, even if he'd been a doomed addition to their not-family when it was already too late to save it. The thought of leaving him wrenched at her.

But yes, she regretted the rest. She regretted ever fancying herself in love with the handsome Italian she'd met in London and followed home – as though she'd been the stray puppy. She'd sunk her last pennies into the B & B and lost everything, whereas he'd always had assets locked up for a rainy day.

They'd never been equal partners. This was *his* home, *his* language. She'd given up everything.

'What does it matter to you if I regret things?' she asked. 'You broke up with me a year ago. I should have left straight away – for both of our sakes.' She'd tried to be reasonable back then, swallow the hurt and the rejection and focus on the business, but she should have got out before she'd paid an even higher price: her pride.

Panic rising up her throat made her slam the wardrobe closed, a few T-shirts still lying, rumpled, on one of the shelves. Arco gave a sharp bark, earning him a glare from Luca.

'You don't speak Italian well,' he pointed out – another pin into her thin skin. 'Where are you going to go?'

'It doesn't matter, as long as it's far away from you!'

His face flattened with a concerning lack of expression that made Jules shudder. 'If you're going to blame me for everything that's happened, then maybe it's best if you go,' he said.

'We agree on that.' She didn't blame him for the business failing, but she had no desire to go into all the ways he'd hurt her over the past year – no, three years – if he didn't already know.

'Wherever you escape to, they'd better accept dogs,' he said, his voice without inflection.

It took her a moment to process what he'd said.

'What are you talking about? I'll be staying somewhere temporary. It'll be no place for Arco, when your mum has a garden.'

'You know Mamma doesn't like that dog.'

The cold spread from her veins into her stomach. How had she been so stupid with Luca? So wrong? She'd left everything and moved to Italy for a man she barely knew and now barely respected.

She wished she could go back in time and convince her naïve, twenty-five-year-old self not to put herself through all of this. *Don't go to Italy, you starry-eyed nitwit!*

With a shot of unease, she wondered if he'd even take good care of Arco.

'I'll come back for him. When I've got somewhere to stay, I'll take him.' She didn't want to know how much sending a dog to Australia would cost, but Arco was up-to-date with his shots. She'd cross that bridge when she came to it. 'Just for a couple of weeks. You have to keep him—'

'I don't "have to" do anything, Jules.'

Go. Now!

Wrenching the drawstring closed, she hefted her backpack with a stumble and dumped it at the door. Stomping to the kitchen, she stuffed a shopping bag full of dog food tins and some biscuits, then grabbed Arco's blanket.

'Here, boy!' she called, her voice quavering.

Burying her fingers in his thick, woolly fur, she was glad at least for the confidence she was doing the right thing: leaving Parma; taking Arco, despite the certain inconveniences. Oblivious to the situation, the dog just gave her a panting look of barely contained excitement at the prospect of a walk.

'This is ridiculous! You'll be living on the street. If you're worried about awkwardness with Claudia, then you don't have to be. I've managed to keep everything separate until now and it was just because of a simple mistake on her calendar that you met her at all.'

Jules was going to scream. Fumbling with Arco's harness and lead in her distress, she managed to get them on and swing her backpack onto her back without keeling over. Storming out and slamming the door would have provided a much-needed drop of satisfaction, but she made the mistake of grabbing her keys, then staring at them with a choke of dismay before flinging them back onto the console table. She didn't have any doors to open any more.

Only after she'd stalked past the pair of palms in the front courtyard did she stop to take a breath. The big old house they'd turned into a B & B loomed silently behind her. She'd always thought it looked a little gothic, especially with the leaves on the wisteria tinted yellow. Even though she'd repainted the white window frames herself, the grey brick still looked forbidding.

She'd mortared and plastered, painted, drilled and polished that house. She'd built her hopes and dreams and little pieces of her heart into their hotel project, trusting that Luca was committed, if not to her romantically, then to the project at least.

But no, he'd been screwing Claudia, an estate agent, and she'd convinced him he should cut his losses and sell, pulling the plug on Jules's own investment.

Walking away broke her a little more, but what difference did that make when she already knew she had to put herself back together? When her steps grew unsteady, she paused for a moment, dropping to her knees to lean her forehead on the top of Arco's woolly head. He pressed himself to her, always greedy for cuddles, this bouncy little dog.

Leaving was the first thing she'd done right in the year since the break-up. It didn't matter where she ended up. She'd only be there until she had her passports and then she'd go home to grieve and heal and start over.

She just had to get through a couple of weeks in any old place – any place that was far, far away from Luca and all their shattered dreams.

'We're both strays now, hmm?' The thought was much less frightening knowing she wasn't alone. 'I'm glad you're with me, pup. I'll take good care of you, I promise. We'll find a way to sort everything out together.'

* * *

It was astounding how much money a single person and a dog could chew through in a week.

Even in a rough hostel by the train station in Bologna, eating only mortadella and cucumbers, her bank balance was setting off even more alarm bells than usual. Jules was glad she and Luca had been meticulous about keeping their finances separate from day one – even more so after their romantic relationship had kicked the bucket – and she could walk away in an instant with full rights to what little she had.

Although, come to think of it, it might have been more satisfying to use a joint account for a decent hotel while she got the hell out of there.

Her mum had offered to send money, but that had to be a last resort, not least because she'd lose a chunk in fees and exchange rates – and a chunk of pride, knowing her parents weren't made of money either. The last message Jules had received from her mum was a link to the 'emergency passport' application from the Australian Embassy in Rome, but she wasn't quite that desperate yet. She wanted to go home, but she had her affairs to settle first with the Italian government.

The citizenship process had been traumatic, with its lineage requirements and official translations and 'Jure sanguinis', which was Latin, for fuck's sake. Luca had tried to tell her what it meant, but she kept seeing 'Law of Blood', which sounded like a fantasy novel. No, to get a real passport in her hand and say, hopefully, a final goodbye to Italian bureaucracy, she would manage for a few weeks – somehow, with a dog, and clothes that were rapidly growing smelly, and a rising sense of panic.

The dodgy hostel was her saviour in the end. A group of French people with dreadlocks turned up on their way to a farm stay somewhere lovely near Florence – a farm stay where they would work for two weeks in return for room and board. A light bulb immediately went off inside her head.

She didn't need 'somewhere lovely near Florence' – that was back in the direction of Parma and she wasn't in the mood for *la dolce vita* anyway – but if she could find a farm as far away from Luca as she could get without a passport, where she could hole up and work in return for food and accommodation, she might just make it on the money she had. Even if it was a run-down farm in the middle of nowhere—

That sounded perfect, actually. The best part was, Luca would never guess where she had gone.

2
_____

Twenty-four hours later, she got off the train at the terminus of an ancient diesel railway with vintage seventies upholstery, in a place called Cividale del Friuli. She was still in Italy – technically. But it was in an autonomous region with borders everywhere: Slovenia was twelve kilometres away and Austria just over fifty, plus the natural boundary of the Adriatic coast.

So many borders she couldn't cross, but with each kilometre she travelled away from Luca, she felt lighter. What kind of idiot stayed with their ex after they'd broken up? Worse, she'd believed that they could amicably run the business together, right up until he'd pulled the plug.

And now she was in a place that had apparently been founded by Julius Caesar, making the small city significantly more ancient even than the upholstery on the train. But at least the B & Bs were such good value she could afford a single room for two nights and a load of washing before she went out to the farm stay in the countryside.

Cividale had unexpected corners and the skewed street layout of a town with mediaeval history – and the concerning cracks to match. Arco was in heaven, poking his nose into damp corners and whining and tugging at the lead whenever he saw one of the many other dogs trotting along between the rendered buildings with coloured shutters. Just on the walk from the train station to her cheap B & B, she'd seen a pet supplies shop and a dog salon, which spoke highly of the population as animal lovers.

Refreshed after a night of sleeping without the rustling and snuffling of ten other people in the dorm, she was looking forward to taking Arco for a walk for once. He seemed gleeful too, as though he knew he would be able to pee on actual grass, rather than in the grotty corners near a train station. She decided to cross the old town once to get her bearings and then walk along the river she could see on the map.

When she reached the main piazza, she marvelled that every single corner of Italy was bursting with charm, as this far-flung town was enchantingly dilapidated. The coloured render ranged from ochre to yellow and everything in between, with contrasting green shutters. Some of the buildings boasted stone porticos with pointed Venetian arches. Cafes sprawled out over the cobblestones.

As she made her way along the main thoroughfare, narrow and lined with shops, she felt as though she were travelling steadily back in time. Faded frescoes adorned one palazzo. Ancient brick houses loomed over the streets and she stared up to see patterned tiles in the wood-beamed eaves.

She couldn't help wondering about the tourism industry in a little place like this, at the edge of the mountains and the sea, but the thoughts were nothing more than habit. One day she'd stop thinking about occupancy rates and giant red numbers in the accounts.

Pulling her phone out, she called her mum as a distraction. While she suspected Brenda would rather be living it up in her retirement than talking her daughter through a crisis, she was only ever a phone call away.

'Jube! How are you getting on, sweetheart? Have you arrived in... wherever you were going?'

'Yes, I'm here. I've organised the farm stay to start tomorrow and it wasn't too difficult to find a B & B that takes dogs until then.'

'I'm still not so sure about this farm work. Shouldn't they be paying you?'

'It's all completely above board. There's an organisation that runs the programme and I don't have to work all day every day. Finding paid work and accommodation for a few weeks isn't that easy.' Her bitten-down fingernails and distressed bank account were proof of that.

'I suppose that's true, especially since you know nothing about farm work.'

'Thanks, Mum,' she said drily. She'd been no good at renovations either, or the hotel business – or learning Italian.

Juggling Arco's lead when they reached a road, she kept him close to her as she negotiated the narrow footpath past a deli where the smell of cheese made him turn in circles, his nose in the air in bliss. Jules happily followed suit.

Her mum continued. 'But you've got yourself out of that... sticky situation and I'm relieved.'

'Yeah,' she agreed weakly, swallowing a grimace. 'No more sticky situations for me. A few weeks of quiet manual labour and I'll be home – maybe even in time for my birthday,' she said with a pang of hope. In the strain of the past couple of weeks, she hadn't allowed herself to picture her birthday beyond the jaded thought that all she'd managed in her twenty-eight years of life was to become a penniless failure.

Passing a bakery advertising something called 'gubana' that

sounded more like a cigar than a bread product, she saw a sign for the 'Ponte del Diavolo' and peered ahead to see a stone bridge, lined with lamp posts.

'Seeing you for your birthday would be lovely!' Her mother kept speaking as Jules listened with only half an ear. On both sides of the road, people stopped and gaped and took pictures, their voices animated.

Jules couldn't see what they were photographing. She wasn't here for tourist sights and Italian flair but when she stepped onto that bridge and caught her first glimpse of the view from the Ponte del Diavolo, she had no choice but to make a space in her poor, tired heart.

Or perhaps the view made space in her heart. The emerald-green river rippled far below, at the bottom of a stony gorge. The coloured houses of the old town perched on the rocks, surely not as precariously as it appeared. Far off in the distance were jagged grey mountain peaks, the nearer hills turning yellow with the onset of autumn.

Everywhere she looked was alive with colour, the green of the river so vivid it didn't seem real.

'Are you still there?' she heard Brenda dimly.

'Yeah,' she said, giving herself a shake. 'It's just... this is a pretty place.'

'Things are looking up then, sweetheart,' her mum said gently.

As Jules gazed at the view she almost believed her. 'I hope so. Chat later?'

Ending the call, she allowed Arco to drag her to the middle of the bridge, where a viewing platform jutted out over the ravine and she could look back at the colourful houses built onto the stone – yellow, pink and orange, with terracotta roof tiles. The crooked bell towers of two churches rose above. She leaned on the concrete wall and settled her hand on the dog's back, needing that uncomplicated presence while her emotions churned.

All her plans, everything she'd pictured about the future, were gone. Luca wasn't just a quiet regret in her life – he was a betrayal, a mistake so big she should have seen it coming. She'd trusted him, relied on him for so long that she was cracked inside – a mess.

But a world where that river, this view, existed couldn't be so bad. Perhaps what she had needed all along was a far-flung town called Cividale del Friuli and some fresh perspective – and then perhaps she could go home in peace.

As if on cue, the hum of an accordion reached her ears – the old-fashioned croon that was so stubbornly Italian, whether you loved or hated it. The October air was still and cool. The world around her seemed big and colourful and fresh with possibilities. What an unexpectedly beautiful farewell to Italy, she thought with a prick of tears behind her eyes.

Arco gave the lead an almighty tug, snapping Jules out of her emotional reverie. She stumbled after him as he pulled her across the bridge with a sharp bark, which dimmed to a wary growl as they approached the other side. A grey stone chapel stood on a hill above a small cobbled square and perched casually on the concrete barrier by the sheer drop into the ravine was the accordion player, head bowed, fingers working over the black and silver instrument strapped to his chest.

'Arooooo,' howled Arco, pulling and jumping in an effort to get closer to... whatever he thought the accordion was. His pack? His mother?

Grasping his harness, Jules held him back as gently as she could, but the animal was determined. 'You weird dog,' she muttered with a dismayed laugh as she stumbled after him.

'Arooo! Arf!'

The longer she held him back, the more the poor dog fought the restraint, leaping in the direction of the music. His strong little body dragged Jules helplessly along. She dimly noticed that they were attracting attention from passers-by.

'Arco, shh,' she tried desperately.

The haunting harmonies of the song reached a crescendo and the dog stopped moving to mournfully join in, his snout in the air as he whined and barked.

It seemed Arco was singing.

'Ar-ar-arooo.'

Jules snorted in disbelief as she crouched next to him, her hand on his harness. He wasn't in tune, but she'd never heard sounds like those from him before – almost musical. Now he'd come sufficiently close to the noise, he calmed down, his nasal howling just as sombre as the melody the accordionist played.

She tried not to laugh but didn't quite succeed. Titters behind her revealed she wasn't the only one amused by Arco's intrusion. Possibly, he was even improving the sound of the whining instrument? At least there was one adoring fan for this wizened old busker.

Glancing up to meet the gaze of the accordion player, she opened her mouth to apologise and...

She hadn't been expecting that. It wasn't a wizened old man. The busker was young – around her age – and he was... Her brain supplied a few unhelpful adjectives, before she pulled herself together and decided to end that sentence with 'very attractive'.

He was smiling at her – well, he was smiling at Arco – a wide, amused grin that was... there went those unhelpful adjectives again.

Ouch, first the view made her cry and now the busker was hot? He had a short moustache and a little goatee. Those were not supposed to be sexy. And since when did she describe men as 'sexy'? That department had never been a particular priority for her and it hadn't been a chore to go without over the past year of platonic cohabitation with Luca.

But suddenly, she was losing her mind over a pair of blue eyes – and a pair of shoulders. They were very nice too – broad and sturdy.

Playing the last few notes with a melancholy vibration of the bellows, he finished to muted applause sounding behind Jules, earning the small group of gathered strangers that smile that she'd stupidly thought was for her a moment ago.

Clipping the instrument closed and shrugging it off those wide shoulders, he set it carefully on the ground and approached, tilting his head, to study Arco. Dropping into a squat, he roughed up the dog with a strong hand.

'Ciao, piccolo. Come sei bello,' he crooned in a deep, smooth voice that scrambled Jules's thoughts again. He met her gaze and asked something, but she had little hope of understanding English at that point, let alone Italian. 'Are you... English?'

She finally managed to react to his statement, if only with a choppy gesture that wasn't quite a shake of her head. 'Not really.'

'Eh?'

She scrambled to her feet. 'I'm Australian,' she explained. 'And I'm so sorry for my dog. He's never done anything like that before.'

His eyes crinkled and a pair of deep, narrow dimples stretched. She also noted hollows under his eyes – deep enough to create shadows, but even that piqued her interest.

'Don't worry about it,' he said. 'I knew a dog who used to play the piano when her owner was out.' He spoke English with barely an accent – another surprise.

'Wow, it's a town of virtuoso canines?'

'Where homo sapiens just plays the simple accordion.'

'Just imagine everything dogs could do if they had fingers,' she quipped, before he could turn away.

'Don't you know about *Wolf*-gang Amadeus Mozart?' His straight face was decidedly wobbly.

'No, but I have heard of Johann Sebastian *Bark*.'

He grinned up at her. Biting her lip as her mind insisted he was flirting with her, her skin blossoming accordingly, she scrambled to arrange her thoughts into something that made sense.

She hadn't thought about being attracted to anyone in a year and suddenly *this*, whatever it was.

A small flirtation with a handsome busker was all it was, she reminded herself.

He stood and she noticed that, on top of the eyes and the smile and the shoulders, he was also tall enough that her eyeline was level with his top lip. Jules was used to looking men in the eye – and the accompanying wariness they seemed to feel in the company of a very tall woman. But the busker had his own oversized proportions and a straightforwardness in his eyes that made her suspect he wouldn't take particular note of her height anyway.

'Do you think your dog will let me keep playing or am I finished for today?'

She glanced guiltily to where the accordion sat. The case was closed and there wasn't even a battered hat to receive donations.

'I think Arco loves the music, but I don't know about the rest of your audience.'

'You think they hate me?'

She nearly swallowed her tongue. 'No! I meant... the doggy duet might not be to everyone's taste.'

'Unlike the accordion,' he added with a wink. 'His name's Arco?'

She nodded.

'He's a sweet dog.' He gave Arco one more rub before turning to retrieve his instrument.

Jules watched him amble away with that same sense of life rolling over her that she'd felt on the bridge. It was one of those moments where you had to roll *with* it.

'Um,' she began inauspiciously, but he turned back, prompting her with a lift of his eyebrows. Then, if he'd had any remaining belief that she was normal, she dashed it with the sentence that flowed out of her foolish mouth: 'Do you want to have dinner with me tonight?'

3

Alex was so surprised by the question that an answer was beyond him. He hesitated for long enough that she turned away and muttered something under her breath, her face contorting into a grimace of embarrassment.

Opening his mouth, he still couldn't decide what to say, as much as he wanted to reassure her that she shouldn't be embarrassed. It was the first time a stranger had asked him out while he was playing accordion in the street, but it was also the first time a dog had spontaneously joined in with his act. He *was* flattered – which surprised him.

'Forget it,' she said before he could pull himself together and respond. 'I don't know what I was thinking. You don't know me from a bar of soap and I'm sure you have better things to do than have dinner with a tourist.'

Avoiding his gaze, she headed for the bridge, urging the reluctant Arco to follow her. She was a tall woman – well above average – with her hair pulled back in a short ponytail that didn't quite contain it. Her jacket was frayed at the cuffs and her sneakers were worn. He had the impression of a person who'd been on the road a long time and just wanted to get home.

She was five steps away, moving swiftly with her chin in the air, when he finally reacted. 'We have a ritual here in Friuli,' he called after her, 'called the "tajùt".'

It was a strange way to begin accepting her invitation, but at least she turned her puzzled gaze back on him. 'Does it involve an accordion? If so, I'm not sure I'm your girl for that.'

'No, perhaps "ritual" is the wrong word. A habit? It's a glass of wine, drunk in an osteria. This... important custom requires company.'

'Ohhh,' she said slowly. 'It's a cultural experience, is it? Not just a glass of wine in a bar?'

He responded to her doubtful smile with an earnest nod. 'Wine is more than culture here. It's life.'

'And you will... donate your time for the sake of sharing the cultural richness of your home?' Her accent was clear now – along with a dry sense of humour.

Alone with her dog, in her shabby clothes and with that tired air, she didn't look like the usual sort of tourist that turned up in Cividale.

He acknowledged her teasing with a nod. 'Have a drink with me. Three courses and coffee might be a risk, in case the accordion player bores you to death,' he added.

'Don't feel obliged. It's weird that I asked.'

'It's a little weird that I want to say yes.' More than a little, but she didn't need his life story. 'There's a bar near the ruins of the Roman baths. Seven o'clock?'

It was her turn to hesitate, but she gave him a slow nod, studying him with a puzzled brow. She had brown eyes, striking in contrast to her blonde hair. Her most prominent feature was probably her pointed chin.

'See you... then,' she said. Giving him a tight smile and an awkward wave, she took off over the bridge after the lively dog.

Alex watched her go, craning his neck to follow her progress back into the narrow lanes of the old town. Even though he wasn't convinced she'd actually come, how soon could it be seven o'clock?

* * *

Surely she wasn't coming.

Alex had told himself exactly that at least twenty times already, but part of him obviously didn't believe it, since he'd returned home, showered and shaved and even spent ten minutes trying to tame the wave in his hair.

And now he was around the corner from the bar near the Roman baths, telling himself firmly that he didn't believe she'd be there anyway, so it wouldn't be a disappointment when it turned out to be true.

The outdoor tables still sat hopefully on the cobbles, even though the evening temperatures dropped after sundown in October. Only a pair of hardy smokers hunched under the awning and Salvino's more sensible customers were inside by the hearth.

Of course she wouldn't come. She hadn't even told him her name and he was unreasonably irritated by his neglect of simple courtesy in not offering his. But perhaps she'd wanted a degree of anonymity. He could relate to that.

Instead of pushing open the door, he peered through the window, past the vintage rotary dial telephone, Roman coins and local embroidery on display. He'd been right. She wasn't there. It was for the best. He wasn't sure what he would have said if she *had* turned up – what *she* would have said, or why he was so keen to prolong their acquaintance.

Checking his watch, he wondered how long he should wait and how long it would be before Salvino saw him and questioned why he was loitering outside the bar. He'd just decided he should go home when he heard a bark, and the joyful ball of curly fluff he recognised from earlier that day appeared around the corner, making a beeline for him.

It was impossible not to smile at the goofy animal, his tongue hanging out as he jumped up in excitement. Alex dropped to his haunches to greet him and Arco promptly perched his front paws on Alex's thighs.

'Ciao, bello,' he said, scratching the dog under the ears as he preened in apparent ecstasy. He was a handsome dog, brown with white markings on his face.

'If you say "Ciao, bella" to me now, I'm going to feel like a dog.'

His gaze snapped up to find his date with a smile on her lips that couldn't quite disguise her uncertainty. Rising quickly to his feet, he held out a hand. 'You can have a Friulian "mandi".'

She took his hand and shook it once, decisively. 'Is that the local greeting? I thought I could understand quite a lot of Italian, but I've disappointed myself around here.'

'Don't be disappointed. Furlan – that's what we call Friulian – is classed as a different language from Italian, an older language.' He cut himself off before he babbled any further. 'I'm Alex, by the way. We... forgot that part earlier.'

'Julia,' she said with an awkward smile.

He caught Salvino's eye as they walked into the small bar, greeting him with a lift of his chin but ignoring his friend's questioning gaze. Perhaps he shouldn't have brought her here – shouldn't have accepted her invitation at all. He knew what his friends and neighbours were all thinking, when they saw him with a woman.

When he and Julia were settled at a table in a corner near Salvino's display of cast-iron cauldrons and teapots, she watched him warily. 'Seriously, you don't have to do this. I didn't even expect you to come.'

'I thought *you* wouldn't be here.'

'Well... here we both are.' Her eyes were guarded under her lashes. 'Are we having that drink? Is there something local you recommend?' she asked, breaking the silence. At least babbling about the local wines gave him something to say for a few minutes.

After he'd called out their order to Salvino, still studiously ignoring the curious looks from his friend he could feel on the back of his neck, he gathered his scattered thoughts.

'Eh,' he began, knowing he owed her an admission up front, but not certain how to explain himself. 'I'm sure you're not interested anyway, but I should tell you that I'm not... that meeting someone romantically is not... available. Not that you're not... It's me. I'm not...'

'Please don't tell me you're married or—'

'No!' he denied immediately. 'That's not what I meant. I'm single. I'm just not...'

'You've said "not" at least six times.'

'I know, it's not coming out right,' he said, rubbing a hand over his eyes. 'I just wanted to be clear that at the moment, for me, a relationship is...'

'Not,' she supplied with a huff of a laugh. 'I hear you, don't worry.' He finally dared to meet her gaze to find shadows at the edge of her expression, making him wonder if 'I hear you' meant 'me, too'. 'I didn't ask you to dinner with romance in mind. Mainly I was just... hungry. Eating alone is awkward.'

'Ah,' was all he initially said in response. And it was a relief – truly, it was – that she wanted to meet him simply to have company for dinner and not because of... anything else. He forced a smile.

'Not that you're not...' she continued. 'Damn, now I'm just saying "not". I mean, it wasn't *only* because it's awkward eating alone. You're also gorgeous.'

Her voice trailed off at the end and the tingle in him bloomed into warmth concentrated in his cheeks.

'I'm leaving tomorrow anyway,' she finished, giving herself a shake.

'Tomorrow?'

She nodded. 'I'm just passing through on my way back to Australia.'

'Australia, yes, you said,' he repeated, his brain still catching up. Perhaps with good reason he'd warned her he might be a boring dinner date. 'I thought you looked travel weary,' he commented, looking up to thank Salvino when the barman placed his beer in front of him. Julia's glass of sparkling Ribolla Gialla arrived as well, along with a bowl of crisps and a basket of grissini. She took a few crisps as soon as the bowl hit the table.

'Travel weary,' she repeated thoughtfully once she'd finished chewing. 'Does that have something to do with bags under my eyes along with all the rest of my luggage?'

'I didn't mean—' Romance or not, he was a terrible date and heat crept up his neck. 'It was your expression, not your appearance. I... like your appearance.' He could do better than that, but he probably shouldn't tell a woman he'd just met that he liked her pointed chin and her wry smile. Releasing a pent-up breath, he looked her in the eye and said, 'I find you attractive too.'

Silence stretched following his confession, long enough for

the air to fizz. Then she smiled – a grin that blossomed on her face – and her nose wrinkled.

'I'm glad we cleared that up,' she choked around stifled laughter. 'We're just two *attractive* people having a drink with no expectations.'

The tension in him snapped as well and he sat back in his chair, matching her grin with an easy one of his own. Lifting his beer glass, he tapped it against hers. 'I'm glad too. No expectations. Salût... Julia.'

'Cheers, Alex,' she responded to the toast and took a sip of her wine.

4

Jules would never in her life forget the moment when the busker with the gorgeous eyes had captured her gaze and said, 'I find you attractive too.'

Although he smiled, there was a seriousness to him that had made those words sparkle in the air around them and mean more than they should have – certainly more than he'd intended, but Jules was determined to treasure them anyway.

Her time with Luca had been a disaster, but a handsome Friulian stranger called Alex found her attractive. A handsome stranger who had been quite nervous at the beginning of their 'not date' but was now speaking animatedly about his accordion while Jules tried not to laugh at his earnestness.

'It's actually more like a clarinet than a piano. The sound is produced by a series of reeds inside the frame.'

'It sounds complicated,' she responded. 'Is it difficult to play?'

'Not at all. To play well enough to accompany a song, it's one of the easiest instruments available, but to play really well takes a lot of practice. You're... not really interested in this, are you?' He fiddled with his beer glass, rough fingers tracing the shape.

She wasn't interested, but she did like listening to him talk while she enjoyed the gentle fizz and soft tang of her wine. 'Your English is very good,' she commented. 'My Italian is terrible. Che peccato!' She added the 'what a shame' with a hand gesture that reminded her of Luca's mother.

'But surely you haven't been here long? I lived in London. That's where I became fluent in English. "Mind the gap between the train and the platform",' he said in a perfect imitation of the announcements on the Underground, followed by a self-deprecating laugh.

'I spent a few months in London when I first arrived in Europe. Did you play accordion on the Underground?'

'I did, actually,' he said, taking a sip of his beer. 'At Tottenham Court Road. It took me years to get the licence.'

Years that he was living in London. She wondered what he'd done there and why he'd moved. Perhaps for love? Had it worked out better for him than it had for her? 'Now you're back here.'

He didn't answer, only gave a nod and a lift of his eyebrows. 'And you're on your way back to Australia. Where's home?'

'Brisbane, on the east coast. I haven't been back in a long time, though.'

'You've been travelling for a while?'

She'd rather listen to him talk about the mechanics of the accordion than explain that she'd been backpacking, fallen foolishly in love and spent three years of her life on a failing business, two of those in a doomed relationship. 'No, I've mostly been here in Italy, making mistakes and speaking bad Italian.'

'Huh,' he responded with another of his half-nods that felt like an articulate language that she just hadn't learned yet. 'Arco is an affectionate sort of dog, is he?' he changed the subject abruptly.

'Uh, yeah.'

Alex shifted, dropping his hand and Jules peered under the table to see Arco avidly licking his knee. He must have been at it for a while, given the wet patch on the denim.

'Arco, stop!' she hissed, fumbling for his harness. She pulled the pup away and gave him a harsh look, but he just gazed up at her, his tongue lolling out of his mouth, no clue that he'd embarrassed his owner.

'I have a cat. Perhaps he can smell it?'

'Really? A cat?'

He gave an affirmative shrug. 'There's a very old proverb here in Friûl: he who loves cats, loves women,' he said with half a smile, before appearing to choke on his words. 'Not that I—'

Jules pressed a hand to her mouth to stifle a laugh. 'It's okay. I asked you out, not the other way around. You clearly like women to an appropriate degree and nothing more.'

The pink in his cheeks was sweet. 'What kind of dog is he?' he asked, peering under the table. 'What breed?' He clicked his fingers and called Arco to him, rubbing his ears.

'He's a Lagotto Romagnolo. We— I took him in after his owner died.'

For a moment, she thought he would ask her more questions, but he seemed to reconsider. 'A truffle dog, no? He must need a lot of exercise,' was all he said.

Exercise she had never been able to give him properly, as all her time had been invested in the B & B. Perhaps that was why he didn't quite feel tame.

'He's a bit unpredictable. His first owner was elderly and could never handle him and, to be honest, neither can I.'

'He's an animal,' Alex said gently, his expression twitching with discomfort a moment later. 'Now he's licking my hand,' he explained, extricating himself with a laugh that made Jules suspect he was ticklish.

'Yeah, a pack animal,' she added, 'and he seems to want you to join his pack.' She froze when the implication of her sentence struck her. 'But you are not interested in joining a pack right now,' she said, meeting his gaze and nodding sagely. 'Don't worry. It came through loud and clear.'

'I didn't mean to sound like such an arse when I said it. He's a sweet dog and you're a beautiful woman and if things were different... We should at least go to dinner. I'd like to and you shouldn't eat alone.'

* * *

'You should have tried the ham.'

'You're treating this like a personal affront, Alex. I'm sure the ham was delicious.' Jules sighed contentedly and gazed up at the strip of clear, dark sky between the wooden eaves of the buildings.

She couldn't really afford a restaurant meal, but thankfully Alex had insisted on splitting the bill, even though she'd invited him, and he surely didn't make much playing the accordion. She was inclined to think the expense was worth it that night. Her belly was just a touch past pleasantly full and the fireplace by their table in the rustic taverna had worked its warm magic on her thoughts and her body.

Everything was going to be all right. She would arrive at the farm tomorrow and get herself in order.

'It's a local speciality,' Alex insisted. 'Prosciutto di San Daniele is famous across the country.' Over the course of the drink and dinner, he'd gone from nervous and earnest to droll, speaking with shrugs and twists of his brow, and Jules could have watched him and listened to him for a lot longer than a few hours on a single evening.

'I understand and appreciate the Italian obsession with local specialities, and that you are proud and defensive because I lived in Parma – whose prosciutto I'm sure is inferior,' she added with a teasing smile. 'But I did not feel like eating ham. Your other local specialities were delicious.'

'But if you're leaving tomorrow, you should have tried the ham,' he insisted.

'You're pouting,' she accused him with a chuckle. 'Stop it. I already give in to Arco's puppy eyes far too often. Another reason he's not well behaved.'

'I don't have puppy eyes.'

Gripping his forearm and peering into his face, she smiled and said, 'You really do. You should be careful where you flash them.'

'I'm sure they don't work on you. You didn't order ham.'

'I've had enough of the ham and I didn't even eat any!'

Arco pulled ahead, finding an interesting smell as they passed under a rugged stone arch. The humpy cobbles dug into the soles of her feet and every corner they turned seemed to take them back another century.

'I do approve of the prominence of cheese and potatoes in Friulian cooking,' she added with a smile. 'The frico was delicious.'

'It was invented as a way to make use of the cheese rinds, but it's definitely comfort food. We're simple people. Put a pig over the fire and add some things we found in the forest – that's Friulian cooking.'

'Sounds like I should try it. I'm a terrible cook,' she admitted, stuffing her free hand in the pocket of her jacket. She wasn't uncomfortably cold, just noticing the nip of autumn in the air, which only added to the scent of change in her life.

Alex had said she looked travel weary and the comment had struck her. She'd only been living out of her backpack for a week, but she recognised a deeper truth to what he'd said.

'How can anyone be a terrible cook?' he asked doubtfully. 'Perhaps you didn't have a *nonna* to teach you, but anyone can learn.'

She grimaced. 'I tried, trust me. I tried all these Italian lifestyle things over the years and I'm just not cut out for them.'

'Italian lifestyle things?'

'You know, fresh ingredients, make-it-yourself, grow-your-own, slaving in the kitchen and pretending to enjoy it – at least that was how it turned out.' She bit her lip, shoving Luca and his criticism forcefully out of the conversation. She didn't want him in her head right now.

'You don't *enjoy* cooking. That's different.'

'Maybe I would enjoy it more if I could get actual results. But I even failed to grow tomatoes and that's probably breaking some kind of law for residents of Italy. I can't believe the government still granted me citizenship.'

'You are Italian?'

'Technically,' she admitted with an apologetic shrug. 'I'm a Volpe from a long line of Calabrian Volpes, one branch of which emigrated to Australia in the fifties. That was good enough for citizenship, after I completed a mountain of paperwork and waited two years for the rubber stamp. Lucky there wasn't a question on the application about tomatoes.'

'Tomatoes aren't the law, but they *are* one of the building blocks of life.' Dipping his head, he gave her one of his eyebrow lifts and she guessed he was joking. He strode off as though he didn't want her to catch his smile.

She hurried after him, Arco bouncing along, thinking it was

all a fine game. Up ahead was another archway, beneath a building with ancient red brickwork and mismatched windows. The cobbled square where she stood was a meeting-point of the centuries: mediaeval brick with vaulted windows, the first floor extending precariously over the street; newer exposed stonework with dark green shutters and a rendered house in terracotta with wrought-iron balconies and herbs growing on the windowsills.

'Are we going somewhere in particular?' she asked suddenly.

He turned back. 'I thought your B & B was this way. I was following you.'

'I was following *you*.'

She adored the puzzled half-smile on his face as he said, 'I think we were both following Arco.'

'He took us for a walk,' Jules said, matching his smile. 'I didn't ask what you wanted to do now. Perhaps you need to...' She couldn't bring herself to say the word 'go'. The evening didn't feel anywhere near finished, but she knew if she checked the time she would have to accept it was past the hour to release Alex back into the wild.

He tipped his head towards the brick archway and didn't wait for her to finish. 'Come and see the river. It's just through here.'

The moisture in the air was more pronounced as soon as they emerged on the other side. The lights of the town stopped abruptly ahead, giving way to the dark ravine and the sound of rushing water. When they stepped up to the stone wall at the edge, the river was only visible in the reflections of the old city on the rippled surface.

Jules leaned out to catch a glimpse of the bell tower of the cathedral, illuminated in a warm yellow glow. She shivered as the damp rose from below and the effects of the fireplace in the restaurant gradually faded.

Alex appeared next to her, his forearms propped on the wall next to hers. With a quick, wary glance he probably hadn't intended her to notice, he came close enough to press his upper arm against hers.

5

'Thanks for asking me to dinner,' he said softly, his deep voice skittering across her skin. She felt that earnestness in him again – the seriousness.

'That sounds like "goodbye",' she mumbled, staring out over the water.

'I suppose it has to be, but I meant I really enjoyed having dinner with you, more than I expected – more than you would understand. I would hate to... have missed out on it, so thank you for asking.'

She peered at him. She couldn't help thinking he was a lot like his instrument: lively notes and poignant refrains and mysterious workings inside. 'You promised to bore me, but you didn't,' she said lightly. 'Not even close.'

Arco whined, as though in a hurry to keep moving. Without the reminder of real life, she would have struggled to take the necessary step away from the unexpectedly lovely evening.

Alex crouched to pat him. 'Look after Julia, eh? Be a guard dog,' he said, giving Arco a stern gaze as he rubbed his ears with both hands.

'Don't worry. He's a good judge of character.'

'Oh, reall—' Before he could finish, Arco barrelled into him tongue-first. Jerking away from the wet swipe of dog-tongue, Alex overbalanced and went down on his bottom, laughing as he fended off the over-affectionate dog.

'Arco!' she called, clicking her fingers and trying in vain to call him away. 'He's a good judge of character, but I didn't say he had any boundaries.'

'Urgh, that feels strange!' Alex chuckled as he batted Arco's nose away with a gentle hand after he'd been thoroughly licked on the ear.

She held her hand out and helped him haul himself up. When he was on his feet again, he was suddenly close, his toes nudging hers. She became aware all over again of how tall he was, how lovely his mouth looked.

She hadn't kissed anyone in a long time. She'd barely thought about it amidst the stress of the business and the angst of working with Luca. But she was definitely thinking about it now.

Their 'not date' had been the best date of her life, a memory she could treasure when she left, a small counterbalance to all the heartache – a little 'what if' to nurture at her lowest moments.

There'd be no harm in a small kiss. She left for the farm tomorrow morning and although it was only a few kilometres out of town, she wasn't planning to come back to Cividale. In a few short weeks she'd be on the other side of the world. She wouldn't see him again.

He stepped away, his hand lifting absently to the back of his head. '*Allora*, I, ehm... should...' He stumbled as he turned away, shoving one hand into the pocket of his jacket.

'Wait!' She took an involuntary step towards him, blood rushing in her ears. He turned back, slowly, his mouth slightly open and his expression dismayed. The thought that she wouldn't see him again echoed between her ears and although she worried she was misinterpreting the signals – she was woeful at signals – she had to try. 'H-how about a k-kiss? Goodbye. A kiss goodbye?'

He returned to her so quickly he tripped again, a smile stretching on his lips. Grasping her face with both hands, he murmured, 'I couldn't think of anything else.' His gaze darting between her eyes and her lips, his smile tipping up on one side as she lifted her chin, he inched closer, his breath gusting as he hesitated.

The tender graze of his fingertips over her cheeks and jaw put her off balance, her skin tingling. He was a stranger. She wasn't supposed to be kissing the random accordion player Arco had accosted in the street – or at least it wasn't supposed to feel like a key in a lock, like finding something that had been lost. Thoughts of that kind were what had got her into Italian-flavoured trouble to begin with.

She met his gaze, sharing a wobbly smile of disbelief. But as they came haltingly nearer, her hand clutching his jacket and his drifting into her hair, a kiss was definitely happening, the pounding of her heart a hint of what was to come.

His mouth brushed hers lightly at first. She could feel the smile in the way he kissed her and all her doubts fled. Returning the soft kiss, she wrapped her arm around his neck and shivered when he dropped one hand from her face to pull her close.

Light kisses with smiling lips slowly became deeper ones, her mouth falling open and her breath short. With an abortive groan, he tilted his head and pressed his open mouth to hers. The sparks over her skin fizzed immediately into heat and she couldn't think, couldn't feel anything except how badly this gorgeous man apparently wanted to kiss her, because his touch had grown rough and a little reckless.

She liked that.

'Do you—' The words began to fall from her lips without thought, between burning kisses. 'I know it's too fast, but—' She kissed him again and her hand had found its way into his hair. 'But I'm leaving so...' It was difficult to pull away for long enough to get the words out. 'Do you want to come back to my B & B? For the night? Don't feel obliged. I don't really know how to... do this, but I'm leaving and I'd rather be with you tonight than not.'

Settling his forehead on hers, he didn't answer immediately, but his unsteady breaths and the way he skimmed his fingers over the back of her neck told her something. 'If you're sure,' he said, swallowing hard, 'I'd love to.'

He smiled again and came back for another clumsy kiss, telling her clearly how much he wanted her.

'Which B & B are you staying at? I should pick up some...'

'The one in Borgo San Domenico, on the corner,' she answered, before taking his hand and heading for the old town, Arco giving an excited bark at this new game.

But Alex stalled. 'Eh, Maria Grazia's place?' he asked.

'That's the name of the woman who runs it, yeah. Do you know her?'

He gave another of those nods with his eyebrows, his expression eloquent with discomfort.

'Oh dear, will she give you the third degree if you show up with me? What about your place?'

'You don't mind coming to my place? I at least have... what we need there.'

Her hair stood on end as she processed his meaning, but his gaze was so earnest as he peered at her that she wasn't put off in the least by the practicalities of a one-night stand, even though she'd never had one before.

'What about your cat?' she asked, gesturing to Arco.

'He's often out at this time of night, but he'd just hide anyway.'

'Then let's go,' she said softly.

If she'd had any remaining doubts, then his giddy smile erased them, as well as the quick, hard kiss he pressed to her lips before setting off again under the soft street lamps.

Five minutes later, he tugged her through an open gate into a crumbling courtyard, hurrying to a door on the right, by a spreading tree. But Jules wasn't interested in the tree – or the rest of her surroundings – pulling his head down for another kiss.

'We'll be inside in a minute,' he mumbled, but kissed her again when she drew back to smile.

'We've only just started kissing. I didn't want to stop so soon.'

'I know what you mean.' He fumbled with his keys as he kept one arm around her. Arco gave a sharp bark and Alex froze, his gaze snapping up to the many windows on the upper floors of the buildings clustered around the courtyard. Shuffling his keys, he searched frantically for the right one.

'Nosy neighbours?' Jules guessed, soothing the dog with a hand on his back.

When he finally got the door open he all but tackled her inside, shutting the door behind them and switching on the hall light. Seeing his sheepish look, Jules burst out laughing.

'They're neighbours, not zombie attackers,' she joked as she unclipped Arco's lead and the dog took off nose-first down the hall.

Towing her close by her jacket, Alex wrapped an arm around her and treated her to one of his broad smiles. 'You don't know these neighbours.' Then he kissed her again, slower, deeper, but no less urgent than outside. He kissed her as though he couldn't *not* kiss her and Jules's head was spinning after the first second.

No one had ever been so impatient to kiss her that they hadn't made it out of the hallway. After his nerves during the early part of the evening and the meticulous courtesy of their 'no expectations' agreement, now they'd decided to take things further tonight, his eager delight was a glorious surprise.

'Ehm, do you want anything?' he murmured between kisses, gallantry not quite abandoned yet.

'No,' she answered, shuddering as his mouth found her jaw and then her neck.

'Just tell me if you need...'

'This is exactly what I need.'

6

If Alex had been able to think clearly, he would have seriously questioned the wisdom of bringing Julia back to his place – for more reasons than just the temperamental cat, who was thankfully nowhere to be found. As it was, he experienced only a vague sense of misgiving as the rest of him was overwhelmed by the lightness in his chest when she pressed kisses to his face.

She was leaving tomorrow, so it didn't really matter what she thought, but he hadn't brought a woman home here since... What if he did something terrible, like call her the wrong name? Were there photos anywhere? Keepsakes? Was there etiquette in these situations?

The few times he'd met someone with the mutual agreement that things would be short and casual, he'd made sure it wasn't here in Cividale, where there were eyes at every window – pitying looks, usually. He hadn't been a monk over the past three years, but tonight didn't quite feel like the other times and Julia didn't feel like a stranger, even though they'd just met.

They stumbled into his bedroom, all smiles and busy hands. He was drawn to the spot where her short hair brushed her shoulders and she gave a throaty, pleased laugh when he kissed her there. He liked the way her voice dropped and roughened.

Items of clothing ended up on the floor – he couldn't quite remember who had removed what – and then he pulled her close and breathed her in. Wow, he'd needed this, to switch off from normal life for a night with no past or future, no consequences.

'Your eyes remind me of chestnuts,' he hummed, kissing her again to cover the words he hadn't quite meant to say aloud.

'Do you like chestnuts?' she asked doubtfully, tugging him towards the bed.

'Love them.' They made it onto the bed and all he could feel was her and it was glorious.

'I've never tried them.'

He reared up on his elbows. 'What? How is that possible? I should find you some right n—'

'Not right now,' she crooned, looping her arms around his neck and dragging him down so her lips were at his ear. 'I'm interested in something other than chestnuts right now.' When she dragged her teeth over his earlobe, goosebumps prickled all over him.

'I could live on chestnuts for two months of the year,' he murmured, digging his fingers into her hair and feathering his lips over her jaw – such a strong jaw.

She grinned. 'Chestnuts and my eyes, right?'

With a deep chuckle, he said, 'Right.'

'My body too?'

'Mmhmm,' he agreed, his thoughts slipping. 'And your jokes,' he whispered, burying his face in her neck until she shuddered.

Her hands touched down on his shoulders, slipping around to his neck. 'I should tell you… it's been a while – for me. Just… so you know.'

'Thanks for choosing me then.' He skimmed the backs of his

fingers over her cheek as he lifted onto his elbows to meet her gaze. 'And tell me if you want to stop – at any time.'

Her hands ventured down his back, as a smile grew on her lips. 'I don't want to stop.'

He lost himself happily with her, almost believing he could be someone else – someone with a different life, another past and a carefree future. She was so soft and strong, open and full of smiles, and she delighted in every touch.

When her fingers gripped his hair tightly as her breath hitched and stalled, he was almost sad this sweet, impatient interlude couldn't last forever, but he was on the edge as well. As the feelings snapped and washed over both of them, he fumbled for her cheek, needing to express... something – something more than how much he liked her chestnut eyes.

But as his breathing finally slowed, the sudden lethargy drained everything out of him and he collapsed next to her.

'Huh, wow,' she mumbled.

'Yeah.' He peered at her from under heavy eyelids. Her smile was smaller now and he would have laughed at her smugness if he had the energy.

'Not bad for an accordion player,' she said softly, pressing a kiss to his cheek that was somehow just as devastating as the deep kisses they'd shared a few moments ago. Her gaze snagged on his upper arm and before he could distract her, she traced a finger over his tattoo. 'What are these?'

'Bay leaves—'

A sudden crash from down the hall made Julia bolt upright. Alex tried to drag himself up, but his limbs felt like syrup.

'Arco?' she cried in alarm, and he pulled himself together to follow her as she snatched up her underwear and stumbled out of the room – too quickly for him to properly appreciate the glimpse of her long, long legs. Wow, she was stunning. 'Arco!' he heard her scolding the dog, a dismayed edge to her voice.

When he arrived in the kitchen, it was to find a windowsill planter on its side, soil spilling onto the floor, and a suspiciously innocent-looking dog hiding under the table, his eyes partially obscured by brown fur.

'I'm so sorry,' Julia said, scooping up soil with her bare hands while wearing only her bra and knickers.

He stilled her with a hand on her wrist. 'Don't worry. It's my fault.' He gestured silently towards the kitchen door – where a fluffy white tail extended from behind the wood, flicking occasionally in apparent annoyance at the intrusion. 'I obviously didn't look hard enough for him when we got home.'

'I suppose I share the blame for distracting you,' she said. 'We're lucky they stayed quiet this long.'

'Very lucky,' he agreed earnestly, only to find her grinning at him with a cheeky smile.

'What's her name?'

'*His* name is Attila.'

'The Hun?'

'I didn't name him,' Alex admitted before he'd thought it through. 'But it suits him.' He continued before she could voice the question he could see on her face. 'Here. You're getting soil everywhere.'

Taking her hands and gently washing them at the sink, wiping the smear from her forehead with a cloth, he pulled her close for a quick hug that was supposed to be tight and friendly, but there was far too much skin in the equation for that.

He didn't have the words to describe what had happened that evening, but he suspected he would never forget it – forget her.

Even her name made him smile. Not the Italian Giulia, but Julia, as though she'd belonged here in a past life. Cividale had originally been named for Julius Caesar himself – Forum iulii. She was leaving tomorrow, but she'd spent tonight with him. He wasn't sure how to explain to her how much he valued the gift of an evening outside of his usual reality.

So, he didn't try. He just said, 'I'll clean it up. You don't need to stand around in my cold kitchen in your underwear.'

She glanced around her as though seeing the kitchen for the first time, her eyes settling on the window and darting away again. Then her gaze fell to his chest, where it stuck for a few breaths until heat rose up his neck. She licked her lips and his skin was tingling and he suddenly had no idea where to go from here, what he wanted.

'Do you want—'

'I suppose I should—'

Her laugh this time was a little strained. She got to the end of her sentence first.

'Go. I should go.'

Brushing past, she shook herself visibly and hurried back down the hall to his bedroom. He hesitated and when he finally made it back to the door to the room, she was stuffing her arms into the sleeves of her pullover. It was for the best.

'I hope you don't...' It seemed he was still incapable of talking in complete sentences.

'I don't, Alex,' she said with a faint smile, looking up. There was something he liked about the way she said his name: softly, almost carelessly, the way people wore their favourite items of everyday clothing.

'Because... thank you.'

'You don't need to thank me,' she assured him.

'No, I mean, tonight... you... Not just sleeping together, although that was...' Putane, sentences were long gone and now even words were a struggle. He took a deep, halting breath and looked away so he could try to explain himself. 'Tonight was the best evening I've had in a long time.'

'Me too,' she agreed quietly.

As she shrugged into her jacket, he picked up Arco's lead from where it lay discarded on the floor by the door and called the dog. Giving him a thorough rub and petting his curly head, he crooned softly to Arco in his native dialect.

'I'm not sure Arco understands Friulian,' Julia joked as she wound her light scarf around her neck. 'I sure don't.'

'I don't know how to talk to animals in English,' he explained with a wry smile and one final pat for the dog. 'I just told him to look after you.'

When she glanced at the dog, her expression tightened briefly with dismay – hinting at the vast array of topics they'd avoided tonight, even though it felt as though they'd shared everything. 'We look after each other.'

Slipping past her to open the door, he only realised when the cool October breeze swept over his skin that he was still shirtless and wearing only his boxer shorts. His arm rose to his chest, as though that would help.

She ran her fingers roughly through her mussed hair and took Arco's lead from Alex's limp hand. 'We won't swap numbers, right? Because we're both "not".'

'That might be for the best.'

'Okay,' she said slowly, as though she was trying to convince herself. 'You... take care of yourself too,' she said.

He just gave a single nod in reply.

Lifting her face, she pressed another kiss to his cheek. With a gulp, she dipped her gaze and kissed him on the lips, quick and sharp, as though she hadn't quite meant to do it.

'Good luck,' he mumbled, words still insufficient.

'Think of me sometimes?' she said in a rush, her voice going up at the end.

'Oh, I will,' he assured her. It was his turn to grasp her jacket at the waist and press one more soft kiss to her mouth before he forced his fist open and stepped back. He stood there, his skin pebbling with goosebumps, and watched as she passed under the old persimmon tree, crossed the courtyard, and walked back out of his life.

7

Jules awoke to her alarm the following morning, fumbling groggily for her phone to switch off the annoying tone. Arco barked for good measure and she rolled over and fumbled to quiet him too. With a flash of goosebumps, her memories of the night before washed over her: talking and laughing; blue eyes she hoped she never forgot; eager kisses and intimacy that had left her drained and melty.

The most striking image was the last: Alex standing in his doorway half-naked, looking lost. It felt strange that she'd never see him again. But at least she'd leave Italy with a favourable impression of one man at least – and an accordion player at that!

After slurping two coffees and hastily consuming as much of the sweet breakfast buffet as she could in half an hour, she stuffed her things into her backpack while Arco wolfed down his own breakfast. Then she hauled the shopping bag full of dog food onto one poor shoulder and trudged downstairs to pay her bill.

She'd chosen the cheapest B & B she could find, but she still tapped her fingers nervously as the payment processed. She had money in her account, but in a few weeks, she'd have to buy a last-minute flight home – for herself and a dog. She didn't want to know how many thousands of euros she'd be on the hook for.

If the sale of the building only covered the debts from the renovation and didn't return any cash, she would be in trouble. Luca's voice echoed between her ears, accusing her of not watching the bank balance. She thought with bitterness that his accusation was true this time. She hadn't been brave enough to check her own balance since she left.

But screw Luca. Counting the pennies wouldn't have made money magically appear and necessary expenses were exactly that. Yes, the business account had regularly been significantly overdrawn, but she'd cut back where she could. He'd kept his day job working at an events company and, while that had kept them fed over the past three years when the B & B struggled to make money, it meant he'd had no idea how expensive it was to run the business – and could conveniently blame Jules.

It was impossible to be financially responsible when there was no money to be responsible with.

Whatever her current bank balance, the payment to the severe-looking Maria Grazia further reduced it, and then Jules was free again, all her worldly goods on her back and the road stretching ahead of her. It was a long road that morning – over an hour's trudge to the farm – but at least, she thought, Arco would get some decent exercise.

While Jules had almost lost track of the days of the week since leaving Parma, for the rest of the world it was a Thursday morning and the lanes were full of people running their errands or on their way to their work. She tried not to search their faces for Alex, but the occasional head of wavy brown hair caught her eye.

Slowing her steps as she approached the bridge, she told

herself he wouldn't be there playing his accordion. He must move around the city and probably take time off – if he could even survive and rent what had been a nice enough apartment just from busking.

Frowning, she realised he'd never said if he played music full-time or had another job and although they'd left each other behind on purpose last night, she suddenly wished she'd asked him all of those questions, even if it had meant sharing her own sorry tale.

Her wondering was in vain, however. The little stone square on the other side of the bridge was empty, no gorgeous man or droning instrument. With a sigh, she paused in the middle of the bridge for a final look at the stunning ravine with its emerald-green water and the view of the colourful little city perched on the rock.

Perhaps the next time she crossed the Ponte del Diavolo, she'd be on her way to the train station starting her journey home.

She shouldn't be thinking about last night. She definitely shouldn't be thinking about Alex and how he'd put her at ease and suddenly come out of his shell when she'd confirmed she wanted to come back to his apartment. She shouldn't wonder why he hadn't named his own cat.

Today, she was headed out to the farm. It was a family operation with a vineyard and an olive grove and a restaurant for tourists that only opened for lunch. The photos online had looked idyllic: a stone farmhouse set in a field with a wooded hill behind; squat, bushy trees with twisted trunks and swing-cap bottles full of cloudy olive oil with handwritten labels.

Thinking of farms just reminded her of the tomato banter from the night before and she shook off those goosebumps again as she walked steadily onwards.

The plain seemed to unfold endlessly once she'd cleared the

outskirts of the city, knobbly hills of vineyards, topped with crowns of forest, stretching to the horizon. Clouds hung suspended in the wide sky. The trees were every shade between green and brown: orange oak, evergreen cypress and yellowing birch trees with white trunks.

There was no footpath to speak of, so Jules had to juggle Arco on a short lead and the bag of dog food that kept slipping off her shoulder. Only her sheer determination and the changing colours of the russet hills kept her spirits up.

She wondered if there were traffic-free footpaths amongst the trees and vines but she couldn't risk getting lost, so she stuck to the road, the cars zipping by too fast, puttering *motorini* – the iconic scooters that dominated Italian roads – and industrial and agricultural vehicles of all shapes and sizes forcing Jules and Arco into the damp grass. Her trainers were quickly soaked, although they hadn't been in great shape anyway.

Roads grew sparse two kilometres out of Cividale, and trees plentiful. She upped her pace even though her backpack had grown heavy and the dog food now sagged in its bag, hanging from her elbow. Her hair tickled her face and her brow was muggy with sweat, despite the cool October day. Dapper and well-dressed Luca would be horrified to see her now.

But hey, she'd had a great time in bed with a guy last night, she thought with a rather manic laugh to herself – or perhaps *at* herself. Alex hadn't minded that her hair could do with a conditioning treatment and a pair of straighteners, and that all her clothes were crushed. Hopefully Maddalena, the women who ran the olive farm, wouldn't mind either.

When she took her last turning – onto a concrete road barely wide enough for a single car, cracked and potholed and muddy – she experienced the first inkling of suspicion that this farm stay might not turn out quite as she'd pictured it.

A faded sign announced her destination: Agriturismo Azienda Agricola Biologica Due Pini. The stone wall along the road had fallen down in places, destabilised by tree roots. Those roots belonged to the farm's namesakes, two tall stone pines, their dark green crowns fanning out so high up that Jules had to crane her neck.

The farmhouse was a large building – possibly an old barn – that had been rendered and painted rusty pink. Wooden eaves and shutters completed the bright picture, but when she looked more closely, she noticed that the render was criss-crossed with cracks and the vintage farm equipment dotting the yard was more of a tetanus hazard than charming decor. There were checked tablecloths hanging from each window and also strung up under the pergola. A goat was gnawing peacefully on the one flung over a bush along the drive.

As she trudged down the cracked driveway, a chicken scampered across her path. A donkey watched Jules's and Arco's progress towards the farmhouse, only flicking its soft grey ear once or twice but otherwise not moving. As Jules spotted the olive trees and several rows of vines, an enormous flock of crows took flight, colouring a portion of the cloudy sky black.

When she'd pictured an organic farm, Jules hadn't imagined the animals would be free-range as well.

'Welcome to Two Pines Organic Farm,' she muttered to herself, holding Arco firmly on a short lead as he skittered restlessly.

Arco was gleefully alert, sniffing under every plant and giving the goat a wide berth, which Jules understood. There was something just *wrong* about goats' eyes.

Approaching the farmhouse, she wasn't sure where to enter, as there were several doors. One set of sliding doors was closed, frilly curtains drawn. A heavy wooden door with a wreath in autumn colours was also firmly shut. But a third door was ajar, a bead curtain moving in the breeze.

The sharp smash of glass breaking – a lot of glass – stopped Jules in her tracks. Cursing in a woman's voice followed immediately, then, drowning out the voice – and the chickens and the goat – came the splutter and buzz of a chainsaw.

With a grimace, Jules gingerly nudged aside the strings of wooden beads and called out 'Hello?' hoping she could be heard over the loud drone of the power tool. Taking a step inside, she startled a woman with greying light brown hair, a wild look in her eyes.

The woman blinked at her uncomprehendingly for a moment, clutching a broom handle and brushing absently at her apron and long skirt.

'Hi,' Jules began. 'Er, I'm Julia Volpe. Are you Maddalena?' She took a step forward to awkwardly offer her hand.

'Stop right there!'

Jules froze, less regimental soldier and more rabbit-in-the-headlights. 'What?'

'Non muoverti! Hold the dog!'

The panic in the woman's voice snapped Jules into action and she snatched Arco off the floor and into her arms, even though her knees complained about his weight, on top of her luggage.

'I broke glass – una damigiana, a *big* glass!'

The back door swung open suddenly and another dog shot in, making the woman shriek again and brandish her broom at the animal. A man tumbled in after the dog, dark hair falling over his eyes.

'Mamma!' he cried, followed by more words Julia struggled to catch, although one of them sounded like 'fiasco' which she thought was rather appropriate.

Arco must have scented the big black dog because he began to wriggle so wildly that Julia was afraid she'd drop him. When he barked, it was loud enough to ring in her ears. The other dog strained at the hold on its collar and the poor woman with the broom swept as though possessed, the clink of heavy glass shards barely audible over the canine chorus.

'I can't hold him any more,' Jules said through gritted teeth just as the woman had contained the shards in one corner of the room and stood guard. Arco leaped out of Jules's arms and bounded straight for the other dog, tail wagging. She stumbled after him, her backpack making her whole body list to the left. Before she could restrain him, Arco had stuffed his nose into the other dog's privates. 'I'm so sorry,' she panted, fumbling with the lead. 'He has no manners.'

Before the man could reply, his dog gave a low growl that quickly progressed to baring teeth and a sharp bark that gave Jules a shower of misgiving down her spine, but it was too late. The black dog raised its paws and snarled at Arco, barking furiously. Arco zipped away, tugging on the lead so suddenly Jules tumbled over, landing helplessly on her backpack.

The other dog shook off the man's hold on its collar and leaped right over Jules, its claws finding grip in her jacket as she cowered, covering her face. To a chorus of howling and barking – and alarmed shouts and oaths from the room's other two occupants – the two dogs nipped and sparred and expressed their clear dissatisfaction with each other.

'Basta, Fritz! Basta!'

Jules managed to unclip her backpack and stand up and then Arco leaped at her. She caught him somehow, despite her shock at his panicked behaviour, and he trembled violently in her arms, whining pitifully.

'Mi dispiace tantissimo,' the man apologised, approaching with a grimace.

The back door banged open again to reveal a man in overalls brandishing a chainsaw – exactly what Jules's day had been missing.

'Nonno!' the younger man exclaimed. 'Metti giù quella cosa!'

Put that down! The man's somewhat standard Italian, even if the consonants sounded a little chewed, made more sense to Jules and she shook her head to clear her thoughts, breathing hard.

The man with the chainsaw flipped open the tinted visor of his helmet to reveal a pair of kind brown eyes and a prodigiously wrinkled, smiling face – in contrast to the power tool held carelessly in his other hand.

'Ah, la signorina!' the old man said, tossing the chainsaw into his left hand to extend his right. 'Mandi! Welcome!'

'Uh,' was all Jules said, rather rudely, although she managed to shuffle Arco in her arms to poke out a hand for him to shake.

'Oh! You are Julia!' the woman said in English, running a hand through her hair in agitation and leaving it standing up in a curly mess. 'I forgot you are coming today. Oh dear, I— Davide, take Fritz away, *please!*'

Mouthing 'sorry,' the younger man shepherded the black dog back outside and shot her a quick smile. She couldn't be certain whether he was apologising for the behaviour of the dog or for leaving her alone with this eccentric pair who were apparently his mother and grandfather, if she'd caught the Italian correctly.

Between the chainsaw welcome, the broken glass and the fierce dog, if she'd had any other options for a place to stay, she would have considered turning around and marching back to town.

'Yes, I-I'm Julia,' she stammered, stumbling as Arco wriggled in her arms.

'I'm afraid I have bad news,' Maddalena said, her eyes a little wild – at least Julia assumed the woman was Maddalena, even though she hadn't introduced herself. Julia's stomach sank as she waited to hear the next stumbling block on the road out of Italy. 'A pipe burst last night and the bunk room was flooded. The wiring is unsafe and I don't know how or when—'

The woman looked entirely at the end of her tether and despite the panic rising in her throat, Jules felt a stab of sympathy.

She set Arco down, keeping him on a short lead. 'Sounds like you need help.'

'You see, Maddalena!' the old man said, raising his hand for emphasis. 'Dut va ben!' It sounded enough like 'Tutto va bene' that Jules assumed the old man actually thought everything would be all right. That made one of them. Putting down his chainsaw, he approached with a wide smile, clutched her shoulders and pressed a kiss to each of her cheeks. 'Juuulia,' he said, drawing out her name almost... fondly? 'We are so happy you are here.'

She blinked at him. She was here for free accommodation in exchange for work. She wasn't a long-lost granddaughter.

'Papà! I don't have a room where she can stay! The wiring is a mortal danger and the floor is more crooked than one of your jokes. As much as we need the help, I have nothing to offer in return. Dear,' she said, turning earnestly to Jules, 'it will be best if you continue with your travels. I'm so sorry.'

Jules allowed her eyelids to fall shut, unbearably weary.

'But she doesn't need to go anywhere,' the old man said, cryptically. Why he was still smiling was beyond her. 'Why stay on the farm here when there's a perfectly *warm bed* waiting for you, eh?'

He patted her arm as though he couldn't contain his excitement and Jules began to wonder if he had a screw loose. Turning to the equally puzzled Maddalena, he said, 'She is the answer to prayer!'

When he continued, his explanation knocked the breath out of Julia's lungs.

'*This* is Alex's girlfriend!'

8

While chaos reigned at Due Pini, business was slow in Luigi's bike shop, where Alex worked. The man himself was out with his friends from the motor club, leaving Alex to ring up the couple of purchases while he kept on top of the repairs in the workshop out the back. Autumn was a popular season for repairs which Alex always felt had some deeper meaning.

Catching himself, he shook off the thought. He shouldn't be looking for deeper meaning in anything, especially not something as prosaic as the changing of the seasons, or he'd soon be off in his own world imagining there was symbolism in his new life repairing other people's brakes and tyres and lamps.

Wow, he'd needed the break from his own company last night. With oil on his fingertips, a multi-tool in his hand and a satisfying project in front of him, he was content, almost... happy. The sex had something to do with his mood, undoubtedly, but he refused to think of that cause and effect. He hadn't slept with Julia to make himself happy. It had just been... the natural next step.

Not for the first time that day, he asked himself where she could be now and what she was thinking about the night before.

The other question that swirled through his thoughts was: had last night been so easy and wonderful *despite* their 'no expectations' rule or *because of* it?

Whatever the answer, he still experienced the occasional shower of goosebumps remembering everything that had happened, and had to shake himself back into the present to concentrate on the bolts and screws and cables.

In the mid-afternoon, the bell over the shop door chimed and he called out a cheerful greeting to the customer while he finished polishing a carbon fibre frame. When he emerged onto the shop floor, he recognised Fulvio Quercig, the father of one of his students – the students old Berengario would probably never take back now Alex had started filling in for him.

He shook hands with the man. 'What can I do for you?' Picking up a battered leather case, the man placed it on the counter and Alex frowned. 'The key stuck again?'

'No, the keys are fine after you fixed them last time, but now it won't shut up. Plays a note constantly. I'm surprised it didn't drone at me in the car all the way here.'

'Don't worry. Sounds like there's a pallet open. It shouldn't be a difficult fix. Leave it with me and I'll take a look tonight.'

'I'm not convinced the thing isn't possessed, to be honest. Gianni joked about it, but barely a week's gone by when this thing *didn't* make some pretty other-worldly sounds – and I'm not talking about Gianni's practice.'

'It's not haunted, Siôr Quercig,' he assured the man with a grin, using the local version of 'signor'. 'If you think it is, you'll have to take it back to Berengario. I don't do accordion exorcism, only repair.'

'You were so busy last time, I tried Berengario, but he said you're the only one who repairs accordions around here now.'

'What?' Alex shook his head with a fond smile, thinking of

the old man who'd taught him everything he knew about the instrument.

'Wants to retire, he said,' Siôr Quercig continued.

'Berengario will never retire,' Alex contradicted him emphatically, picking up the leather accordion case and stowing it behind the counter to take home with him later.

'He probably just had a date with Elena,' the other man said with a wink.

'Or with a friend and a bottle of wine,' Alex agreed, although the man was right that Berengario and Elena had been inseparable since they'd officially become a couple, as juvenile as that expression sounded for a pair in their eighties.

'At least you're taking over the business,' Siôr Quercig said, slapping him on the arm before turning to leave.

Alex's mouth dropped open to protest, but the man was already walking away. He wasn't taking over from Berengario. His old mentor was part of the musical fabric of the city, while Alex was... a bicycle repair man who dabbled in busking and teaching accordion to the awkward kids at school. Cividale had got on fine without him during the years he'd been away.

Luigi appeared with a cigarillo hanging from his lips just before closing time, helping to bring the bicycles for hire back inside for the night and counting the money. He shooed Alex out of the shop twenty minutes before the end of his shift.

'I'm lucky to have you, boy, and I see you have a hot date tonight.'

Alex's gaze shot up, a denial on his lips. Had Luigi found out about Julia somehow? But he wasn't seeing her tonight – or ever again. He was gripped by a sudden panic that someone might have seen them, and the news would be across town by the end of the night as all of his friends and acquaintances discussed his miserable love life over their tajùt on the piazza. For a moment, he wished he *could* meet Julia again tonight for another drink, as consolation for being the object of pity and gossip.

But the panic ebbed again when he saw Luigi's eyes on the accordion case behind the counter. Those were his usual evening plans: a date in front of the TV with his pliers and screwdrivers and beeswax and someone's grandfather's instrument.

It was a miracle he hadn't bored Julia stiff the evening before. Perhaps she'd just been nice about it because she wanted to get into his underwear. He could live with that.

Hefting the old case, he gave Luigi a lazy salute and called out the usual 'Mandi,' because the shop was proudly Friulian and '*Ciao*' was only for customers from the rest of Italy. The last rays of the sun painted the sky with slivers of orange as he stepped out of the shop and the wrought-iron street lamps of the old town switched on, illuminating his short walk home.

He wondered if Attila was still angry with him for inviting a dog to his house last night. The cat had regarded him with distinct dissatisfaction that morning, even eating his breakfast with his tail curled in clear disdain. Although Attila was a Persian mix and always looked mildly peeved, even when he was content.

Waving to the owner of the pet salon as she shut up shop for the evening, he wondered what Arco was doing right now and who he was licking. He'd probably already left Italy with his mistress. Given the position of Cividale, she could be in any number of countries: Austria, Slovenia, Croatia, Switzerland, Germany – even Bosnia or Hungary were possibilities.

All of which made it seem strange that he hadn't crossed a border in three years. He didn't need to, he assured himself. Udine was a big enough city for practical errands, the beach at Grado was only half an hour away for a summer dip, and in winter he had the Dolomites to the north. He wasn't stuck; he was home. He needed that now.

Elena was at her window when he arrived at the gate under the archway but she disappeared inside her apartment before he could call up a greeting or ask after Berengario, her beau, who was undoubtedly in the apartment with her.

The windows of his building were at least eighty years old and everywhere paint was peeling and wood and glass were warped. Perhaps it was for the best that Julia had arrived here in the dark – and he had kept her effectively distracted.

But that evening there were people by the persimmon tree – three people even, not just Siôr Mauri puffing on a furtive cigarette while his wife wasn't looking. Make that three people and a dog. Alex froze, concern and anticipation prickling up his spine. He recognised those sneakers, the short ponytail – that place on her *neck*. He'd spent all day reminding himself she was gone, but... here she was.

Arco saw him first, giving a bark and turning in an excited circle. Alex snapped himself into action when he recognised Berengario with them. He didn't want to be caught staring, nonplussed, at Julia when she was supposed to be a stranger. But what was she doing there? With *Berengario,* of all people? Or was it a coincidence that his old mentor was here as well and... was that Aunt Maddalena?

While he absently greeted the ecstatic dog, Maddalena and Berengario both attempted conversations with him at once.

'There he is!'

'Alex! We were starting to think—'

'—you didn't say anything about your *young woman*—'

'—except there was a burst pipe and—'

'—it's none of my business why she's not staying with you, but she—'

'She can stay with you, now.'

Alex struggled to decipher the rush of words, but his thoughts got stuck on the ones that didn't make sense: *his young woman?* And Berengario admitting something was none of his business?

Julia turned slowly, a pained expression on her face, and only then did he notice that her hair was limp and knotty, a smear of dirt was on her cheek and her old jeans were caked in mud. When she lifted a hand to swipe at a strand of hair, he saw her skin was raw.

'What happened to you?' he asked, peering into her face. Only belatedly did he attempt to soften his expression. Her only response was an overwhelmed look in the direction of the two older people. Maddalena's question finally penetrated his thoughts and he glanced back at his aunt. '"She can stay with me"?' he repeated, dumbfounded.

He mustn't have quite achieved the disbelieving inflection he'd been aiming for, because Maddalena sighed with relief. 'Oh, grazie al cielo, I felt so bad for her and I didn't know how I would manage—'

Berengario stopped her with an affectionate whack with the backs of his fingers. 'I told you everything would be all right. I suppose these things might be complicated if you haven't been together long,' he said, peering between Alex and Julia with the warm smile of a priest at a wedding. Switching to English, he said, 'Alex is as good as they come, Giulietta,' with a glint in his eye that swung Alex's thoughts back to the other confusing part of the chaotic conversation.

'But she's not—'

Berengario leaned close and said, 'Your *fantate* is tired and hungry, young man,' in a low voice, using that suggestive 'your' in front of the even more suggestive 'young woman' in Furlan. 'If it weren't for her today, Maddalena would never have managed, so take her inside and deal with yourself later.'

Alex was even more confused now, but Berengario was right

about one thing: he had to speak to Julia without an audience if he was going to get an answer that actually made sense. He unlocked the door and allowed Berengario to usher him inside. After pressing a quick kiss to Aunt Maddalena's cheek in hello and goodbye, he then found the door closed firmly in his face, Berengario's worryingly mischievous grin the last thing he saw. He wouldn't have been surprised to hear the bolt slipping into place to lock them in together – except that would be pointless, since he had a key to his own house.

After taking a moment to breathe out heavily, his hand resting on the door, he glanced up at Julia. Still wearing her tatty backpack, a bag falling down her arm, she looked as bewildered as he felt. And pretty, with her lips pressed into half a smile and her hair mussed. He found memories of last night on every inch of her face – memories that made him a little light-headed.

But it also made him woozy to think that Berengario knew he'd slept with someone, although how the old man had met Julia was still a mystery.

'I'll leave as soon as they've gone.'

He snapped back to the present with a frown. 'What do you mean? I thought you needed to stay here tonight.'

'I can go back to Maria Grazia's place. Maddalena just felt bad because she couldn't offer me any accommodation.'

His brow drew even tighter. 'Wait, *you're* the temporary worker at the farm? You said you were leaving.'

'Take it easy. I didn't mean to come back! And I didn't know that out of the hundreds of farms in the area, I happened to end up with people you know. It was all an accident, okay? I know we weren't supposed to see each other again after last night and now we'll *really* never see each other again. I promise.'

He panicked when she headed for the door, rushing to stop her with his hand splayed on the cracked blue paint. 'Look, you can stay for a night. Berengario said you worked hard at the farm today and it's the least I can do... for Maddalena. You're supposed to be paid in accommodation and food, right? You're a volunteer on that programme?'

She nodded, her eyes flitting around the hallway as though deciding whether to run.

'If you stay, I don't mean in my bed— There's no expectation of a repeat—' He gulped.

'What?'

'There's a separate part of the house you can stay in,' he managed more comprehensibly. 'I'm not suggesting we...'

Her shoulders dropped a fraction, making him wonder what had brought her to this far corner of Italy. She wasn't the backpacker he'd taken her for. Perhaps she'd left as much out of their conversation last night as he had. 'At least you aren't making assumptions,' she mumbled.

'Was there some kind of misunderstanding? About us?'

'Oh boy, was there ever!' she said emphatically. 'I tried to clear it up, but they wouldn't listen! I wanted to knock their stubborn heads together!'

He smiled faintly. 'You sound like you've got to know them well already. But I don't understand why they think you're my... you know.'

Her brows rose. 'You can't even say the word "girlfriend"?'

'Apparently not,' he said flatly.

'It was not my fault,' she insisted. 'We were both clear what last night was about and it wasn't a grand romance. But I assume you were right to be wary of your nosy neighbours? Berengario said he saw you... in the doorway as I was leaving. Does he live here or something?'

Mortification shivered down his spine. 'No, but *his* girlfriend does. *Damn it!*' He should never have brought Julia back here, even though the alternative would have been the walk of shame past Maria Grazia.

'I told them it was just casual – I even said "just sex" at one point because they didn't seem to be listening.'

Alex choked, imagining how that one had gone down with Berengario – and Maddalena! Puh, it was a mess! He'd been trying for years to get them to stop worrying about him and now this!

'Perhaps it would have been best if we hadn't—' He cut himself off when he caught the flinch she tried to hide. 'I didn't mean it like that,' he tried – but how had he meant it? 'I am... happy to see you again,' he added, rather annoyed to have to admit that to himself when he'd been stuffing those feelings away in favour of something more constructive.

She chuckled as though she didn't believe him and patted his arm. 'Yeah, sure. It's okay. If you have a spare room, then I'll stay tonight, but I'll get out of your hair tomorrow.'

'Get out of my—?'

'I'll find another solution in the morning.' Her voice trailed off as she spoke.

'A solution to what?'

'My life!' she said with a groan.

He eyed her, picking up on that world-weariness again, along with a hint of desperation that disturbed him. 'There's plenty of space upstairs,' he reassured her. 'The only thing is—' Ah, he hadn't thought this through properly. 'The plumbing up there isn't working.'

To his surprise, she laughed – full and throaty, bringing back memories of the night before. 'What is it with the plumbing in this place? No water will be an improvement on too much water at Due Pini. I can come down here for a tap.'

'The bathroom too. You'll have to use mine.'

'I promise to use water sparingly and not leave my shaver lying around.'

'That's not what I—' He cut himself off, catching her twitch of a smile. 'Let's go find you a room.'

'Thank you,' she said through pursed lips. 'Just for tonight – I promise.'

He glanced over his shoulder as he grabbed a set of keys and headed for the stairs. 'This is the second night in a row you've promised to leave tomorrow.'

Her response was a sigh. 'I didn't imagine leaving could be this hard.'

9

After the shades of vexation she'd seen on Alex's face that afternoon, Jules was deeply uncertain about whether she should have taken him up on the offer of accommodation. Her bank balance would thank her, but his reluctance to play host couldn't have been clearer. Her decision to come to the middle of nowhere appeared to have backfired spectacularly, and it took constant effort to stuff back down the panic when she was reminded that her free accommodation had fallen through.

She'd never guessed that the whole building was Alex's home – although he hadn't mentioned if he owned or rented it. Three more floors existed above the small apartment she'd glimpsed last night between kisses – kisses she needed to stop thinking about, so they could get back to being 'not' anything before more of his acquaintances came to the wrong conclusion and refused to be talked out of it.

Alex was obviously embarrassed that there had been witnesses. It was a shame, since she had some rather nice memories of his bare chest from last night. In fact, it was rather distracting, watching him climb the stairs in front of her. He was wearing a pullover that was fine enough to show the lines of his shoulders and from there, her brain skipped right back to the memory of him shirtless.

At the top of the stairs, they arrived in a dim corridor with a creaky wooden floor, lined with furniture from several past lives, including a globe that looked old enough to show Australia as New Holland and a rocking chair that would probably disintegrate into wicker shards if anyone actually sat on it.

Alex breathed a sigh of relief when the hallway sconces flicked on, although the light was weak and dim. It was cool up here – cold, even, now the temperature outside had fallen after the mild autumn day. Peering into the room he unlocked, Jules only saw a bed, and she could have wept for joy after the ways she'd imagined seeing out this night.

But Alex closed the door again quickly. 'Not that one,' he said, locking it again.

'Is that where your housemate the vampire lives? The one that protects you from the zombie neighbours?'

'You're going to give yourself nightmares,' he commented, giving her a dubious glance that had no business looking so good on him. 'I haven't aired any of these rooms in…'

She waited for him to finish, but he just got a dismayed look on his face and stopped talking.

'Don't worry. I can air it. And I can pay for—'

'Don't even suggest it,' he said, his tone so sharp it made her stand up straight. She wasn't sure what he'd done with her smiling co-conspirator from last night, but this serious, rather bossy version of Alex was… actually just as attractive, unfortunately.

'This house used to be a B & B, but a long time ago,' he explained.

'Now it's musty, but allows you to take in stray women whose dogs are your biggest fan.'

Moving to the next door, he said, 'You make it sound like it's happened before, but *nobody* has been in here for years.'

She waited as long as she could, but he didn't elaborate. 'So the vampire thing could be true. You don't know for certain.'

He wisely ignored her, opening the next door after trying out several different keys. When he switched the light on, dust motes swam in the air from the frilly fabric lampshade. An equally frilly bedspread covered the bed and a dark hardwood wardrobe filled one corner. Arco immediately went to work learning the smells of the room.

'I suppose I can go to Narnia if all else fails,' she mumbled to herself, running her fingers along the rustic joinery.

'Better than Transylvania?' Alex replied with a frown, as though his own joke were an unwelcome surprise. There was a heaviness to him that definitely hadn't been there the night before. Had he had a bad day? 'I'll get you some fresh bedding and air out the room while you shower if you like?'

'I can make the bed,' she insisted as he wrestled with the stiff fastenings to open the double windows and then push out the shutters. She dumped her backpack, taking her battered laptop case carefully out of the top and placing it on the bed before rummaging for fresh undies and her threadbare pyjamas. 'Thanks for this. Really,' she added without looking at him.

'Psht,' was his only response. 'I'll find the Wi-Fi password for you. And I'm not sure how well this radiator works. You'll have to let me know if you're cold.'

'Thanks. I'll be fine.'

Half an hour later, she tiptoed out of the bathroom feeling slightly more human and ready to collapse into bed and sleep off her bad decisions. Her stomach rumbled, but she didn't have the energy – or the cash flow – to go out and find something to eat.

The kitchen door was open a crack, sending a narrow shaft of light into the hall. A little wet nose appeared and Arco nuzzled his way out, tail wagging as though she'd just made his day by appearing after an absence of ten minutes. As soon as she stroked her hand over his woolly head and neck, he pressed himself into her, demanding more petting.

'We'd better get you some dinner,' she crooned.

'He's already eaten the cat's food.'

She glanced up to find Alex standing in the kitchen door, a tea towel over his shoulder and another frown on his lips.

'Oh, shit! I'm sorry!'

'You'll have to apologise to Attila, not me,' he said. He gestured into the kitchen with a lift of his chin. 'Come have something to eat.'

Opening her mouth to protest that he didn't have to cook for her, she instead took a breath of the most divine scent of red onion and salted meat, and nothing could have stopped her feet from taking her straight into the kitchen.

'We shouldn't be taking advantage of you,' she insisted weakly as she took a seat at the small table. 'Or Attila,' she added, looking around for the cat, but there was no sign of his bushy tail.

'It's only polenta soup. It's no trouble to reheat a little more broth. And the cat has gone out to terrorise the night-time wildlife.'

'Broth? You make it sound like food for needy orphans, but it smells like paradise in here.'

'You're my needy orphan for the night, hmm?'

He placed a ceramic bowl in front of her, full of creamy soup topped with pancetta. The bowl was painted with tiny blue flowers and beige stripes and had two little handles on the side.

Grabbing the spoon like a starving woman, she nearly dug in then and there, but she felt Alex's gaze and remembered her manners, setting the spoon down again, her cheeks hot.

'Bon pitìc,' he said with a hint of a smile – the closest he'd come to one since she'd seen him again that evening. 'Our version of "buon appetito". Don't wait. You look like a wolf.'

'A dog, a cat *and* a wolf. You've got a menagerie tonight.'

She sipped her first spoonful and stifled a groan. 'Wow,' she mumbled, taking another spoonful. 'This soup could put the entire world to rights.'

Alex took his seat opposite her with a doubtful smile. Tugging a cork out of a bottle of white wine that was already open, he poured a small amount into two glasses. 'Cure the world with polenta and radicchio? You sound like an Italian grandmother.'

'Radicchio? Is that the taste I couldn't work out? I didn't think I liked it.' With a pinch of discomfort, she remembered Luca's mamma constantly trying to educate her palate.

'It has the amaro taste – bitterness. Perhaps it takes some getting used to. Cooking it takes some of the bitterness away, but I enjoy it raw.'

'Perhaps I have enough bitterness,' Jules joked, taking another spoonful of soup and hoping he didn't ask why.

'Here in Friûl we appreciate bitterness,' was all he said, propping his chin on his fist. 'Sometimes life is hard. Bitter is one of many natural flavours.' With a thoughtful frown, he picked up his wine glass for a sip.

She took note for the first time of the strange wine glasses. Although the stem was conventional, the top part was made of green glass. Peering at her own, she said, 'Are these genuine seventies vintage? It kind of looks like we're drinking absinthe.'

'They came with the place,' he explained. 'The bowls too, although none of them match.' He gestured to his own soup bowl which was decorated with colourful, swirling flowers and leaves, along with a sentence in a straight, sharp script.

'Benvignûts in cjase nestre,' she read out, squinting. 'Benvenuto in casa nostra?' she guessed.

'Benvenuti a casa nostra in standard Italian,' he corrected with a nod. 'Welcome to our house – or *my* house in this case.' The smile he gave her was tight and puzzling.

'Well, thank you for putting me up for the night,' she said, raising her glass. 'So, this place was a B & B? How did you end up here?'

'I inherited it,' he explained. 'But it's a long story. It's been nearly ten years since the business operated.'

'Have you thought about starting it up again?' Not that it was a simple thing to just open a B & B, she thought bleakly.

His grimace seemed to match her thoughts. 'Sometimes it's easier to leave things be.' He sipped his soup without looking at her, a shadow over his eyes that made Jules think about 'nots' and bitterness and hard times. He was a puzzle of a man. His fingers were blunt and his hands a little raw, with specks of something dark under the fingernails. He'd arrived home with an accordion case and he'd inherited an old B & B from someone he didn't want to mention and his family – at least she thought he'd called Maddalena 'zia' for aunt – seemed keen to imagine him together with any old stranger who turned up in his life and insisted they'd only had casual sex.

Perhaps he was right and it would have been less awkward if they hadn't slept together the night before. Now her stomach was full, her mind kept snagging on the memory of his mouth on hers until she was worried she was staring at his lips. They were nice ones – the bottom lip full and soft – contrasting with the light scratch of his trimmed moustache and beard.

'What about you?' he asked.

'You mean why am I at the very edge of Italy with all of my physical possessions stuffed in a backpack and only a dog for company?'

'Exactly.' Propping his elbows on the table, he leaned forward, his expression making her wonder again where his smiles from last night had gone.

'That's also a long story,' she mumbled, eyeing him pointedly. 'But I'm trying to leave Italy.'

'Trying to?'

'I told you I lived in Parma for three years... well... now it's time to go home, except I'm at the mercy of the government. I don't have a current passport. I'm officially Italian now, but I only have a certificate to prove it. It should only take two weeks to process the application once I've got an address for them to send it to, but until then I'm in a bureaucratic black hole with no savings.'

'Which is why you were supposed to work on Maddalena's farm.'

'Yeah,' she agreed with a sigh. 'But apparently the room for workers at Due Pini could electrocute me, so that won't work out. I just seem to stumble from one disaster to another. I spent today hauling water so the group booking at the restaurant could go ahead. I didn't sign up for a bodybuilding boot camp.'

She flexed her arm for emphasis, but he ignored the joke.

'Wasn't there someone in Parma you could have stayed with?'

'Well that someone is the reason I'm "not",' she said, catching his eye.

'Ah.' Alex looked as though he wanted to say more, his lips moving from uncertainty to a concerned pout. 'He didn't... Are you all right?'

'Yes, I'm not on the run. You don't need to beat anyone up.'

He choked on a sip of wine.

'We wouldn't want you to damage those accordion hands.'

This time he coughed and spluttered.

'Do I need to pat you on the back?' she continued while he got his breath back. 'I thought you liked my jokes.'

When he met her eye, instead of the warmth from the night before, there was a sheen of dismay over his expression that made her neck prickle with disappointment. 'I use these hands for lots of things – not just playing the accordion, you know.'

'Oh, I know,' she teased him with a wink, even though she knew she was poking the bear. Apparently he *didn't* like her jokes today.

'That— I... That wasn't what I meant. I just thought I should mention my real job. I work in a bike shop – bicycles. I repair them.'

'I thought you were a bad busker!'

'Thanks,' he muttered.

'No, I mean you didn't even have a hat set out for money.'

'It's one of the places people don't usually mind me practising. Siore Cudrig – Signora Cudrig – in the building across the court-yard yells at me if I play here when she's trying to take a nap.'

'She must be one of the vampires! Have you ever actually seen her in daylight?'

'Yes, I have. She hangs her washing every Wednesday after-noon at one o'clock.'

'She probably also saw you half-naked in your doorway last night, right? I bet she wanted to put her fangs in that!' She should probably have taken pity on him and stopped cracking jokes, but she was too tired to filter herself.

Then he laughed. It wasn't much more than a chuckle, but when relief washed over her, she realised how much his reserve had confused her.

'Don't come running to me when you wake up from your bad

dream,' he said drily, as though he didn't realise what pictures that put into her head. 'So, you're an Australian-Calabrian Volpi just waiting for a passport so you can leave your ancestral home again?'

'Volp*e*,' she corrected him glumly, staring into her soup. 'A homeless, penniless, jobless Australian-Calabrian Volpe.'

'Julia Volpe.' It felt as though he were trying out the shape of her full name on his lips. Giving her a short, rueful smile, he held out his hand over the top of their bowls. 'Nice to meet you properly, Julia Volpe. I'm Alessandro Mattelig.'

She took his hand haltingly. 'Huh. Wow.'

'Hmm?'

She should let go of his hand but her thoughts had got stuck. 'I suppose I... Last night was so wonderfully out of normal time, I keep assuming you don't exist except as a perfect figment of my imagination, like I've hit rock bottom, so I invented you to make me feel better. But you have a full name. You exist.'

'I do,' he ventured doubtfully. 'At least, I think I do. Are we ever really certain about that?'

'I couldn't have made you up.' She hadn't imagined after the past year that she could still feel that warm tingle when she looked at someone. She didn't have the optimism for that. 'I've never heard your surname before, so I couldn't have made it up.'

She was relieved Alex didn't look concerned that she'd lost her marbles. He just studied her and said, 'I know what you mean. Last night felt imaginary. But here you are – again.' He didn't look happy about it and she wished she weren't so disappointed that he hadn't been as drawn to her as she'd been to him.

'I really appreciate you putting me up for the night,' she said, pulling her hand back from his warm, rough one. Standing, she took her plate to the sink and turned on the tap.

'Don't worry—'

'You cooked, so I should clean up,' she insisted.

But he reached around her and turned off the tap, and all she could do was go still and try to stop her knees from giving out when his presence seemed to melt her from the inside. She remembered him holding her in this kitchen last night, before she'd bolted.

'Go to bed,' he said gently. 'You've been at bodybuilding boot camp all day.'

The joke made her drop her guard and she looked up at him – bad idea. He was standing far too close and her memory was too good. Jules had made so many bad decisions in recent years, but she'd be gone for real tomorrow and what was one more kiss?

Lifting her palm to his cheek, she leaned close to press her lips softly to his.

She didn't know what she'd intended, but she hadn't expected his hand to slip around her back and haul her closer after he'd been a frowny grump all evening. But the grump kissed her back.

The kisses started slow – teasing even – but it wasn't long before she had her fingers twisted in his hair and they were both gasping for breath. He nudged her chin up to kiss her neck, a shudder racing through him. She had to fumble for the kitchen bench as her spine melted.

'Why does that feel so good?' she mumbled, her eyes falling shut.

She shouldn't have said anything because he stopped abruptly, pressing his cheek briefly to hers before drawing away.

'I don't know,' he said flatly. 'I didn't mean to do that again.'

His words prickled over her with misgiving and she dropped her hands, grasping his pullover to steady herself – steady both of them. Glancing at the kitchen window with its gauzy lace half-curtains, she almost expected to see Berengario peering in.

Alex was real – a man with his own life and family, his own

secrets. He wasn't an anonymous accordion player whom she'd asked out on a whim and then had the most unexpected, wonderful date with.

'We shouldn't then,' she forced out, stepping away firmly. 'Thank you for dinner. Goodnight,' she murmured and ran for her room before she did something else stupid.

Tucked up in bed fifteen minutes later, she congratulated herself on her sensible behaviour as consolation for the cold and rather lumpy bed. The radiator was more lukewarm than hot, but she couldn't go back down and ask Alex or she might find him half-dressed and looking ridiculously attractive. Arco lay across the door which would have been sweet if it had been out of protective instincts, but Jules suspected it was because he wanted to go back downstairs into the warmth – maybe even to Alex, the traitor.

Despite her conviction that she'd done the right thing, she slept poorly. She awoke several times thinking she heard the faint ghostly humming of an accordion. Once she dropped into a deep sleep, she had vivid dreams, although whether they were of zombies and vampires she didn't remember in the morning.

All she did have when she woke up was the lingering panic about the state of her life and the stab of regret that she'd stopped kissing Alessandro Mattelig.

10

———

Alex snapped awake quickly the following morning, relieved to hear the thump of footsteps above him. Good, she hadn't left yet. By the time he'd pulled on some clothes and wrenched his bedroom door open, she was coming down the stairs, backpack in place, holding Arco's lead.

'Where are you going?' he blurted out. *Without saying goodbye.*

'Arco needs to go outside so I thought I'd just...'

She looked pale, with shadows under her eyes, as though she'd slept as poorly as he had. She had a lot on her mind. It probably wasn't because he'd been monosyllabic with her and then made a U-turn and kissed her like a fiend.

Although beating himself up for his own behaviour was probably better than the urge to look after her that kept assailing him. Right then it was the desire to make her coffee and breakfast.

He shook his head firmly. 'Go sit in the kitchen and use the Wi-Fi to make a plan for where you're going. I'll take Arco out.'

She looked at him warily, but just responded with a dry, 'Yes, sir,' and handed over the lead.

Annoyed that he felt a thousand contradictory things at once,

Alex wrenched open the apartment door with a little too much force and nearly walked into Berengario, whose hand was raised halfway to a knock.

'Oh good, I caught you,' Berengario said with a smug grin that only annoyed Alex further. 'Are you taking the dog to work? That's a good idea. Davide was at the farm yesterday and Fritz scared the life out of the poor thing.'

'What?' Alex snapped. 'The shop doesn't open for another two hours. The dog just needs to do his business, but Julia is looking for somewhere else to stay.' He glanced at the kitchen window.

Berengario's smile vanished. 'What do you mean? She's staying here. I came by to see if she wanted a lift to the farm with me this morning.'

Alex was getting very sick of being the last to understand people's stupid assumptions. 'I thought the room flooded. She can't stay at Due Pini.'

'Uffa! She is staying with *you*! Didn't you notice the woman in your home last night?'

'The woman *you* invited to stay here.'

'You looked quite happy about that last night after dinner!'

Alex's mouth snapped shut and he gritted his teeth, resisting the urge to whirl around and scowl at the kitchen window with its inadequate curtains. 'I'm getting proper blinds,' he grumbled. 'I should never have introduced you to Elena, old man. You're around too much.'

'Only when you need a kick up the arse. You're allowed to start a new relationship.'

'How many times do we *both* have to explain this: she's not my girlfriend!'

Berengario's response was an inarticulate grumble that sounded concerningly like 'We'll see about that.'

'She's leaving,' Alex insisted. 'As soon as she gets her passport, she's leaving the country.'

Berengario was undeterred. 'Until then, you have a place where she can stay.'

'Do you mean you thought I offered to have her stay here for *weeks*?'

'Of course. Why not?'

It took all of Alex's effort not to repeat Berengario's words at the top of his voice. Lifting a hand to his hair in agitation, he allowed the bouncing dog to drag him to the persimmon tree, its branches hanging low with ripening orange fruit. 'Berengario,' he said sharply, 'you know why I can't have Julia staying with me.'

'Stupido! It's been three years, son!'

'It doesn't matter if it's been three minutes! I don't want her in Gigi's house, with Laura's things.'

'Shh, she'll hear you!' Berengario said in a severe tone. 'Where's your hospitality? She has nowhere to go and Madda needs all the help she can get on the farm. You obviously like the woman,' he added with a pointed scowl.

Alex opened his mouth to protest some more, but he couldn't tell his mentor that *liking* Julia was part of the problem. That he didn't want to play house with someone warm and funny who'd made him feel something good despite his best efforts to the contrary.

But he hadn't wanted her to leave that morning with nowhere to go. It was selfish not to help her – and Aunt Maddalena – because he was still a mess. It was only two weeks – not long enough to tear him open again, surely.

Besides, she was on the rebound from what had probably been an important relationship. He wasn't the only one who couldn't embark on something... romantic. They could be friends. As long as he made sure not to kiss her against the kitchen bench ever again, he'd find a way to sleep – or at least sleep just as badly as he usually did.

'Good man!' Berengario said before Alex had even expressed his agreement. 'When the two weeks are up, you won't want her to go!'

Berengario's comment caught him in the ribs.

'Let's go tell her the good news!'

'Wait a moment,' Alex said, grasping Berengario's arm to stop him. 'You can't just tell her she can stay here. I should offer – as though it were my idea.' He stifled a grimace.

'Don't worry. I have more tact than you do.'

Berengario's idea of tact wasn't always the same as everyone else's, so it was clear what Alex needed to do. 'I'll talk to her. How about you come back in half an hour to take her out to the farm?'

'I knew this would all work out,' the old man said, the disturbing twinkle back in his eye.

When Arco whined to go back inside to his mistress, Alex headed into the house, arranging a smile on his face. The scent of coffee reached him and when he opened the door to the kitchen, Julia looked up from where she had been studying the moka pot.

'I never got the hang of these things,' she said with a grimace.

'I thought *that*, surely, would be on the citizenship test,' he said lightly, earning a scowl. She reached to take it off the heat but he shook his head and caught her forearm to stop her. 'Not yet.' They watched the moka pot together in awkward silence until it made the first gurgle. 'Now it's ready.'

She took the pot gingerly off the stove. 'Sorry that I rummaged for the coffee without asking.'

'Don't worry about it. I hope there's some for me in there?' The pair of lime green ceramic espresso cups on the table answered his question. The domesticity of the moment threatened to choke him in memories, but he pushed them away.

Julia had made coffee for him – something any of his friends would do without a second thought. It didn't mean anything.

'Right,' she said with a sigh, after taking her first sip of scalding coffee as she studied her laptop screen. 'I've found a farm not too far from here, in Veneto, but I'll have to contact them to ask if they have a space.'

'I have a suggestion,' he said, 'Maddalena needs you. I have space here. Why don't you just stay?'

She went still, her gaze wary and her mouth hanging slightly open. She had such strong features – in the way that strength and beauty were somehow on the same spectrum.

'Are you inviting me to stay *here*?'

He gave half a nod. His eyebrows wanted to betray his conflicted feelings about the invitation but he hoped he kept them still.

'Did Berengario force you into this? I saw him outside.'

'No!'

She crossed her arms and gave him an assessing look. 'Did he guilt you into it, then? You don't even need to answer that. I can see the truth in your face.'

That was concerning.

'It's all right,' she continued. 'I'm not your responsibility and I don't want to be a burden. I'll go back to Maria Grazia's place until I can find another farm—'

'Your accommodation *was* Maddalena's responsibility and I am happy to help.'

'You sound really *happy*, Alex.'

Her tone made him uncomfortable, but after everything they'd shared, it was difficult to hide the truth. 'I have a lot of space. Just stay here. Nothing else makes sense.'

'I assume you're suggesting the same sleeping arrangements as last night.'

'Of course,' he answered immediately. 'We're not... You said it too.'

Her shoulders rose and fell on an enormous sigh. 'We nearly screwed that up last night.'

He gave a cough to clear his tight throat. It was so damn flattering to think that she'd kissed him even though she hadn't meant to. That some stranger found him irresistible was both incredibly gratifying and utterly preposterous.

Oh, God, he should have made sure she stayed a stranger.

'Is the accidental kissing what you're worried about?' she prompted.

Yes! 'Of course not. A housemate arrangement is entirely separate from... that.'

For a moment, he thought she would argue and he nearly broke out in a sweat. But then she said, 'You're right,' and he could breathe again. 'I'm sure you can't be irresistible, especially since everything I do seems to make you angry.'

'I'm not angry. I'm just used to my own space to...' *Wake up in the middle of the night and wander the halls like a ghost.* '...play the accordion. It's not a peaceful instrument.'

She gave him a smile – a touch sceptical, but she didn't seem keen to ask more, which he was grateful for. 'For free accommodation, I'll put up with a lot more than a bit of hurdy-gurdy.'

'A hurdy-gurdy is an entirely different instrument. It has strings, not reeds, and you turn a crank to play it.'

She snorted a laugh. 'Sorry, I didn't mean to offend you. I didn't know a hurdy-gurdy was an actual thing.'

The tension in him slowly letting up, he managed a smile in response. 'I'll play you some recordings over dinner,' he promised with mock earnestness. 'Mood music.'

'I'm assuming the mood of a hurdy-gurdy is not calm and soothing?'

'I just hope you don't like it more than the accordion.'

'We don't need to eat dinner together. Maddalena will give me lunch at the restaurant and I'll sort myself out in the evening. I'll start my passport application tonight and I should be gone again in two weeks – three weeks tops. I won't take advantage of you and you won't even know I'm here.'

That sounded like wishful thinking. 'You're not taking advantage of me. Maddalena and Berengario are, but they're allowed to.'

'She's your aunt?' she clarified. 'Does that make Berengario your grandfather?'

'No – well, not really. But they're definitely family.' Which was what made the situation with the one-night stand all the more awkward.

He glanced at the kitchen window, wondering if Berengario could see inside from Elena's apartment. What did the old man really think of him sleeping with a stranger? Yes, Berengario was family, so he would always be too invested in Alex's life. There were times when that interest pinched.

'But you might be right,' she added, absently patting the dog's head, where he'd laid his chin on her thigh. 'If we settle in as housemates – temporarily – then we'll probably find that all the kissing and... stuff... was so intense because of the element of mystery. Before too long we'll be arguing about how to pack the dishwasher.'

'I don't have a dishwasher,' he deadpanned, waiting as long as he could before allowing himself to smile. 'But I like the fridge arranged a particular way.'

'Oh boy, am I going to drive you crazy.'

'I'm... looking forward to it?' And unexpectedly, he really was.

11

If it was possible, Due Pini looked even more run-down than it had the day before. When Jules had imagined an organic farm with vineyards and an olive grove, she'd pictured autumn sunshine on golden leaves, smiling workers calmly going about their business and... okay, she'd had woefully little idea what awaited her.

Instead of sunshine, a heavy autumn fog settled over the vines and instead of bushy, profuse olive trees, they were wizened, squat and ghost-like in the mist, some trunks split in two with branches sticking out in all directions. Perhaps there was some truth to the notion that Friuli was not quite the same Italy as the rest.

And the happy workers? From the grumpy Maria Grazia to the austere barman the first night to blunt, straight-talking Berengario, Jules was beginning to wonder if Friulians had their own way of smiling that she hadn't decoded yet.

Even Alex, who'd been so open and laughed so much that first night, had turned into a scowling housemate, although she couldn't blame him. He hadn't expected a houseguest and even if it had pricked her to see him so obviously arguing with Berengario in the courtyard, it was his right to feel put out by the intrusion – his right to privacy.

Jules was here to earn her keep, especially now Alex had offered her somewhere to stay despite the inconvenience. She would make it worth everyone's while to host her. Maybe she could even clean up a room or two at Alex's place in the evenings so he could rent them out. She would be *useful*, damn it!

The thought of more renovations made her shudder, remembering everything that had gone wrong at the B & B. Alex probably didn't want her sloppy paint job. Tonight she'd sort out the paperwork for the postal redirection and start on her passport application. She would do her best to stay out of his way and not be any trouble.

The plumber – another wrinkled, unsmiling man – had arrived at Due Pini to look at the burst pipe, but Jules still had to haul water first so the cook could start work on lunch. Juggling Arco's lead, she almost wished she'd walked all the way to the farm that morning to run off some of his excess energy instead of accepting a lift from Berengario.

After Jules had filled the bottles and tanks in the kitchen and fetched the eggs from the tumbledown chicken coop that reminded her of the meaning of her Italian surname – fox – Maddalena hurriedly pressed the handle of a manual lawnmower into her hands and sent her off into the olive grove with harried instructions to cut the grass. As Jules made her way towards the spooky, twisted trees, she looked up to see a figure coming towards her out of the mist.

Jumping in surprise, she told herself she was being silly for thinking the figure was Death himself, complete with scythe propped over one shoulder. She thought of Alex's warning about bad dreams and she gripped Arco's harness tightly as the figure approached, wondering who Death would be coming for.

But as the face came into focus, she recognised Berengario and released a long breath.

'Are you coming?' he called out.

Approaching hesitantly, she pointed to the fierce blade hanging casually over his shoulder. 'What is that?'

A deep frown marked his brow. 'A falcet,' he said as though the answer was self-evident. 'For cutting grass. I don't know what it is in English.'

'Ah.'

'What did you think it was?' His English was surprisingly good given his age and the fact that he used a scythe like a peasant from a hundred years ago.

She couldn't exactly explain to him her weird image of Death, just as she hadn't admitted to hearing ghostly accordion sounds overnight. Her sudden departure from Parma had obviously dealt her a shock that she was still recovering from and her landing in this weird place with spartan accommodation and grumpy locals hadn't been the softest.

Except for the part where she'd landed in Alex's bed.

'I couldn't see it properly in the fog.' With a shiver, she followed Berengario into the mist, the sun creating a smoky halo over the shadowy hill.

'Are you cold? Although we are close to the sea, we have some bitter winter days here when the wind comes down from the mountains. Perhaps you need a good coat – and some better shoes.'

'Bitter,' she repeated thoughtfully. She'd never heard that word as much as she had over the past two days. 'But it's only autumn and I won't be here long.'

'If you say so,' Berengario said, his words sending another

shiver down her spine. 'But we hope the weather improves before next weekend.'

'Next weekend?' she asked as he turned back.

'The harvest!' he called over his shoulder.

Walking into the grove after him, she imagined entering a portal, emerging in an alternate timeline. Perhaps in this world Luca was a stranger to her. How wonderful that would be, if she could just erase the past three years and her youthful stupidity.

Olives hung heavy on the trees, in shades from yellowish-green to light purple. Her companion squeezed the occasional berry absently as he passed.

'I cut the long grass, you cut the short grass, hmm?' was all he said before he picked a spot and set to work.

Berengario made operating the scythe look effortless, clutching the handle halfway along the pole to slice the blade through the wet grass. Jules found the hand-push lawnmower difficult to steer and it required a shove to get it moving. Her arms ached before she'd cut a single row. To make the work even more difficult, Arco snapped at the machine every time she pushed it, making her worry that he'd cut himself. But she struggled on, knowing how desperate Maddalena and Berengario were for help.

'Try more gently. You want to keep your elbows, yes?'

Her only response was a sigh.

'Alex should have taken Arco to the shop.'

'He's my dog and Alex has already done too much for me.'

'Alex likes to help people.'

'That doesn't mean people should take advantage of him. You do understand that I'm not his girlfriend, don't you? We only just met.' With a gulp, she realised how that sounded, given everything Berengario had witnessed. 'But don't judge him for that either. It was my idea.' Eek, now she'd never be able to look the man in the eye again.

His chuckle behind her was deep and reminded her of Alex's voice. He'd said Berengario wasn't his grandfather. Perhaps he was a great-uncle or something. 'Brava! I like that, Giulietta. An audacious woman.'

His statement didn't do anything for her embarrassment, but his choice of words made her laugh. 'Reckless' was the word that had come to her mind, but 'audacious' sounded less like making mistakes and more like derring-do, as though she'd bravely – rather than awkwardly – asked Alex out on a not-date and begged for a kiss.

When they trudged back for lunch, Jules was damp to her bones, her hair plastered to her face. Stepping into the farmhouse was a blessed relief. There was a fire on the hearth in the dining room, warming the handful of lunch guests who had braved the fog.

It was a funny fireplace – surely not compliant with anyone's ideas of building regulations. Raised to waist height on a brick dais, the flames were open on three sides with a giant plastered flue hanging above. It reminded her of the fireplace in the taverna where she'd eaten with Alex.

She expected to be tucked in a corner of the kitchen and fed vegetable stew, but Berengario led her to a table in the dining room. A relieved Arco ducked under the table, bumping the chairs as he wriggled in a few circles and then plonked himself down to sleep with a doggy sigh.

'Give me your jacket,' Berengario instructed gruffly.

Shaking her head, she pulled it around herself and shivered. 'I'll keep it on.'

'It's wet. Let me put it by the fire.' Then he raised his voice and shouted something indecipherable – to Jules anyway – after which Maddalena poked her head around the archway to the kitchen and nodded in acknowledgement.

The day's special was giant slices of spiced sausage called muset and lightly fermented cooked vegetables that spoke directly to her comfort-seeking soul and even made her forget about her icy feet. After Maddalena had hauled a few more buckets of water for the cook, she appeared with a bundled-up brown canvas jacket.

'Put this on, dear. It might be a bit small, but wearing your wet coat is no good. You can borrow this.'

When Jules stuffed her arms into the thick jacket, lined with wool, some of her stress faded instantly. The sleeves were too short and it was a bit tight in the shoulders, but she could get it closed. 'Thank you. This feels so much better.'

Maddalena smiled – a tight smile that showed up the fine lines of age around her mouth – and squeezed Jules's arm before hurrying off again.

Bolstered by the cosy new jacket, Jules set to work with determination that afternoon, raking furiously to tidy up the grass they'd cut in the morning. By the time the sun was low in the sky, she was sweaty and sticky and smelled of grass clippings and hard work, and her toes were squishy and clammy and probably covered in wrinkles.

Although the sun had burnt off the fog in the late morning, damp hovered over the plain. Berengario showed no signs of leaving and she didn't want to presume he'd give her a lift, so she waved goodbye to Maddalena and headed to the wonky gate by the two pines, Arco frolicking in front of her as though he hadn't spent the whole day on a long leash sniffing around the olive trees.

Light rain fell as she trudged back along the road to town. She was so tired she understood that thing she'd read about people in mediaeval times going to bed early and then waking up in the middle of the night to socialise instead. As she glimpsed the Ponte del Diavolo ahead and the cluster of houses on the rocks, she could almost picture the people here in those times.

She needed a shower too much to live in mediaeval times though, a thought that kept her lifting her exhausted feet, one in front of the other, until she'd reached the archway into the court-yard with the broad tree laden with orange fruit – and Alex's door.

* * *

Alex was about to call Maddalena to ask what had happened to their guest when he heard the rap of the old brass knocker. He opened the door to a gust of damp wind – and a bedraggled woman and her dog. He wouldn't have been surprised if she'd keeled over right on the doorstep.

Arco leaped up in excitement, scratching at Alex's thighs and barking a joyful greeting – and leaving dark smears of mud on his jeans. That was when Alex noticed Julia was shivering – violently – and she was wearing a jacket that made his stomach drop to his toes when he recognised it.

For a moment, all he could do was stand in the doorway, paralysed.

'Can I come in?' she asked in a withering tone that finally snapped him out of his confusion. It wasn't her fault an item of clothing made him see a ghost. 'I'm a bit cold.'

'Sorry, yes. Come inside.'

His gaze kept snapping back to the jacket, noting the way the sleeves cinched an inch above the bone of her wrist. Julia had longer arms. She was taller, so it made sense. The comparisons prickled over him and he didn't want them, any of them, but he also felt terrible for Julia.

The shadows around her eyes were pronounced and her lips were cracked and wobbly, even though she kept her head high. The wary look she gave him made him suspect some of his dismay showed on his face and he swallowed the discomfort to help her out of the jacket – not *her* jacket. Hanging it on a hook next to his, the image struck him and he had to pull himself together before she started asking questions.

'I just need a shower,' she insisted after she'd slipped off her shoes. 'I'm staying out of your way. I'll just borrow your bathroom and go to bed.' Her eyes glazed over at the last part. Shaking herself, she lifted one finger and added, 'After I change my address and look at my passport application.'

She looked so tired and defeated, and he didn't like that she'd misinterpreted his wariness. But he also couldn't discuss his numerous triggers in casual conversation, especially since he'd managed to convince her so far that he was mostly normal. Settling his hands gently on her shoulders, he turned her towards the stairs. 'Go get warm. I'll feed Arco.'

With an exaggerated nod and mumbled thanks, she hauled herself up the stairs, leaving wet prints from her drenched socks on the scuffed wood. Alex frowned at the prints, which turned into a grimace when he retrieved one of her trainers from the shoe rack and found it soaking wet.

After noting the size and sending Berengario a quick message, he set Julia's shoes by the stove in the kitchen and stoked the fire. Arco inhaled his food and then scraped the bowl along the floor as he tried to lick every last morsel from the bottom. Then he settled on his blanket, peering up at Alex, his brown eyes glazed with adoration.

'He's just an animal,' Alex muttered to himself, but he smiled down at the contented dog. 'You've discovered the best place in the house. Attila isn't going to be happy.'

He considered lighting a fire in the grate on top, but that seemed excessive. Setting the frying pan back on the cooker, he quickly mixed another omelette, arranging a side plate of Caprese salad and a glass of water at the end of the table by the fire. So much for her insistence that he didn't have to feed her. When she arrived home in that state, he couldn't *not*.

When the door of the kitchen opened suddenly, he arranged a guilty expression on his face and clasped his hands, turning to face her.

'I—'

'Sorry to bother you but—'

'—wasn't supposed to but I—'

They both stopped talking.

She glanced at the table and seemed to pull herself together. She clicked her fingers to call Arco to her and the dog dragged his feet and hung his head as he left the warmth of the stove.

'I just wanted to ask if there was a way to turn up the radiator. It doesn't seem to be working very well. But... I don't want to interrupt your dinner. I'm fine after my hot shower and I'll probably just go straight to...' Her gaze snagged on her shoes, sitting neatly to dry. 'Thank you for that. You didn't have to. I'll just—'

'Wait!' He stifled a grimace. Maybe what she'd meant when she'd instructed him not to feed her was that she wanted her privacy. That was fair enough. They were *housemates*. She could do whatever she wanted. She didn't have to sit by his hearth and eat his food and she was capable of looking after herself.

'Please, eat your dinner. I don't want to disturb you.'

'You're not. I've already eaten,' he explained with an apologetic shrug. 'I know you said you don't need to eat here but cooking for one is... Allora, just have this omelette.' He flipped it hurriedly onto a plate and set it at the table with the salad, drizzling a little olive oil on both. He held out her chair, belatedly realising that was definitely too much.

She took the seat, giving him an uncertain smile while Arco joyfully curled up again by the stove. 'Thanks.'

'I'm sorry about before,' he blurted out when he couldn't stand her doubtful glances at him.

'It's okay. It's your house. You can be grumpy in it if you want.'

'No, but it's nothing to do with you,' he assured her.

Drawing herself up straight, she eyed him where he stood leaning against the kitchen bench and said, 'You don't have to apologise, Alex, and I don't want to eat your guilt food.'

'Guilt food?' he repeated.

'You're feeding me to make yourself feel better. Actually I am going to eat your guilt food because I am starving and this looks like the tastiest meal I have ever eaten.' She cut a strip of omelette while he tried not to smile and eventually failed. 'And I had those amazing sausages for lunch, so that's saying something.'

'It's not guilt food,' he insisted, although he was wondering if she was right. 'You're no use to Maddalena tired and hungry. We have to keep you healthy until the olive harvest. And there's cheese in the omelette too. I know how much you like cheese.'

She stuffed the first bite into her mouth and sighed deeply, her shoulders drooping as she chewed. 'God, this is perfect: the protein; the cheese; the fire – wow, the *fire*.' Tipping her head back she slumped in her chair, visibly relaxing.

'The fireplace is the heart of a Furlan's house,' he commented.

'Well, thank you for inviting me into your...' She wisely let that sentence go.

'We have a special word – fogolâr – for the old open fireplaces,' he continued, trying to cover her faux pas. 'We don't have fancy dining rooms for guests when the best place is here in the kitchen,' he finished, averting his gaze from her soft, tired features.

'Why does this omelette taste so good? What's that zing in it?'

'Forest garlic,' he supplied. 'We pick it in spring and freeze it for the rest of the year. There's a patch at Maddalena's and in the woods nearby.'

'Forest garlic,' she repeated, peering at her omelette before placing the next piece in her mouth. 'I don't even know what that is.'

'We call it bear garlic too, but I don't know the name in English.'

Glancing at him as she fumbled to cut another piece of omelette, she said, 'Are you going to sit down or just talk to me from over there?'

Despite the awkward domesticity, the uncertain friendship, he couldn't pull out the chair fast enough. Perhaps the guilt food was working.

12

Jules collapsed into bed as soon as she made it upstairs. Arco settled on his blanket and she thought, as she sank into drowsiness, that at least being bedraggled and smelling faintly of grass and nearly falling asleep at the table made kissing less of a temptation for both of them. It was only a shame that in return, he'd cooked her comfort food and stoked a fire that had felt like a hug. Except there hadn't been any hugs. Only a horrified look when he'd seen the borrowed jacket and his obvious reluctance to share why.

She didn't mind the guilt food thing. It was kind of sweet that he took care of her to make up for being less than hospitable, and she truly didn't blame him for occasionally resenting his unwanted guest and being reluctant to tell his life story to a stranger. If only she hadn't been so sleepy she could have looked into her passport application. Perhaps she'd wake up early and make a start.

But instead of waking refreshed with the first streaks of dawn sunlight, she roused in total darkness at some point in the night – freezing cold darkness. She'd forgotten to get Alex to look at the heating. The night-time temperature had dropped, and whatever radiant warmth the stove in the kitchen had sent up the chimney breast in the corner of the room was long gone.

Paralysed in indecision for a moment, she eventually accepted that she was wide awake and needed to at least pull on another jumper. When she slid her legs to the floor, the edge of the bed was so cold it gave her a shock. The radiator wasn't working at all.

Tugging out her thickest fleece and an extra pair of old, loose tracksuit bottoms, she padded downstairs to the bathroom, trailed by a curious Arco, and she imagined they both threw a longing glance at the kitchen door, even though that blessed fire in the stove wouldn't be flickering any more.

On her way back upstairs, she heard the ghostly hum again and froze. It sounded like an accordion, but distant and eerie, as though heard through a portal in time. Even though she called herself all kinds of idiot for feeling spooked, the hairs on the back of her neck stood on end, and images of the twisted olive trees and Berengario with his scythe and Alex's pale, stunned face when she came home in that jacket, mixed with the wheezy, breathy accordion soundtrack until her heart pounded.

A sliver of light shone under a door in the hallway she'd not taken note of before and with the vague sense that she was in a dream, she headed for it and gave it a sharp knock, turning the handle and peering inside.

'Julia? Everything okay?'

It took her eyes a moment to adjust to the light and then... Oh dear, she needed to wake up from this dream. Alex wasn't supposed to keep getting *more* attractive the longer they lived together. He sat on a stool at a scratched and pockmarked table, a set of tools laid out – apparently for performing surgery on accordions, if the one flayed open in front of him was anything to go by. He held a tiny screwdriver in one hand and a complex-looking wooden frame in the other. His wavy hair was mussed, his old sweater looked soft and had a couple of inviting-looking holes. And he had a pair of wire-rimmed glasses perched on his nose.

Just when she'd thought this man couldn't get any cuter, she discovered he wore glasses.

Arco trotted over to him and began enthusiastically licking his knee while Alex peered doubtfully at him with a puzzled smile on his lips – a gorgeous, puzzled smile. With a blur of white, the cat jumped down from the table and fled past her ankles.

Only when the silence stretched and Alex's gaze returned questioningly to hers did she remember he'd asked her a question.

'Yeeeessss, I'm fine, just... seeing things and—' Seeing things like Death in the mist and an adorable accordion doctor with fine, strong hands and bright blue eyes. She shook herself.

He rose and came around the workbench to where she was standing. 'Do you have a fever?'

'No,' she insisted, 'I—' His fingers on her forehead stole any words she might have uttered in explanation. What did come out of her lips was something entirely unhelpful. 'Those glasses look so hot on you.'

His gaze flew to hers in surprise as she clapped a hand over her mouth. 'I took my contacts out.' Tugging the glasses off, he rubbed his forehead self-consciously.

'No, keep them on,' she insisted, the damage done now so she might as well make it worthwhile. He eyed her as he slipped them on again, and even that was attractive. 'What are you doing still up? I don't even know what time it is.'

'I'm trying to repair this for a student,' he explained, taking the opportunity to step safely behind the bench again. 'It's making a phantom sound.'

Jules burst out laughing and he stared at her again, mystified. 'A phantom sound is a very good description. I heard it last night too and it put me in the weirdest mood. I'm imagining ghosts everywhere.'

He gave her a strange look that reminded her of the way he'd looked at her when she'd arrived home from the farm that day. 'You're not the first person to suggest this accordion is haunted,' he muttered. 'But I think it's only haunting me.' He stretched, making his sleeves pull up over his forearms. 'There must be a stuck pin somewhere but there are so many little things out of place in here I can't find it.'

She peered at the carcass of the instrument, spread out on the table. The bellows, the vinyl concertina part in the middle, had been set carefully to one side and the two wooden ends taken apart to reveal a complex mesh of pins and valves.

'These are the reeds,' he explained, pointing to a set of metal strips in a wooden frame. 'When the air moves along them, they vibrate and that's how the sound is produced.' Picking up one end to show her the grid of round buttons, he pressed a couple and little hatches opened and closed on the other side. 'The pallets control the air flow to the reeds and that's how you choose which note to play.'

'It's like a little machine and you're a midnight mechanic.'

He gave a shrug in agreement.

'At least your workshop is warm,' she commented, pressing the backs of her fingers to her cheeks.

He glanced up sharply. 'Your radiator wasn't working. You said something earlier and I forgot.'

'I forgot too,' she admitted. 'And I fell asleep fine at first.'

'But now you're freezing,' he finished for her, getting to his feet again and selecting a pair of pliers from the toolbox on the workbench. 'I hope it's just the valve. Let's have a look.'

While Alex inspected the radiator, Jules's gaze wandered to his hunched figure in her room, drawn to study him. As she leaned over to peer at what he was doing at the radiator, she noticed he had an indentation in his earlobe, suggesting he'd had his ear pierced at some point, which only reminded her of the many things she didn't know about him.

He got the knob of the radiator off and tugged gently at the pin with the pliers. The radiator gurgled and then warmth began to flow into the unit – to Jules's relief and also, she guessed, to Alex's, if his deep exhale was anything to go by.

Glancing over his shoulder at her, he froze to find her leaning close. Jules told herself sternly to move away, except her brain was sluggish with questions about why he was awake in the middle of the night, why he looked at her with such a pained expression sometimes, when she'd thought they'd had fun the night they'd been together.

She was so close she saw his throat move as he swallowed and could pick up the scent of him. *Move away.* She was supposed to be granting him privacy, not smelling the mix of woodsy cologne and old accordions that she found strangely compelling.

He drew back so suddenly that she had to clutch his sleeve for balance, then prised her fingers open again before he thought she was trying to pull him closer. He stood as soon as she released him.

'I—' she began, as she scrambled to her feet as well. 'Sorry I was—' Running an agitated hand through her hair, she noticed his eyes drift there and suspected she looked desperately unkempt – even more of a mess than she usually did. 'I was just —' She tried again, but with him regarding her expectantly from behind those gorgeous glasses, she could barely remember what she'd been doing leaning so close. '*Smelling the scent of old accor-*

dion and sexy cologne on you' wouldn't do. 'I was watching so I can fix it myself if it happens again. I don't want to be any trouble.'

His brow knit and his sigh came from deep inside him as he rubbed a hand over his face. 'It's not your fault,' was all he said.

'I know, but I still don't want to be a burden.'

'You don't understand,' he continued. 'I lost someone – important. It was a while ago, but it hit hard and I needed to be alone—'

He looked so dismayed that Julia's stomach twisted and plummeted. 'You don't have to talk to me about it. Something to do with the jacket, right?'

He nodded.

'I'll give it back to Maddalena tomorrow.'

'God, no! Use it. And don't work yourself to the bone like you did today. I don't want to feel guilty about that on top of everything else.'

It was a shame he was such an adorable grump. Something of her thoughts must have shown on her face because he bolted for the door with a mumbled, 'It's warm now.'

'Are you—?' she began before she could stop herself. He turned to her warily. 'Are you going to be able to sleep?'

His answer was an eloquent shrug, his fingers open and hesitant and although Jules didn't know his situation, the vulnerability in the gesture was clear and shot straight to her heart. 'We'll see,' was all he said.

'Buonanotte,' she said, hurrying him off before she started wishing he'd stay.

'Buine gnot,' he replied quietly, turning away before she could ask him to repeat the words in Furlan so she could learn them.

When she was wrapped in blankets in bed and trying to stop her thoughts from spiralling with suspicions and assumptions, she glanced at her phone, charging on the bedside table. It was past two o'clock.

* * *

She tiptoed downstairs the following morning, a pacifying hand on Arco's back to keep him quiet, but despite her attempts not to make any noise, they were greeted in the kitchen by a hiss and the clang of pots and pans as the cat ran for his life, zipping past in a furry white blur.

'Shit,' Jules muttered, righting the pans and glancing warily back down the hallway. When Alex's door opened and he appeared, utterly rumpled and wearing only a pair of loose cotton boxer shorts, she felt triply guilty for enjoying the sight.

Wrenching her eyes away, she hurriedly set the coffee on, determined to get out of his way as soon as she could. He didn't come into the kitchen until fifteen minutes later, when she'd grabbed some toast and slugged her coffee. Slipping past him into the hallway and definitely not noticing the scent of his soap, she legged it for the door, pausing only to give him an awkward wave because it felt rude not to acknowledge him at all.

Safely out at Due Pini, she accepted both her mission for the day – which would mostly involve washing and sterilising steel tanks in preparation for the new oil – and a pair of worn, sturdy boots that belonged to Maddalena's son, Davide. She hesitated before heading into the storage lean-to by the farmhouse – long enough even for Maddalena to notice.

'What's wrong, dear?' the older woman asked.

'Are you sure it's okay for me to borrow this jacket? I got the impression from Alex... Now you have that look on your face too. I don't want to keep reminding people of someone who—' Oops, she was making it worse, if Maddalena's stricken expression was anything to go by.

'Alex told you? About Laura?'

'He...'

Maddalena grasped her arm in a firm grip. 'He needed to. If he's going to keep living in the past like this, then at least he should explain himself. We've been so worried about him, but it's not your fault.'

'That's what he said,' Jules mumbled, feeling that somehow the opposite was still true.

'We just all want to see him smiling again. It's been so long.'

'He smiles,' Jules insisted. Her memories of their not-date were vivid and he'd definitely smiled. She could still remember the way his deep laugh had tingled over her skin. 'At least I've seen it on occasion,' she added – just no occasions since she'd moved in with him.

'Good,' Maddalena said with a look that was a touch too hopeful. But before Jules could protest – again – that there wasn't anything romantic between her and Alex, the older woman continued briskly, 'I'm glad the jacket is useful. You've been such a help already. I don't know what we would have done without you.'

If Maddalena only knew how good those words made her feel. A grin spread across her face – which abruptly died when the older woman continued with a humph, 'And it's not as though my sister will come back for the jacket.'

Her sister... If she was Alex's aunt, could Maddalena mean his *mother*? He'd inherited the building, returned home from London. If Jules lost her mother, she'd be in a state too. She had suspected something else, but losing his mother made sense.

But it was clear that Jules should keep her questions to herself and get on with work – and her escape from Italy. This family's grief wasn't any of her business.

13

———

Julia was avoiding him.

While Alex could see it was only natural, given his inability to deal with the various sources of awkwardness with his new housemate, he was disappointed every time she quickly escaped the dinner table and when she disappeared with Arco all of Sunday. His disappointment made no sense, because he didn't want the domesticity to begin with, and he only cooked for her because he wasn't certain she'd eat a thing if he didn't.

She appeared at the door of his workroom on Monday evening and he stood in surprise almost as quickly as Attila leaped, panicking, off the table and out of the room.

'I never see him properly,' she commented. 'I wouldn't recognise him in a missing cat poster.'

'I hope he never goes missing,' Alex blurted out.

'Oh, shit. Oops, I'm sorry. Nothing's going to happen to your cat. Sometimes I think I can see ghosts, but I can't tell the future.'

'You can see ghosts?'

She groaned. 'I'm joking. It's Halloween soon and there must be something in the water. Is the haunted accordion still haunted?'

'It's not working yet.'

'I won't take up too much of your time, but I need a little help with the Italian on my application form. It'll get me out of here sooner.'

With a disapproving huff at her continued insistence that she was a burden, he nodded and followed her into the kitchen, where she'd set up her laptop.

'I've requested a postal redirection because changing my address would require official proof that I live here. I can do the application now. I've completed the form for my Australian passport renewal, which was complicated enough, but this Italian one...'

'Okay. I'll make sure your name is on the post box – and the doorbell, just in case.'

'Thanks. You know how to spell my surname by now?'

He nodded. 'Calabrian Volpe. Did you come to Italy because of your family history?'

She glanced at him as though surprised he was making casual conversation, but he didn't want to pretend he wasn't interested. 'No,' was the only answer she gave initially. With another wary glance at him, she continued bitterly, 'I came to Italy for a man.' Clearing her throat, she pointed out the instructions causing confusion. 'I'm not sure what I'm logging in for here.'

Skimming the text, he said, 'You have to make an appointment with the state police in Parma.'

'Damn it,' she whispered, rubbing the heel of her hand over her forehead. He noticed an angry red mark on her thumb, probably from a popped blister. He frowned at the evidence that she was still working too hard in a position she wasn't being paid for.

'If you make an appointment for the afternoon, you can probably go and come back in one day. Look, there's one available next week. I can take care of Arco.'

'Oh, God, of course I can't take him to the appointment. But he's got his passport at least – his EU dog passport,' she joked. She paused, biting her lip, then muttered, 'Thanks for offering to help. Maybe I should have stayed in Parma, rather than cause all this trouble.'

He wondered briefly how he would have felt if he'd been stuck in London after everything had gone wrong. 'Sometimes reacting is all you can do.'

Her expression was pinched. 'Yeah, but there are constructive reactions and irrational reactions and coming here to the middle of nowhere is feeling more and more irrational.'

He couldn't resist chiding her gently. 'The middle of nowhere is somewhere for the people who live there.' He was rewarded with an apologetic glance from her pretty eyes.

'I didn't mean to imply otherwise. But I survived a year of living with him after we broke up and surely I could have survived another two weeks for the sake of my bank account.'

'You lived together after breaking up?'

'That awkward situation is what I got for moving to a foreign country for a brand-new relationship that wasn't ready for that step. Everyone I knew in Parma was a friend of *his*. I didn't have anywhere else to go – as I've unfortunately proven by getting into this mess! God, I hope I don't run into him.' She dropped her hand and Arco came immediately, nuzzling her leg. 'That's what I got for moving to Italy for *love*.'

The disdain in her voice as she said that last word was clear and he wasn't sure what to say in reply. A haze at the edge of his vision warned him against drawing parallels, even though his heart wanted to remind him of what he'd done for *love*, especially during the worst moment of his life.

His gaze zeroed in instead on the form she was filling out in her browser. 'Your birthday is November 12? That's soon.' He wondered why she'd felt so much younger when he was only three years older than her nearly twenty-eight. To be honest, everyone felt younger than him most days – even Berengario, with his new girlfriend and the spring in his step.

'If I'm still here then, you'll be desperate to get rid of me!' Her sigh was deep.

'If you're still here then Due Pini will be spotless with everything in working order,' he commented lightly in reply. When she stared at him blankly, he brushed his thumb over the raw patch of skin on her palm. 'Don't work yourself too hard.' He dropped her hand again in a hurry.

'I think you overestimate the contribution I can make,' she said drily. 'Do you know why I chose Due Pini from the list of farms to contact?' she asked. 'Because it was the farthest I could easily get from *Italy*, while staying in Italy.' Her laugh was pained. 'As far away as I could get from *him* without crossing a country border.'

'The rest of Italy might view Friuli as the middle of nowhere, but the Furlans know this is the crossroads of Europe. And your problems don't worry us. We have a word, cumbinìn. It means we join together and find a way. You're helping us. Let us help you.'

He'd said too much. She was watching him with so much scepticism in her gaze that he wondered what her ex had put her through before she'd been brave enough to leave.

'Do you need help with the rest of the form?' he asked, needing to change the subject before the glint in her smooth, brown eyes took him right back to their not-date. 'Look, colore occhi: eye colour,' he pointed out absently on the screen. 'This says you need to put "M" for "marroni".' A faint smile touched his lips. 'Do you know, as well as meaning brown, "marroni" is a word for the very sweet chestnuts?' His smile faded as soon as he realised what he'd said.

When he risked a glance at her, she lifted her eyebrows and gave him an amused smile that sent heat up the back of his neck. He was surprised he'd managed to sit next to her for this long and continue breathing normally, so the tightness in his chest shouldn't have been unexpected.

He stood to put some distance between them. 'I'll... um... The accordion? You don't need any more help, do you?' He barely waited for her to shake her head before he bolted.

When he escaped the kitchen and saw the jackets hanging on the hooks by the door, the sight stopped him cold. He'd managed to *forget* for a moment why he shouldn't risk getting attached to Julia. The guilt that washed in with that realisation was almost as bad as the ache when he saw the jacket.

No matter how many times Berengario winked at him, even if her eyes were pretty and his skin tingled every time she was in the room, the best thing for both of them was to get her out of Italy before those tingles turned into something real – something that could hurt.

* * *

He took Berengario to task on Thursday evening as they drove to choir rehearsal. 'Do you have any idea how tired she is every evening? Does Maddalena? She's working too hard – for no pay!'

'Are you sure she doesn't have Friulian heritage?' was all Berengario said in reply.

'No, Calabrian Volpe apparently.'

'I think she has Friulian heritage. Hard worker, that girl. Like she belongs here.'

Alex stifled a groan.

'If not with you, maybe with Davide.'

Not Davide... He'd never got on well with Maddalena's son and he couldn't help thinking Davide wouldn't appreciate Jules, but Berengario knew that. God, the old man knew how to press his buttons. 'She's not here for your matchmaking service.'

'It's not impossible that she'd fall in love with Davide. It was quite funny when they met. The dogs went wild and she fell over. It would make a good story to tell their grandchildren. Perhaps a little matchmaking is a good idea.'

'She's not falling in love with Davide or anyone else!'

The small smile Berengario didn't manage to hide showed Alex he'd fallen into the trap. 'But I thought you two weren't together,' he said smugly.

'We're not! But someone has to show some casual concern for Maddalena's labourer.'

'Casual "concern" is it? I thought it was casual something else.'

'Ha! Can we change the subject?'

'*You* brought her up. You've talked about nothing else since we got in the car.'

Was that true? Alex certainly thought about her too much. 'She has no one looking out for her.'

'I won't be on the farm after the harvest, by the way. I've got plans with Elena.'

'On top of everything, she'll have to walk there?' He could take her. Perhaps he should, although she'd probably get up early and walk just to prove she didn't need his help.

'Julia's hardy, a Furlan Volpe. She'll be fine,' Berengario insisted.

'When did you last get your hearing tested? I said her family is from Calabria.'

'When you admit you like her, I'll hear it crystal clear.'

Alex gritted his teeth so hard that Berengario could probably hear *that*. 'You know it's not that simple. Stop pretending it is.'

'Alex!' he said, his voice high, as though he was the frustrated one in this conversation. 'We all lost her! Don't you think *she'd* want you to find love?'

'Do you want me to have the guilt of disappointing a dead person as well as everything else? Of course she would want that. But *I* don't. I won't go through that, especially not with someone who's determined to leave the country as soon as possible!' He sounded desperate even to his own ears. 'It's not the first time I've slept with someone, if you really want to know,' he added, hoping to shock his friend into silence.

Of course it backfired. 'But it's the first time you've wanted to take care of someone.'

'Because she has no one else,' he insisted. 'Do you know she moved to Italy for a boyfriend and then had nowhere to go when they broke up and stayed living with him for a whole year? Her family is half the world away.' Cutting himself off when he realised he was babbling about Julia again, he could feel Berengario's gaze, even though he kept his own firmly on the road.

'It's not because she's alone,' the old man contradicted gently. 'You want to take care of her because you're waking up again – because it's who you were before...' Before everything he'd had to do *for love*.

'I know you mean well,' Alex said quietly, 'but this isn't going to happen. She's not staying. She has to have a day off next week for her passport appointment and she won't be here long after that.'

'Anything can happen in a few weeks, especially in the autumn.'

Alex glanced at his friend and he did not like the glint in the other man's eye.

14

Jules only worked half a day the following Saturday. Maddalena sent her home early, which Jules appreciated. The restaurant was open Thursday to Saturday for lunch and after helping out two days in a row, she decided she preferred the place without the pressure of impatient customers who didn't appreciate the effort that went into growing and preparing their food.

The hard work usually kept her mind off the limbo she'd found herself in, but that day her insufficient Italian had made it difficult to help the waitress, and the huffing of the customers as she painstakingly tried to communicate only reminded her again of Luca's lack of patience with her.

The waitress, Alina – a teen with dyed black hair and a ring in her lip – offered Jules and Arco a lift back into Cividale in her old Fiat Panda. The girl seemed to be in a hurry, so Jules told her to drop her off on the main road and she dawdled along the foot-path towards home, thinking guiltily that Arco hadn't had a proper walk that day, since she'd been busy indoors.

It had been a week full of blue skies over the Friulian plain, leading to frosty mornings and bright afternoons. The yellows in the hills seemed to shimmer with a hint of red. Something about the gentle slopes and thick woods called to her, as though from another life.

As she always did when she crossed the bridge, she stopped to gaze at the river and the grey stone peaks in the distance. In the lovely weather, she almost felt like lazing on the white stones down in the ravine as the emerald water rushed past. She had a whole camera roll of photos of this one spot, but every time, she wanted to take another, to capture something she might have missed.

The view also reminded her she hadn't called her family since that first day in Cividale, so she paused to chat briefly to her mum, who was about to go to sleep.

Just after she crossed the bridge, the sound of a deep voice, speaking with rare animation, made her freeze, pulling Arco's lead short. Down a side street was a shop with a row of bikes lined up outside – where Alex was talking to a customer, a smile on his face.

Dropping into a crouch, he inspected the bike the customer held steady, producing a tool and making some kind of adjustment as he continued to converse. She didn't understand much of the clipped dialect, but that smile took her right back to the first night, when he'd barely been able to stop talking.

After spending a week excusing his grumpiness, she was miffed to see him smiling naturally. Maybe she'd been wrong about him, as she'd been wrong about Luca, and he'd just spared her feelings when he'd told her she wasn't a burden.

Even more discouraging was the prick of longing she felt as she watched his blue eyes light up and his soft lips, framed by his trimmed beard, curving for the customer. Turning away with a huff, she marched blindly down the opposite side street, the poke of the cobbles into the soles of her feet now familiar.

Past the gates of the old monastery and under ancient stone archways, she reached the road along the river – the place where she'd stupidly asked for a goodbye kiss – and continued furiously, without even stopping to admire the water. She didn't pause until she reached a narrow street of tiny, well-kept terraces with stone windowsills and brown shutters. Some had small gardens perched on the rocks over the river, many with the now-familiar silver leaves of an olive tree or two.

She began to calm down just as Arco grew suddenly boisterous. He barked and pulled and a moment later, a woman appeared, walking an impossibly white poodle – a series of fluffy clouds joined together, with a dog under all that fur somewhere.

Jules stammered some poor Italian, asking permission for Arco to approach the other dog several moments too late. Her cheeky pet had already stuck his nose under the poodle and was sniffing rudely. 'Sorry,' she mumbled in English.

But the other woman smiled. 'It's okay. Is that... Arco? And are you Julia?'

Her gaze snapped up, taking in the woman for the first time. She was slim and slight, with curly brown hair that looked effortlessly stylish – but probably required about as much grooming as the dog – and a cropped jacket. She had a belt around her waist with a pouch of dog treats and a loop to attach a lead, which Jules noted as something useful for farm work when she couldn't let Arco run free.

'How do you know who I am?' Jules asked.

'It's a small town. I'm Marisa. I own the dog salon near Alex's house.'

'Ohhh,' she said, unable to stifle a smile. 'Your dog is a wonderful advertisement for your business.'

'I watch a lot of TV while I groom Chanel,' she said with a chuckle. 'Arco is a Lagotto? Or a mix?'

'He's a Lagotto. I might need to make an appointment with you in a few weeks—' *If I'm still here.* 'He'll need a trim.'

'I'll give you my card and in the meantime, if you need anything, give me a call. Or if you want to go for a walk – or a drink.'

'A tajùt?' Jules suggested with a smile, before remembering where she'd learned that word and heat pooled in her cheeks. She wasn't sure she'd take the stylish woman up on her offer, not when she spent her days getting dirty on an organic farm and she'd never understood much about fashion – at least that's what Luca had said and her threadbare wardrobe certainly suggested he was right.

'Esatto,' Marisa said with an approving nod. 'Give me a call.'

As Marisa was about to continue on her way, Jules asked, 'I was thinking of walking in the forest, but there are no trails marked on the map on my phone. Do you know a route I can take?'

'There are lots of paths in the hills. Maybe you need an app for hiking?'

When Jules downloaded a different app, the blank space on the map suddenly became criss-crossing trails – and the promise of a long walk to clear her head.

'These ways are also used by mountain bikers, so keep Arco on the leash.'

After saying goodbye to Marisa, Jules took a deep breath and headed out of town. The path was steeper than she'd expected and she was puffing and almost regretted her decision, but a sudden glimpse of the plain and the distant, sparkling sea caught her interest and she kept climbing in earnest.

The speckled sunlight under the yellow leaves glowed warm, like breathing out before the cold of night, and she was struck by the notion that these few weeks of spectacular autumn were a gift, a cosy period of rest and plenty before the onset of winter.

In that reflective state, she stepped on something small and hard that made her thankful again for Davide's sturdy boots. Peering down, she found a spiky case, split open to reveal the polished curve of a rich, brown chestnut.

She couldn't help thinking it *was* very close to the colour of her eyes.

Reaching for it, she discovered the spikes were not joking and gasped at the painful prick, grimacing when she saw she'd drawn blood. But her curiosity was stronger and she tried again more carefully, tugging the sides of the case apart to reveal two shiny little nuts. They felt so smooth and gratifying in her hand that she kept them, twirling them along her palm like stress balls, as she wandered behind Arco under the canopy of trees.

It wasn't long until she saw another little pouch. Tucking the first nuts into her pocket, she opened the next one, still pricking her finger, but not as badly as the first time. The next one she found was rotten, but around a corner, the path was suddenly strewn with cases – hundreds of them.

Remembering Alex's comment about being able to live on them for two months of the year, she set to work. Within twenty minutes, her pockets were sagging, her fingertips were raw and she'd trained her eyes to seek out the freshest-looking cases.

Straightening, she had to press a hand to her aching back and she realised she'd been doggedly collecting on her haunches for a few minutes too long. Even after she told herself to stop, she looked longingly at each spiky little package she passed and she couldn't resist opening a few that looked particularly plump. But she kept walking, only pausing occasionally to forage a few more.

By the time she emerged from the forest into golden vineyards and sweeping views of the plain before her, a looming chain of mountains to the west, the sun cast low rays over the landscape and her stomach was rumbling, despite the hearty meal at the restaurant at lunchtime. Even Arco seemed worn out.

But the walk had done her good. The forest had shared its bounty with her – and its autumn beauty – and it didn't matter so much any more what Luca had thought of her, or how bad her Italian was, and what she was going to do with her life when she left this place.

She felt silly when she arrived back at the door of Alex's house with pockets like a squirrel's cheeks. She didn't even know what to do with the chestnuts, since she did at least know they had to be cooked before eating them. Did people even collect the wild ones, or were they too dirty or poor quality?

Foraging was not something she'd ever done. She'd never known the right places in Parma and she'd only ever learned in Australia that anything she collected might be poisonous. Oh well, there was no way she'd just bin her forest treasure, even if she had to work out how to make a fire and roast them herself.

With that conviction, she turned the key in the lock and stomped through the door. Alex emerged from the kitchen immediately, his brow furrowed.

'Where have you been?'

'Hello to you too.'

Alex slowly blew out the breath he'd been holding and squeezed his eyes shut for a moment. He'd been worried sick and she looked bright and fresh and rosy with her hair coming out of its short ponytail and her eyes... It was best not to look at her eyes right now.

'Sorry, I was cooking and then I didn't know when you'd get back.' He scratched the back of his neck. 'I called Maddalena and she said you left after lunch.' He'd started worrying in earnest when the first hints of dusk tinged the sky outside the window.

He'd pictured Alina's car flipped and twisted, ambulances, police and... hospital beds.

'I didn't realise I needed to tell you when I'd be home.'

'You don't,' he snapped, trying to clear his head now he could see she was clearly fine. 'I hope you weren't staying out because of me.'

'I hope you weren't staying out in the evenings all last week because of *me*,' she responded.

'Of course not,' he said gruffly as she shrugged out of the jacket and placed it on the hook.

'It wasn't anything to do with you. I was exploring the forest.'

He hadn't expected that. 'The... Did you get lost?'

'I am capable of reading a map,' she grumbled.

'I wasn't suggesting you can't,' he said with a tight sigh.

'It was just a long walk.'

There was something she wasn't saying and the strain between them frustrated him. It was growing unbearable, this housemate arrangement where so many topics were off limits – and so many feelings.

'Come and eat, then.'

She looked about to protest – as usual – but her gaze slid to the jacket and a small smile touched her lips. 'I actually brought something home to contribute to the household.' The smile grew wider, her lips pressed together and he was charmed all over again, flummoxed by how easily he fell under a spell she didn't know she was casting.

Rubbing his chin in chagrin, he asked, 'Contribute? Did you go to the greengrocer? The market! Did you go to the market this morning?'

'I should do that one time, but no. I, uh...' Biting her lip, she dug into one of the pockets and produced a handful of chestnuts.

Colour spotted her cheeks. 'There are quite a lot of them. I don't really know what to do with them.'

Struggling against an amused smile, he said, 'You'd better bring them into the kitchen then.'

There were indeed a lot of nuts. 'This must have taken you a while,' he commented mildly, running a few under the tap and then fetching the paring knife to score them.

'Once I started, I couldn't stop,' she explained, watching him cut a cross into the skins with interest.

'I know the feeling.'

She turned to him in surprise. 'You do?'

'It's an instinct perhaps. And chestnuts are soul food.'

'Soul food,' she repeated softly. 'Definitely.' He got the impression she'd been thinking about her ex again. He would never actually punch someone, but joking about it was certainly one way to release the frustration he felt when she beat herself up about the relationship.

She turned on the tap to wash her hands and he frowned, grasping her wrist. 'You didn't wear gloves!' He inspected the raw skin of her fingertips, dotted with tiny puncture marks. 'Let me check that none of the spines broke off. It can get infected if you're unlucky.'

Her gulp was audible as he swept his thumb carefully over each finger, wishing there was more he could do to ease the discomfort she must be feeling.

'I'll get you some salve after dinner, although it will be difficult on your fingertips.' He glanced up to find her watching him, her eyes wide and wary. He blinked and then looked away in a hurry, placing her hand gently on the table.

In the silence that followed, where he wondered whether he should apologise for being short with her when she got home, her stomach rumbled loudly enough for Arco to lift his tired head where he was stretched out in front of the stove.

'Thank you for cooking,' she said softly.

'Thank you for eating,' he said in reply, his expression slipping when he realised how strange that sounded. 'I mean, let's eat. I'll put a few of these in water and we can roast them after dinner.'

'Really?'

He eyed her as he fetched a jug and filled it with water. 'Yes. Did you want to hang them on the wall like a trophy?'

'No, of course not!' She gave him a chiding nudge. 'But I didn't expect I'd actually done something right in Italy.'

He dropped the handful of nuts into the water with a loud plop and leaned heavily on the bench, pausing before turning to her forcefully. '*What?*'

15

'Chill out, Captain Cranky,' Jules said, putting her hands in the air. 'No need to get defensive.'

'I'm not defensive,' he snapped, pausing when her lips wobbled and he listened back to what he'd said. 'Okay, that was defensive, but you'd better explain what you think you do wrong.'

He poured two glasses of wine and, as he'd hoped, she followed the wine to the table and sat down – with enough stifled groaning to suggest she'd been on her feet too long that day, again.

'There's no "think". I was *told* often enough that I was doing things wrong.'

'Your ex-boyfriend,' he said grimly as he fetched the risotto off the stove and set it onto the painted tile in the middle of the table.

'And his mother, yes. If I ever hear the phrase "brutta figura" again, I will punch something. How was I supposed to know that yellow flowers are for jealousy and hanging the washing out in my old tracksuit wasn't allowed?'

He stifled a grimace. 'Okay, I'm starting to understand.'

'It gets worse!' she said, her mouth full of risotto. He was kind of touched that she felt so comfortable in his kitchen. 'He said I had cheap taste,' she said with a false laugh. 'At first I thought he meant it fondly, but we were running a B & B together – or trying to – and he said I always bought the wrong things, inferior products that the guests would notice as cheap substitutes. To be honest, I wouldn't know Maddalena's fresh, organic olive oil from the supermarket own brand.'

'Of course you would!' he scoffed.

She paused shovelling the risotto in to give him a pained look. 'I know nothing about olive oil.'

'You don't have to *know* about it. You just have to taste it – at least, that's the way it works around here. And Siore Cudrig across the courtyard hangs her washing in her dressing gown with curlers in.'

'While you kiss strange half-naked women in your kitchen with the neighbours catching glimpses,' she teased. But she continued before he could blush. 'I didn't even think to wait until I had gloves to collect chestnuts.'

'You didn't have any with you. I'm impressed you managed to bring so many. You went into the forest and you came back with food. You're turning into a real Furlane.'

As he'd hoped, she snorted a laugh at that. 'I spend enough time with my hands in the Friulian soil. Maybe some of it is rubbing off on me. But it's Furlan-*e* not Furlan-*a*? The female form of Friulian, right?'

He nodded. 'Furlane. It's different from Italian.'

'You've made that abundantly clear,' she said with a dry smile.

'Berengario thinks you can do no wrong and Maddalena might actually have time to sit down for once because of you.'

'Yes, well, I didn't do very well helping out at the restaurant today. The farm work is better. I don't know whether things are really different here in Friuli or whether the expectations are just different. I suppose it's not very challenging work.'

'What do you mean? I've seen you this week. You've been ready to drop dead every evening. How is that not challenging?'

'You barely saw me all week! The instant I came home, you had to rush off somewhere – which was very suspicious! But you know what I mean. I'd hate for my ex to see me, now, confirming all his thoughts about how incompetent I am. He probably wishes he'd given our relationship a merciful death sooner.'

Alex choked, the shot of panic at her choice of words taking him by surprise. He set his fork down with a shaking hand and gripped the edge of the table.

'Are you okay?'

He nodded, willing that to be the case before she asked more questions. Damn it! He'd been enjoying the conversation and lulled himself into a false sense of security, but he didn't have emotional security – not any more.

She sighed deeply, making him look up and distracting him from the ache. 'Do you have an accordion to urgently tune?'

'Hmm?'

'You rarely last this long in a conversation with me.'

He stood suddenly, feeling trapped. 'I'll put the chestnuts in the fire.' Telling himself firmly to pull himself together before he made her feel even worse, he fetched the wine out of the fridge to refill her glass. But when he turned back, he found her halfway to the sink, dinner plate in hand. 'Sit down!' he said – again, too harshly. 'I mean, wait for the chestnuts. And have some more wine if you want.'

'I should be contributing to the wine budget, if we're real housemates.'

'It's okay.'

'I don't want to rely on you.'

He looked up from pouring wine to find her stubborn jaw set. He really liked that jaw. 'You're not relying on me,' he insisted. 'Or rather, we all rely on one another.'

'I didn't mean to suggest that Maddalena and Berengario did basic work, by the way. I can see how complicated it is to run that place. I was only talking about myself. I studied International Relations at university – feels like a long time ago, now. I was just going travelling for a few years and then I was going to go back and do a Master's or join a graduate programme or something, but...' Her sentence trailed off.

'How old were you when you left Australia?' He busied himself arranging the wet chestnuts in a cast-iron pan and placing it carefully on the coals of the little fire in the stove.

'I was twenty-four,' she answered. 'I'd just turned twenty-five when I moved here. At first, I was certain I'd perfect my Italian in six months and apply to the University of Parma, and in five years I'd work for the European Commission or something.' Her laugh was bleak.

'Why didn't it work out like that?' he asked carefully.

'It was never going to work out like that. I was an idiot for thinking it would. I never perfected my Italian, even in three years.'

'Did he help you?'

Her hesitation vexed him even further. 'Yes, he did,' she began, but she didn't sound convinced. 'He had to. You don't understand what it's like to be completely dependent on someone else. He had to come with me to every official appointment, all the bureaucracy, the tax, healthcare, business permits – everything. I didn't understand enough Italian and when some words started making sense, I didn't know how "things worked". Every time I filled out a form, I did it wrong somehow. I was different and I couldn't communicate with his friends. It wasn't at all like either of us had pictured.'

'Life rarely is.'

She'd taken a breath to continue but paused, slowly deflating as she released the breath. 'I suppose you're right.'

'Are you going to continue your study when you go home? Is that your plan?'

'Oh, God, I have no idea. I haven't thought that far ahead. And "International Relations" sounds like a bit of a joke now. I don't know if I could handle going back. So much pressure.'

'If you can handle the chaos at Due Pini, you can handle anything,' he said lightly. 'Did you know Maddalena used to work a corporate job in Verona until she decided to come home and buy the farm? It's the most honourable work you can do, producing food and taking care of the land for the future. Like collecting chestnuts, there's something calming about it.'

'Meaningful,' she agreed. She toyed with the stem of her wine glass. 'It seems to be what I need right now. What about you? How long have you worked at the bike shop? And what were you doing in London when you weren't playing the accordion?'

'I worked as a technical designer for an engineering firm,' he said carefully. 'That's my profession. I've been at the bike shop for... nearly two years?' How had it been that long?

'That's when you came back from London?'

He shook his head. 'I was having some problems when I came back from London.' He looked up suddenly to force her to meet his gaze. 'I know what it's like to rely on others too. I don't know where I would be without Maddalena and Berengario. That's why I will help you with anything you need – not because I think you can't look after yourself.'

Her jaw moved and her eyes asked a hundred questions he

wouldn't answer. He thought about that jacket, the one she'd filled with chestnuts almost until the pockets burst. There was something new here – inside him too. For the first time, he wondered if it might be something good, even if it wasn't forever. He knew nothing was.

Nodding slowly, she said, 'Thanks. I appreciate the explanation. I'm oversensitive today.'

'Oversensitive sounds like me. I'm sorry I snapped at you when you came home.'

'I obviously should have showed you the chestnuts first, since they seem to have made everything better.' She gave a little toss of her head and the cracks inside him glowed with heat. She was so... *alive*, which broke his heart. He wanted to pull her into his lap and kiss her until her ponytail was a mess and she'd forgotten all about this guy who'd stolen her confidence, but every time he looked at her, he was also reminded of everything he'd lost. It didn't make sense.

A subtle sweet scent and the faint smell of burning reached his nostrils and he stood to check on the nuts, glad to be out of her gravitational pull. Over his shoulder, he said to Julia, 'Can you get that tea towel and put water on it?'

Tugging the pan out of the fire with a pot holder, he gestured for Julia to set the wet towel on the bench and then poured the nuts onto the towel, wrapping them up while they cooled.

'You really haven't ever tried chestnuts?' he asked, his ears hot, remembering the moment she'd told him that.

'Really. We don't have the trees in Australia – definitely not in Brisbane. We don't even have autumn where I'm from. I saw the sellers in the street in Parma, but never tried them.'

'Well, it's an honour to share your first ones with you.'

'I'm sure it won't be life-changing,' she said with a chuckle.

He gave her a look that suggested otherwise, making her laugh again. Unwrapping the bounty with a flourish, he tested a nut and picked it up when he was sure it had sufficiently cooled. Cracking the shell and rubbing off the inner skin with the ease of many years of practice, he held it out to her on his palm while he reached for another with his other hand.

She took it with a doubtful look and bit it in half, chewing thoughtfully. 'Wow, it's...' She popped the other half in her mouth. 'Mmm. It's like a savoury dessert, sweet without being sugary, definitely comfort food. God, how did I live nearly twenty-eight years without tasting these?'

He stifled a smile, inspecting the next peeled nut before lifting it to his mouth, only to pause when he noticed her greedy gaze on his fingers. Lifting his brows, he offered it to her. 'You wanted this?'

'I foraged it.'

'You did,' he said, handing it to her with a laugh. 'You foraged them, so I'll peel them.'

'You can have the next one,' she said magnanimously. 'I'm not going to eat all of them, not after that delicious risotto. What will we do with the rest of them?'

That little 'we' crept up on him, but he was sick and tired of everything she said triggering him. 'Roasted, boiled, in soup – the only thing I can't do at home is grind them into flour.' He popped the peeled nut into his mouth, stifling his own groan of enjoyment. There wasn't anything to compare to fresh, warm chestnuts, buttery and rich.

'Now I see why you were willing to accept rent in nuts.'

'Get some gloves next time though. Speaking of which...' He fetched a tube of antiseptic ointment, noticing Attila skulking inside through the cat flap when he headed back to the kitchen. The cat followed him in casually, his tail rubbing against Alex's leg, but stopped suddenly, hackles up, when Arco pricked up his ears.

A second later, the cat was gone again.

'That poor cat,' Julia said with a grimace.

'He'll be all right,' Alex assured her, his jaw tightening when he appreciated what he hadn't said— *He'll be all right when you're gone again.*

Pulling his chair to hers, he took her hand and dabbed drops of ointment onto her fingertips, glancing up in concern when she hissed at the sting. Her skin was dry and there was a little dirt under her fingernails and— He should stop studying her hands.

But when he lifted his head, her *face* was right there. He couldn't stop thinking about how they'd kissed by the city wall as the river rushed by, how she'd told him she wanted *him*. That evening had been everything – but it had to be nothing.

Kiss her again and all this guilt and confusion would only multiply. She deserved so much more than his bad-tempered hospitality, but he still didn't draw away.

She did. With a light pat on his cheek, she gave him a tight smile and said, 'Thanks – for everything. I'm going to take a shower.'

He nodded mutely, letting her brush past. Arco lifted his head and watched his mistress leave the room. When the dog hauled himself to his feet, Alex assumed he was going to station himself outside the bathroom door to wait, but he plonked himself down next to Alex's chair and rolled over with his feet in the air.

'Why are you so determined to be friends with me?' he asked the dog. But he leaned down and gave him a thorough scratch on the tummy.

16

———

Jules went to sleep full – her belly, her mind and also somehow her soul. When she awoke in the night for a sip of water, she heard movement downstairs and that twinge in her heart made itself felt. Before she managed to fall back to sleep, her thoughts settled once again on Alex's comment last night that had made her heart beat strangely.

I was having some problems when I came back from London.

His haggard expression had revealed more than he'd meant to, she guessed. Yes, he'd lost someone, but something had happened to him too and she couldn't bear thinking about it, but she also couldn't stop wondering about the significance of that small confession and the shadows in his gorgeous eyes.

The following day she had no plans and swung her stiff legs over the side of the bed slowly. After wrestling with the latch, she pulled open both sets of windows to the seep of frigid air, making her shiver as she pushed the creaky shutters. The church bells rang out into the stillness of the cool Sunday morning where no one ventured out of the house unless they had to. The afternoon would be soon enough.

But to her surprise, when she trudged down the stairs in an extra pair of socks, the cuffs of her threadbare hoodie over her hands for warmth, Alex was already up and preparing to leave.

'I made you a coffee,' he said, his expression hesitant.

Something had shifted last night and she wasn't sure where they'd go from here. 'Thanks.'

'Umm, I'm going to the market.'

'I thought the market was on Saturday.'

'Not that one,' he said, scratching his head. 'Il Baule del Diavolo – the devil's... suitcase? It's the monthly antiques market.'

'You want another accordion?' she teased, enjoying the flash of a smile over his lips.

'Always.' He paused, turning to her with his coffee cup halfway to his lips. 'Do you want to come?'

'Sure.'

She didn't overthink it. She quickly fed Arco, attached his lead and followed Alex out into the sunshine that was already burning off the chill of the morning. Walking with him through the old town reminded her of their first date, but she stuffed her free hand into her pocket and refused to dwell on that.

'How are your fingers?' he asked as they passed the main piazza where the cafes were opening up.

'Better – thanks.' She wanted to ask him how he'd slept, but suspected that topic would be off limits.

When they emerged from the narrow lane, the square beside the cathedral was filled with market stalls, from tables and gazebos to the occasional simple blanket on the ground – all of them crammed with tarnished, faded and downright old... stuff.

Alex waved to a stallholder with a series of antique glass lamps and then glanced awkwardly at Jules. 'Eh, you don't have to stay with me. The accordion talk might bore you.'

'Where have I heard that before?' she teased, before she'd thought better of it. It was nearly worth the ache of memory to see his cheeks blossom pink. She turned to the nearest stall, pretending to be interested in... Wait, was that a real cat in a wicker basket?

Quickly leading Arco away, she wandered the stalls, admiring the old canvas-bound books she couldn't understand, the painted, gold-trimmed soup tureens, endless plates and teacups, doilies and table runners and rocking chairs. She could picture all of it at Alex's place – and she knew exactly how much Luca would hate it all, which brought a smile to her lips.

A flash of colour partly hidden in a pile of woollen jumpers caught her eye and she reached for it absently, pulling out a chunky knit cardigan that looked as though it had once belonged to a Sherpa. It had rainbow stripes in thick wool and a baggy fit and she was certain the person who wore it could be outdoors all day and never grow cold. It was rough-hewn and rugged, words she suddenly felt could describe *her* and she just *had* to try it on. If it fit, she would buy it.

The owner of the stall, it turned out, was from over the border in Austria, but spoke Italian and English fluently and directed her immediately towards the full-length mirror, and even took Arco's lead for a moment so she could tug on the heavy cardigan. What she saw in the mirror made her grin.

She might never find the starry-eyed Jules she'd been fresh out of uni, falling in love with a handsome Italian, but she liked the woman in the old, colourful cardigan – the woman she would be. Perhaps she was sometimes 'brutta' – and bitter – but that was authentic.

'Fifteen euros,' the stall owner said to her. 'It's pure wool.'

Even if it hadn't been an eminently reasonable price, she

probably would have bought it, her dwindling bank balance be damned. For pure wool and a glimpse into her own heart, she happily handed over two banknotes.

Wandering the rest of the market, it became clear she truly was visiting a place at the crossroads of Europe. There were woodcarvings from the Alps, Murano glass, Russian orthodox crosses in gold, Meissen porcelain – and Limoges porcelain and Bohemian porcelain – and coins and notes from the former Yugoslavia.

When she spotted an accordion, she got so excited, she had to admit to herself that she'd been looking for an excuse to go and find Alex. Except she'd drifted a long way from where she'd said goodbye to him in the Piazza del Duomo – and they somehow still hadn't exchanged phone numbers.

Dodging meandering punters, relaxed Sunday locals and tourists who distinguished themselves by speaking other languages – or standard Italian – Jules picked her way back in the direction of the cathedral, keeping her eyes up. She should have realised it wouldn't be too difficult to find him. Not far from the statue of Julius Caesar, she caught sight of his curly head, several inches taller than everyone around him.

'Alex!' she called out, rushing in his direction. Arco picked up on the game and frolicked ahead, his tongue lolling. 'Alex!'

He whirled around. 'What? What's wrong?'

'Nothing! Don't worry,' she said breathlessly. 'I found you an accordion.'

His smile stretched slowly. 'You did?'

She grasped his hand without thinking. 'It's this way! Come on! Before someone else buys it.'

'I don't think we need to worry about that.'

When she turned back, he was studying their joined hands and she hurriedly dropped his. 'You can't be certain!'

'All right, I'm coming,' he grumbled, but this time with a smile that reminded her of sitting by the fire in Maddalena's dining room – or roasting chestnuts on the stove.

As she was having a day off from her money worries, she insisted on paying for it, calling it 'rent' just to make him roll his eyes. But she suspected that if she'd divulged her real reason for giving it to him – so he'd have something to remember her by – he wouldn't have accepted it.

By the time they returned home for lunch, he was the proud owner of a red and gold Fantini piano accordion, only slightly not working. And Jules had started to wonder what the future version of her would have to remember Alex by.

* * *

On the following Tuesday, Jules made her mad dash to Parma for a ten-minute passport interview at the local police station, while Arco stayed rather too happily behind with Alex. She wore her new cardigan, freshly hand-washed, and arranged her hair in a messy ponytail, just in case she had the opportunity to disappoint Luca's mother one more time.

But the closer she got to her old frazione, the part of the city where the B & B was situated, the smaller she felt. What if the bureaucrat in the interview took issue with her misshapen old cardigan? She could be too colourful for the country of Gucci and Dolce & Gabbana. And if Luca saw her, his mouth would twist in a sneer she still sometimes pictured in her dreams – her bad ones.

Returning to Parma also made her realise she'd been avoiding thinking about the sale of the building. Luca hadn't contacted her even once, which she would have thought was a good thing, except she didn't know what that meant for her investment.

With a shot of panic, she realised she would cut her losses and run so she never had to face him again. She wished she could have brought Arco with her – but no, he would have drawn attention to her and she couldn't risk Luca seeing her.

She got through her appointment with a combination of blank smiles and 'Puoi ripetere, per favore – lentamente,' to have the important bits repeated slowly, then she bolted for the train back home.

Home?

The journey passed in a blur, even though it took five hours to travel between Parma and Udine – longer that day, as one of her trains was delayed. She had her e-reader with her, but she couldn't have said what happened in the pages she apparently read. All she knew was that the fog in her brain gradually cleared the farther she got from Luca, and she asked herself if perhaps she was in a worse state than she'd realised.

I was having some problems.

Her mind had been in such a tangle that it was only when she arrived at the station in Udine and went to buy a ticket for the retro diesel railway that chuffed east to Cividale that she realised how late it was and that she'd missed the last train.

After a leap of panic up her throat, she took a deep breath and considered her options. It was past eleven o'clock. She refused to disturb Alex, Berengario or Maddalena so late – which meant her only option was a taxi.

When the taxi pulled up at Alex's courtyard, she placed her card on the reader with dismay, imagining her meagre balance ticking down by another thirty euros she'd never see again. Stepping under the low brick archway, she felt as though she'd been gone much longer than a day, although the tree looked the same as it had that morning, the plump orange fruit more prominent now more leaves had fallen. She shivered with the sudden cold of the late evening.

It was nearly midnight and although the shutters in the court-yard were all firmly closed – except her own on the first floor of Alex's building – she suspected someone would still hear her footsteps.

And Alex was probably awake.

But she fetched her key quietly, just in case. Of course, it wasn't quietly enough. An alarmed bark sounded, followed by frantic scratching. Before she could even turn the latch, the door flew open and Arco made his best attempt to bowl her over.

'Hey, boy,' she crooned, dropping to a crouch to give him a thorough rub. 'I missed you too.' She let him give her a gentle lick on the chin and looped her arms around his little body. Boy, she'd needed a hug. 'I bet you had a nice day at the bike shop.'

'He did.'

Her gaze snapped up to see Alex leaning in the doorway. He wore a tight cotton undershirt and baggy tracksuit bottoms that hung loose and, with his forearm propped against the frame and his other hand on his hip, Jules could do nothing but appreciate the definition in his arms, his big-knuckled hands, the height of him.

Wow. The attraction was really not going away.

Then her eyes lifted to his face and she scrambled to her feet. 'Were you asleep? God, I'm sorry. My train was delayed and then I had to find a taxi and I really didn't think I'd be home this—'

'You should have called me.'

'Alex, it's nearly midnight. If you were asleep—'

'I wasn't asleep – well, not properly.' His hair was unruly, his cheeks stubbled and his eyelids heavy.

'Were you waiting for me? I should have sent you a message—'

'Eh, shh,' he said, rubbing a hand over his face. She should have felt insulted at his brusque interruption, but it was somehow preferable to Luca's smirk, which she'd been seeing behind her eyelids all day. 'This is your house too. How I sleep shouldn't concern you.'

That was the problem: she was concerned, even though she tried not to be.

'Can I...?' *Have a hug?* She swallowed. '...come in?'

He straightened in surprise. 'Of course. Sorry. Maybe I *am* half asleep.'

As she brushed past him, a creak from across the courtyard made her glance up to see a shutter closing and she froze, remembering all the witnesses they had. Alex was looking in the same direction and with both of them squeezed in the doorway, she couldn't help thinking about giving the nosy Signora Cudrig more of a show. She could just slip her arms around his waist and—

Arco jumped up, scratching at her hip as though to remind her that he was supposed to be part of any snuggling that happened. She stumbled into the doorway, tripping over Alex's foot and grabbing his shirt for balance, as he scooped an arm around her and staggered in after.

In a split-second decision she would never have made with a clear head, she leaned into him, pressing her cheek to his shoulder.

Breathing out for what felt like the first time that day, she didn't even mind if he pushed her away after a second. His soft shirt, the warmth of his body was what she'd wanted and she'd found it.

But he didn't push her away.

The arm around her tightened, then another joined it. He shuffled them inside and toed the door closed, sagging against the wall in the hallway, his head falling back. She wasn't even sure if they were friends, but he definitely hugged her back – soft and real.

'Today—' he began, and she had to give him credit for picking up on her weird mood. '—was it...? How did it go?'

'Fine. Processing the application should take about ten days.'

'Ah.'

Those two words, *ten days*, seemed to be hanging in the air.

'Did you see him?'

She shook her head against his chest. 'Thankfully not. It was bad enough knowing he was there.'

'It's over. You did it.'

'We still have to sell the property. I'll have to call him soon.' She wished her voice didn't sound so thin.

'If you want me to beat him up before you leave...' He lifted his hand and flexed it and she couldn't help but laugh.

'Attila would probably do a better job of beating him up.'

'True.' He wiggled his fingers, his smile tight. 'Accordion hands.'

She peered up at him without removing her cheek from his shirt. 'Have you got the new one working?'

Shaking his head, he said, 'I only just finished my student's instrument.'

'I think that one needs an exorcism.'

'Speaking of which...'

She jerked her head up. 'Do I want to hear what you have to say?'

'Yes,' he said, stroking a soothing finger along her temple before snatching his hand away again as he realised what he'd done. 'There's a walking tour of Cividale on the evening of the 31st of October. You should keep it free. Berengario is taking one of the routes. There'll be some music afterwards.'

'Sounds great. The olives will be harvested by then. Hopefully Maddalena will take her foot off the accelerator.'

'She rarely does that.' His arms tightened again. 'It's a shame you'll miss San Martino. We have a big fair with craft stalls and local businesses – and eat pumpkin and drink wine.'

'Any excuse to drink wine?'

'You don't need an excuse to drink wine,' he quipped. Stifling a yawn, he sighed deeply enough that Jules felt the movement against her cheek.

'Are you going to sleep?'

'Bed? Yes. Sleep? I never know,' he said with a tight smile.

'Want to keep doing this... horizontally? Just the hugging? Nothing more,' she managed to say, even though the words were pulled out from under her mortification like a magician's tablecloth.

'Julia...' he began.

'I think you should probably call me Jules,' she mumbled into his shirt. 'No one actually calls me Julia.'

'Jules,' he said experimentally, his deep voice forming the syllables with a devastating ruefulness. 'I don't think that's the best idea.'

'Of course it's not the best idea! But I thought—' She drew away, ignoring how cold she suddenly felt.

'I only meant...' He dropped his hand from where he'd clutched her arm for a moment. 'You know I don't sleep well. I wouldn't want to disturb you.'

'What if I don't mind being disturbed?' she said, but her voice was tentative. She wasn't sure if they were talking about cuddling all night or Alex finally telling her what had happened that made him think he had to be sad and crabby all the time. She still wasn't sure if she really wanted to let him tell her.

But he shook his head with a faint smile. 'You're leaving soon.

Get your sleep – upstairs. Berengario will be coming to pick you up early as usual.'

As she followed his instructions and trudged upstairs to the soundtrack of Arco's claws clicking and the wood creaking, all she could think was how much she wished she'd kissed him first.

17

The sunshine held out until the end of the week – a welcome blessing for the olive harvest at Due Pini – and the cold mountain breeze gave way to milder conditions on the plain from the Adriatic. Jules had grown used to the chafe on her cheeks from spending so much time outdoors and she'd rarely been so well-fed, between lunch at the agriturismo and dinner by Alex's fireplace.

As harvest weekend approached, Due Pini was even more chaotic than usual, now with stainless steel tanks called fusti piled up ready to be sterilised and filled with oil at the mill. Jules had washed and dried her share of fusti, as well as several bulbous flasks in green glass like the one Maddalena had broken the day Jules had arrived at the farm.

She got up early each morning to travel to the farm with Berengario, who spent the ten-minute journeys listing Alex's many virtues: he was the type to settle down; he could fix anything with a paper clip; he'd won all the mountain-biking competitions in the area when he was a teenager; he cleaned up really well – even his ear piercing had closed up over time.

Jules didn't have the heart to point out that the saintly Alex could also be bad-tempered and curt, although after he'd hugged her on Tuesday night, she was ready to overlook a lot of his flaws.

She might even add his early-morning bed hair and the sleepy gravel in his voice to that list of virtues, although he now put a shirt on before emerging, unfortunately.

He'd been busy avoiding her as usual during the evenings – in the poorly kept garden behind the building this week, which she thought was a rather extreme and uncomfortable way to avoid her. He came back in late, shivering and peeling a pair of fine workman's gloves off his hands.

But on Saturday, he surprised her by coming into the kitchen fully dressed in worn work trousers and a rough wool pullover with a couple of holes in it.

'Does the shop open early on a Saturday?'

He looked up from his coffee in surprise. 'I'm coming out to Due Pini for the raccolta – the harvest. I thought I told you?'

'No, you didn't mention it.'

'I'm going to drive us. Berengario won't be at the farm next week, by the way. But we'll think of a way to get you there.'

She opened her mouth to insist she didn't need help, but she paused as a ripple of self-consciousness made its way through her with the sudden suspicion that Berengario had talked at length about her in the same way she'd heard nothing but Alex from the old man.

'I understand you can walk, but you never know what the weather will do at the end of October.'

Alex's car was parked in a lot that backed onto the crumbling city wall. They reached it under another archway off the courtyard, passing the small allotments with plants wilting and turning brown after the cold snap. The ancient Fiat 500 looked as though he might have inherited it along with the building.

Arco found plenty to sniff after he leaped into the footwell in the back.

After a few attempts, the engine coughed and caught and Alex manoeuvred the little car out of its space, craning his neck and draping one long arm over the back of the passenger seat because he didn't seem to quite fit in the driver's seat. Jules sat frozen, leaning forward slightly in case his thumb grazed the back of her neck, which she unfortunately pictured in enough detail that she thought he'd actually done it once or twice.

As usual, she pressed her nose to the window as they took the main road over the river. The vivid yellow of the leaves – now with deep reds and oranges as the season progressed – contrasted wildly with the bright turquoise water rushing over the rocks. The Friulian plain extended out in front of them and she always felt as though she could see so far that she might even find the future somewhere in the distance among the little hills. The looming mountains to the east made her think of Alex's words about Friuli being the crossroads of Europe. Sometimes it seemed as though this pocket of Italy could contain the whole world.

She felt Alex's gaze on her and thought she might have given a contented sigh as she stared out at one of her favourite views, but when she returned the glance, he looked away quickly. She imagined the day ahead, picking olives together, with some trepidation, but a bigger dose of anticipation. One day in each other's company wouldn't get them into too much trouble.

They arrived at Due Pini to find a collection of cars parked on the hard standing in front of the farmhouse and a group of at least thirty people, including Berengario and his girlfriend Elena, Alex's lively, grey-haired neighbour. She also spotted the barman who'd witnessed their not-date and the older man with wild hair and ripped jeans whom she occasionally saw emerging from the tattoo parlour around the corner.

'Arooo!' Arco bounced even before Jules let him out and his excited howl was echoed by yips and barks from an array of other dogs. To her dismay, Jules noticed the big black one from her chaotic arrival at Due Pini two and a half weeks ago.

But Arco made a beeline for another dog first – the downy white poodle belonging to Marisa, the owner of the pet salon. While the poodle made a vain attempt to maintain its dignity, Arco sniffed enthusiastically, no idea how badly he was embarrassing his mistress. But Marisa greeted her with an airy kiss to her cheek and a laugh.

'He really likes Chanel,' Jules said ruefully.

Marisa glanced over Jules's shoulder and her expression brightened. 'Alex!' The stab of discomfort at her tone caught Jules by surprise and she gave herself a stern talking-to as she pointedly ignored the kisses on the cheek they gave each other in greeting. Alex gave Marisa a smile and that only unsettled Jules further. So much for Maddalena's insistence that he never did that.

She couldn't understand much of the conversation between them, only that the owner of the pet salon had her hand curled around his forearm and was standing close and Jules was dismayed that their interaction bothered her. She was supposed to be keeping out of Alex's way and that included leaving him to be fawned over by local women he could perhaps have a real relationship with.

Except, she hated the idea. And she had to admit that Marisa wasn't fawning. Jules was being oversensitive.

Berengario appeared next to her and she greeted him with a quick kiss on the cheek and a smile. 'Come and meet Davide properly,' he said. 'My grandson.'

'Eh, Berengario!' Alex hurried to catch up with them. 'Are you sure that's a good idea after what happened with Fritz?'

'You two really have been talking about me,' she accused.

'He doesn't *stop* talking about you,' Berengario said gruffly, which stuffed any further words she might have said back down her throat. He *what*?

Alex's ears were pink, but it might have been from the chill.

She was about to ask him if Davide was his cousin, but Alex abruptly offered to take Arco and then stalked away, rubbing a hand over the back of his head, leaving Jules mystified – and a little miffed.

Davide seemed a lot more straightforward than her grumpy host, with a wide smile to go with his shiny, dark hair. He wore a turtleneck that, while obviously worn, still gave him a dapper appearance. 'I'm so sorry about what happened on your first day. I wanted to meet you properly then, but I hadn't taken Fritz for a walk yet and he was unsettled. I've just moved back here from Rome and allora, it's nice to finally meet you.'

Jules smiled in return, but struggled to think of anything to say – especially because Fritz seemed determined to make paw prints all over her jeans, desperately snuffling after Arco's scent on her.

Davide scolded him and tugged him off with an apologetic glance. 'Should have kept up with puppy school.'

'I know what you mean,' she said wryly.

'Are you going to show Julia how we harvest?' asked Berengario, slapping Davide on the back. 'We need teams of three. At least she's nice and tall.'

'She's standing right there, Berengario! Talk *to* her, not about her,' Alex called from several metres away, where Arco was sniffing at a potted palm.

She was a second away from calling back an indignant response, but Berengario continued. 'The three of you, then. Good, that's one team.'

Jules looked from one of the three men to the next with a faint suspicion of some subtext she didn't understand, but the group moved off before she could bug Alex for answers.

At the edge of the grove, they gathered around a rusty pickup truck to collect equipment while Jules put Arco on a long lead. She tugged on her gloves and took the little rake Davide held out to her, along with a couple of collapsible baskets, while the two men lugged a roll of plastic netting.

Jules took a moment to study her first specimen. While the olive trees were squat and wizened compared to the towering stone pines, they were still twice as tall as a person – or perhaps a little over one-and-a-half times taller than someone of Alex's proportions. The trunk was wide and knotted and the whole thing leaned far enough for her to wonder if it would one day just teeter to the ground.

The fruit was plentiful, green to light purple ovals hanging richly on every branch, smooth and plump, with a soft coating on the skin.

Davide and Alex rolled out the netting beneath the tree, talking only in clipped sentences that Jules couldn't understand. Fritz was running around off the leash and Jules decided that Arco must know his way around by now and might be more confident meeting Fritz running free, so she unclipped him too, keeping a worried eye on him as he tore off after the big black dog, bounding happily.

'I suppose that means he's not afraid,' she said thoughtfully.

Davide looked uneasily at the two dogs, but quickly recovered his smile. 'Here, let me show you how to use the rastrello.' He brandished the small handheld rake while Alex strapped a battery pack to his back and hefted a long pole. 'The idea is easy: just pull this over the branches as you reach them and let the berries fall into the netting. Alex will agitate the higher branches.

Just make sure he stays on the other side of the tree from you or they'll fall on your head.'

'Okay,' she said, a little daunted.

'But you'll find nothing is quite as easy as it should be in Friûl.'

She shot Davide a puzzled look as she grasped the first branch and tugged the rake over the silver leaves. One rosy olive fell obediently onto the net, but the firm green ones refused. She tried again, but it wasn't until the action was more wrestling than raking that she had success with the more stubborn berries.

'Let me guess, tough Friulian olives?'

'Exactly,' Davide said with a laugh. 'No fruity Tuscan ones that come sweetly off the trees. Here, try one!' He tossed her a berry and she fumbled to catch it.

'Don't eat it!' Alex called out from the other side of the gnarled trunk. Ducking below the foliage, he explained, 'They taste terrible fresh.'

'I know,' she assured him. 'But I'm kind of curious.'

'Don't say I didn't warn you.'

Remarking absently to herself that she was supposed to be getting better at heeding warnings, she still took a reckless bite – and immediately spat out the tough flesh, Davide's laughter ringing in her ears.

'Urgh,' she gagged, poking her tongue out as though that would help to banish the lingering taste. 'It's like... tree bark dipped in acid. It's foul!' The bitter texture still coated her tongue and she met Alex's sympathetic glance.

But Davide clapped her on the shoulder. 'Everyone has to do that at least once.'

'Once will definitely be enough,' she said emphatically. 'It's difficult to believe they're so tasty when they've been processed. Are they even ripe though?'

'They taste foul even when they're dark and ripe. That's the magic of growing olives,' Davide explained. 'The best oil comes from olives that aren't ripe. You have to pick them at the right time and then press them immediately. The frantoio – the oil mill in Cividale – will be working twenty-four hours a day for the next few weeks.'

'Are these ones particularly bitter? For you bitter Furlans?'

Davide gave her a puzzled glance, but Alex answered, 'All olives are bitter. This variety is called Bianchera – a very hardy variety, resistant to cold. They grow like the devil.'

'And they're a devil to pick,' Davide added. 'But the flavour is worth it. Once you've tasted the spice of this oil on bread, fresh in the autumn – you don't need any other food.' He kissed his fingertips.

With another awkward glance at Alex, she decided not to resist temptation. 'I've heard that you can live on just chestnuts in autumn too.' He coughed at the awkward memory and looked away.

'Yes, they're delicious,' Davide continued, oblivious to the undertone. 'Another food that the Tuscans domesticate that we still collect wild from the forest. You know the difference between castagne and marroni.'

It was her turn to clear her thick throat. Everything seemed to be a minefield when it involved her and Alex. 'I've heard about it. Which ones do you collect from the forest here? Castagne?'

'Yes, castagne are the wild delicacy that are free, but you have to work for them. Marroni are farmed. They're bigger and sweeter. We should take the dogs into the forest one time and collect some together,' Davide suggested. 'And find some mushrooms as well. Mamma is always after me to go gathering mushrooms for her.'

The idea appealed strongly to her new-found foraging

instincts and she was about to agree enthusiastically when Alex warned, 'Jules works on the farm most days,' in a low voice.

'Maddalena said we wouldn't be so busy after the harvest,' she countered, giving him a measured look. 'And I thought you said I was working too hard!'

He glanced darkly at Davide and then away, not meeting her gaze. 'You're right. You should do it. You'll love gathering mushrooms.'

I'd rather do it with you, you idiot. Instead, she resumed her work on the olive branch she was raking, ignoring Alex entirely. 'How old is Fritz?' she asked, watching the two dogs chase each other.

'He's only two. What about Arco? Have you had him long?'

'He's three, but I've only had him a little over a year.'

'How does he get on with Laura's cat?' Davide asked with a chuckle.

In her peripheral vision, Alex bolted upright, cursing as he hit his head on a low branch.

Davide continued, oblivious to Alex's reaction. 'I can't imagine Attila would be happy about a dog coming to stay.'

Jules glanced warily at Alex, but he had turned away. 'Attila is very good at hiding from Arco, but the first time they met—'

Alex whipped around to face her just as she realised the night she was referring to and cut herself off. She didn't like how dark his expression was, when she knew how much he'd enjoyed that night too. But they'd gone from 'Thank you for the best date ever,' to 'I wish I'd never met you.' She knew him well enough to understand that he wouldn't injure her on purpose, but that didn't stop it hurting.

And who was Laura? Jules tried to tell herself Davide probably would call his aunt by her first name. She could be Alex's mother, as Maddalena's words had suggested. Those reassurances didn't quite plaster over the cracks of suspicion Jules had been harbouring.

'Poor Attila,' she finished. 'Lucky for him I'm not staying long.' She could almost feel the tension in Alex's jaw from where she stood several metres away. Turning to Davide, she asked, 'So are you two cousins then?'

Davide gave Alex a sidelong glance before he answered. 'Only by marriage.'

'Oh.' The answer explained why they didn't seem close, but the more she thought about it, the more confused she became. 'Whose marriage? His mother's? But wait, Maddalena said her sister was... But if...'

Both went still, Alex turning white. The worried look Davide sent him confirmed that Jules was ignorant of something important – something Alex really should have told her, even if they were only platonic housemates, something she had perhaps already suspected, but hadn't wanted to know for certain.

With a sigh, Davide turned to her and muttered, '*Alex's* marriage. To my cousin Laura. You didn't know?'

She could barely think for the tide of emotion welling up, embarrassed that Alex had kept silent, afraid of what that meant for their already awkward cohabiting situation – but more afraid of what she could already feel was the truth.

The shadows...

Licking her lips, she forced out the question that needed to be asked: 'She died?'

18

Alex definitely should have explained sooner. Jules was looking at him in horror, as though every conversation between them had been a lie. He certainly felt as though he'd been lying to her for weeks and now she knew it too.

'How long has it been since she died?' she asked. He was also very familiar with that cautious tone from others.

'More than three years.' He looked away, refusing to wonder what she thought of those three years. His grieving wasn't her business.

'Um, okay. Now I—' She cleared her throat. 'Right. I under-stand. I mean, of course I can't really understand—'

He cut her off. 'You don't need to say anything.'

'Of course. Okay.'

With a deep sigh, he returned to harvesting. He meant to give her some relief from the pressure of sympathy or condolences or whatever she felt was the right thing to say – which wouldn't be the right thing. But the easy conversation under the olive tree was gone for good.

She barely looked at him as she raked at the leaves until she was cradling her wrist in her hand and her cheeks were pink and her hair filled with twigs. He'd thought he'd wanted her to keep her distance, but as the day of harvesting wore on, he couldn't stand it.

He enjoyed the relief of a few moments alone as he stacked crates of golden-green olives onto the back of the truck in the afternoon.

'Feels like she's always been here, hmm?'

Berengario's voice cut into his thoughts, making him realise how deeply he'd descended into his own miserable mind when he usually enjoyed the camaraderie of the raccolta. 'What?'

'Julia.' Berengario gave him a nudge and Alex glanced over to see her in conversation with Davide as they laid out the nets for the next tree.

'Hmph,' was all he could say in reply, especially when he saw her smile at Davide. In the afternoon sun, she'd taken off the jacket and wore a peach-coloured hoodie that seemed to accentuate the contrast between her blonde hair and dark eyes. Wearing work gloves, her sleeves pushed up her arms and her wide-leg jeans drawing attention to her height, she made a picture he could have gazed at for a lot longer than he would allow himself.

'I'm heading to the mill with the first load of berries,' Berengario continued.

'Va ben,' he responded automatically in the affirmative.

'Can you stop by the mill on your way home? Maddalena promised Gabriella the fresh oil for her event tomorrow. You can take it out to her.'

That got his attention. 'Gabriella? Can't Davide take it?' Gabriella was a family friend who ran a restaurant up in the hills.

'He's bringing the second load to the mill and then he has to get home to Palmanova. Gabriella's place is close to Cividale. Take

Julia. She hasn't seen enough of the area and she'll want to see the old chestnut.'

Alex must have been imagining that Berengario knew the nonsense he had spouted about Julia's eyes. He gave his old friend a measured look. 'It's half an hour away and it'll be dark.'

Berengario shrugged. 'Take a torch. The tree's not far off the road.'

Stifling a grumble, he nodded and went back to work with Julia and her new best friend, Davide, even more annoyed with himself for making too much of... everything. If she liked Davide then it was none of his business, and if she wanted to go and collect mushrooms with him, that was *wonderful*. She'd love it.

The sun had just dipped behind the distant hills when the harvest party packed up for the day and Arco was the first to bound back to the car. Although it wasn't the car exactly that he returned to – it was Alex. He gave the pup a reluctant smile and a rub.

'He's had a good day,' he commented when Jules approached, tugging her gloves off. She stretched and groaned, teetering as she worked the kinks out of her sore muscles. Watching her made his throat thick and he turned his attention back to Arco. 'This is the happiest animal I think I've ever seen.'

'And you have the grumpiest cat?'

His gaze snapped up. Her quip was a return to familiar ground, but there was a catch in her voice that hadn't been there before. When he met her gaze – briefly, because she quickly looked away – he could see she was still working through what she'd learned about him that day. He hadn't intentionally kept the information from her, but— Actually, perhaps he had. He hadn't wanted her to know and now she did.

'I'd say our pets copy our personalities, except that I know I could never be as purely happy as that,' she continued as she slipped into the passenger seat after closing the door behind the contented dog. 'And I know you aren't always grumpy,' she added, but he wasn't sure she'd intended for him to hear.

Or perhaps he was just avoiding the conversation they should probably have. The prickle of emotions ran up to his hairline again when he remembered Davide casually explaining Alex's connection to the family.

'She died?'

A two-word question and a simple nod. So little for someone who held such an important place in his life.

'What are we doing here?' she asked when he turned into the parking lot at the agricultural school that housed the small mill on the outskirts of Cividale.

'Come inside. I have to deliver some oil to a friend of Maddalena's.'

'The oil has already been extracted? Oh, I bet Arco can't come in there. He'll panic if I leave him in the car.'

'I'll just grab the oil then. But tomorrow we can leave Arco at home and I'll show you around.' There was that easy, familiar language again that had been kicking him in the shins all week, but he shouldn't let it bother him so much. Something had obviously changed between them now she knew about Laura.

'Are you sure I wouldn't be in the way?'

'You have to taste the oil fresh from the frantoio – the mill,' he insisted. 'It's a rule.'

'Well in that case.' She gave him a tentative smile. 'You'd better go get the oil.'

'I won't be long.'

He should have expected Berengario to fill a vintage damigiana with fresh oil and he lugged the bulbous green glass bottle laboriously back to the car, clutching it carefully with both hands. Tapping on the passenger-side window, he gestured urgently for

Jules to open the door, heaving the bottle into her lap. Thankfully it was a ten-litre vessel instead of the larger ones which he wouldn't have been able to lift.

She fumbled for it in surprise, her hands covering his for long enough for him to come up in prickles again.

'Sorry,' he said, out of breath, as he withdrew his hands. 'It weighs a lot.' Closing the door firmly behind him before he was tempted to pull the twig from her hair and brush back the strand that had fallen into her face.

Without looking to see what he suspected would be her pinched expression, he started the car and turned onto the main road out of town. Only when they reached the Ponte San Quirino, the border between Friuli proper and the Slovene-speaking Natisone Valley, did she sit up suddenly and peer out of the window.

Orange clouds glowed above the hills and the river rushed over stones, deep below the bridge, its signature aqua waters glowing pale in the evening light.

'Where are we going?'

Guilt washed through him at her short tone. He deserved it. He'd been just as touchy as Attila – for days now. 'Delivering the oil. I should have offered to drop you home. Berengario thought...' He trailed off. Berengario hadn't been serious. He'd been pushing Alex and Jules together again, the wily old man. 'He said that you haven't seen enough of the area.'

'I suppose that's true.' She peered out of the windscreen at the rusty hills, dimming rapidly. 'But how far is it?'

'About half an hour's drive.' He hesitated, wondering just how much she didn't want to be in the car with him. 'Maddalena's friend Gabriella is hosting a special lunch to celebrate the fresh oil tomorrow. She runs a small restaurant near a historic chestnut tree.'

'A historic chestnut tree?'

'It's a coincidence,' he hurried to assure her.

'I didn't think you'd told Maddalena what you said about my eyes while we were in bed,' she replied drily.

He swallowed a reluctant laugh. 'To be honest, I think Berengario set us up and I fell into his trap.' He snapped his mouth shut, not sure he'd intended to admit that – or admit to himself that he hadn't resisted the trap at all.

'What are you talking about?' was all she said in response.

He clenched his jaw as heat crept up his neck. He hadn't expected he could feel even more embarrassed and out-of-place next to her. 'He's matchmaking,' he muttered quietly.

Feeling her eyes on him, he gazed resolutely forward. 'But… why?' she asked.

'Damned if I know,' he answered tightly. 'I've told him over and over again that we're not together and that you're leaving.'

'No, I mean he's your wife's grandfather. Isn't he still grieving? Like you?'

He responded before he'd thought it through. 'Maybe he should be.' He gripped the wheel tightly.

She obviously picked up on his guilt and confusion, because she said, 'I'm sorry. It's none of my business.'

But he wanted to explain. The urge was unexpected. 'Her death was… hard.' Ah, that flicker of pain was why he never talked about it. 'It's complicated,' he finished instead.

'Seriously, you don't have to explain.' Was she relieved? He certainly couldn't be considered the life of the party these days. But the dynamic between them felt wrong and he wanted to right it, as much as that would be a pointless exercise in the long run. She continued. 'I should have guessed. I just felt a bit stupid. That's all. You don't have to confide in me. It's fine.' It didn't sound fine.

'I am sorry you felt stupid. It wasn't my intention.'

'I know,' she said softly.

He took a sharp turn-off and the road narrowed between the hills, the towns little more than small clusters of houses with polished wood shutters, crumbling stonework and rusty farm equipment under corrugated-iron shelters. The signs announcing the names of the settlements were in both Italian and Slovene: Crostù/Hrastovlje; Cosizza di Sotto/Dolenja Kozica.

Jules peered out of the window, taking in what details she could in the fading light. 'We're really in the middle of nowhere.'

'There was a hard border not far from here for decades. Some of the most popular hiking routes now were used by smugglers – or partigiani, the resistance during the Second World War. There was a lot of fighting around here, occasionally even among the different resistance groups, against one another.'

'Is that where this Friulian appreciation for bitterness started?'

'No, that was much, much earlier. When you're invaded as many times as this area has been, you start to be stoic about it.'

'Because *you've* experienced invasion so many times,' she said drily.

'I do remember when the border opened. I was at secondary school. But memories are long around here. The Slovene minority remembers when they weren't allowed to use their language for official purposes and everyone still shudders when you mention Yugoslavia. There was a lot of emigration from this region – to Australia too. Maybe that's why Berengario keeps insisting you might be a Furlan Volpe.'

The sky ahead was turning rapidly navy as the hills grew steeper, with glimpses of mountain pastures in the distance.

'Berengario isn't... He wasn't really...' Jules began, scrunching her eyes closed as she searched for the words. 'He's not really matchmaking, is he? I thought for a moment today that he was giving me nudges and winks about Davide. He's protective of you.'

With a grumble, Alex explained. 'He was trying to make me jealous.'

'He was not! What makes you even think that?'

The hair on the back of his neck stood on end as he thought back to his conversation with Berengario on Thursday on the way to rehearsal. *You're waking up again.* His friend had hinted that he wasn't above using his own grandson to make Alex see what was right in front of him.

But Alex saw her. That was the problem. She made him want to laugh and think of sweet things instead of bitter ones and discover every little detail about her, touch her just for the joy of it. She made him want to be the man he'd been their first evening together.

Except, he wasn't that man. Life had given him a different set of circumstances. And wanting only made him feel guilty – and bitter – and that's why he was in this stupid state, avoiding a person he got on well with, arguing and silences when he should have been a polite host, constantly denying what was obvious every time he looked at her. He was exhausted – even more exhausted than usual, and for once not only from lack of sleep.

'I know he was trying to make me jealous,' he said grimly, flipping on the indicator as he approached the turning where they headed up the switchbacks through the villages clinging to the hillside above. 'I know, because it *worked*, damn it.'

19

Jules sat in stunned silence as the Fiat climbed – and climbed. She had the impression of a wide valley beyond the sharp drop-off at the side of the road. Every few hundred metres, Alex slowed and then carefully swung the car around another tight bend – calmly, as though he hadn't just admitted that he'd been jealous of Davide.

Jealous, when she'd barely listened to Davide, she'd been so caught up in her confusion. When she'd barely been able to look at Alex all afternoon because of the mess of thoughts and feelings about *him* that could go nowhere.

The worst part was that she *had* known, on some level, that this thing between her and Alex was causing problems. She'd just pretended she hadn't – and hoped her suspicions about his great loss weren't true.

She closed her hand around the grip on the car door, as though that could steady her light-headed emotions. Her other hand was curled around the cool glass bottle of fresh olive oil that was slowly making her legs go numb.

The road was so narrow she didn't know how another car

would pass without one of them tumbling into the valley. But people obviously lived up here. Every few minutes came another little settlement, houses with stone detailing and clay roof tiles and wooden eaves like the ones in Cividale.

She should say something, but she was torn between wanting to grumble at him for being hot and cold and apologising herself for intruding on his grief. Certainly, in comparison to her own recent misfortune, he deserved understanding.

That's what she'd been telling herself all day anyway.

Before anything inside her had settled – and her stomach was roiling from more than just her emotions after all the hairpin bends – he finally pulled the car to a stop near a woodpile opposite a rendered building with the shutters closed. The verge was narrow and he had to park on a steep angle, tugging the manual park brake hard.

The last glow of light was rapidly disappearing over the mountains far in the distance and when she pushed open the car door, the cold rushed quickly at her skin. Alex got out and tramped up to the building, knocking at a blue door set under the weathered wooden balcony. The house was decorated with rusty old farm tools and woven baskets. A carriage wheel and an old barrel wine press stood on a small terrace by the door.

There was apparently no answer to Alex's knock and Jules struggled out of the car, lugging the heavy glass. Worried she'd drop it, she dumped it into the footwell, hoping Alex would be able to heft it back out.

'It doesn't look open,' she pointed out as she released the bouncing Arco from the back seat, attaching the lead.

'They only open for lunch for day trippers. There are very few people around here in the evening.'

'I noticed,' she commented drily.

He knocked again, leaning his other hand on the lintel as he did so. He'd probably have to duck to get through the door. With a frown, he turned back in time to see her shiver.

'I don't have Gabriella's number, but I'll call Berengario. Put your... coat on.'

She grabbed the jacket self-consciously, trying not to dwell on the fact that it had belonged to his dead wife Laura.

He called the old man several times, but there was no answer and when he glanced up and met her gaze, the memory of what he'd told her in the car hung between them: Berengario was matchmaking.

'I'll call Maddalena,' he murmured. That conversation was animated – and punctuated by deep sighs and an exasperated, 'Che cosa?' When he ended the call, he was still grumbling to himself. She caught something that sounded like, 'Madonna,' but was definitely not a prayer. 'She says she arranged that the oil would be collected tomorrow morning. No idea where Gabriella is.'

'Berengario has definitely been up to no good,' Jules said flatly.

'God, I'm sorry.'

'It's not your fault,' she pointed out.

'It *is*. I knew what he was doing and I still brought you all this way for nothing, after such a long day. I'll find a place to leave the oil and we'll go home again. Make sure you stay warm.'

She watched him as he hauled the bulbous bottle out of the footwell and stomped up the concrete stairs to the back of the building. He seemed to be even grumpier than he'd ever been with her.

He ran an agitated hand through his hair as he flung the car door open again and she rushed to close Arco into the back and climb in herself. 'There's nothing lost, Alex,' she assured him. 'It's interesting for me to see this place.'

That only seemed to make him grumpier. 'Merda,' he cursed, leaning over her to rummage in the glovebox. He came away with a small torch. 'I was supposed to show you the monumental chestnut.'

'We can just go. It's almost completely dark,' she pointed out.

'You don't want to see it? Then I really have brought you out here for nothing.'

Confusion rippled over her skin again seeing him so worked up. He'd admitted he was jealous of Davide, had willingly allowed Berengario to trick them into spending time together, and yet he was moody and prickly, as though he couldn't get away from her fast enough. 'Fine!' she threw back, lifting her hands in exasperation before reaching for Arco's lead once more. 'I want to see the tree!'

In the daylight, the narrow paths between the run-down stone buildings of the tiny village would have been charming. Even at night, the place was atmospheric, especially with the mist beginning to swirl as the temperature dropped. She couldn't see many lights on – and the shutters of most of the buildings were firmly closed – but there were street lamps set at intervals and Jules had that feeling again of travelling back in time with each step. Unlike Cividale, with its ancient roots in Roman and medi-aeval times, here she could imagine the hardy farmers from the previous century holing up and preparing to defend themselves from a variety of powers, all of them foreign in this isolated valley.

They took a paved walkway with grass growing through the stones, heading steeply up behind the town, and Jules followed as Alex took long, impatient strides. Arriving in a clearing, she saw the silhouette of a craggy tree trunk that split in two about halfway up. It wasn't enormously tall, but so wide her outstretched arms wouldn't even span half of it. She stayed close to Alex – to the light – as they took the makeshift stairs of earth and wood and Arco bounced happily ahead of them in the dark.

The tree was perched on a slope facing the wide valley behind. Without daylight, the view was more a sense of openness and the glint of white on a distant mountain top. The sight of snow gave Jules a start – a reminder that winter was coming, time was passing, faster for her than for this wizened old tree.

Alex moved the torchlight over the trunk and she skimmed her fingertips along the crevices in the bark, taking in the jumble of knots and shoots and the vine growing up the middle.

'It's about four hundred years old. So at one time, this tree was a citizen of the Republic of Venice,' he said softly.

'I wonder if the Doges liked chestnuts.'

He peered at the ground, then twisted his foot carefully in front of him, before bending to retrieve something. Opening his hand in front of her, he held two smooth, brown nuts in his palm.

'I doubt it. Chestnuts were always considered peasant food, although that could be true for most delicacies in Friûl.'

He continued to hold his hand out, so she reached hesitantly for one of the nuts, brushing her fingers over his rough palm. The nut was smooth, curved on one side and flat on the other, where it had nestled against the second. She glanced from the grand old tree clinging stoically to the mountain to the cold evening glittering with mist and broken by spots of light from the hillside settlements.

'It's so isolated, but you can tell that many people have visited this place.'

'Chestnuts are also a symbol of endurance,' he continued quietly. 'Sometimes we call it the bread tree.'

'Emergency rations from the forest,' she mused.

'Exactly.'

'Maybe Berengario had a good idea,' she commented, appreciating the stillness of the cool evening, the feeling of being far away from the real world. A smile on her lips, she glanced at Alex to find him studying her warily. She gulped. 'I meant suggesting you bring me here. This is why I came to Europe in the first place: to explore and see new things. I didn't mean the matchmaking.'

'Of course you didn't. Should we go back?'

She glanced doubtfully at him, wishing she could make out more of his expression.

The darkness had drawn in on them as they stood contemplating the ancient tree and she had to stay close to Alex or risk tumbling head over heels down the hillside.

'I can't see,' she explained when he appeared unnerved by her snuggling up to him. 'Take it easy, Alex. It's not my fault that you don't want to hang out with me.'

'What?' There was an edge to his voice.

'I know you'd rather I weren't gatecrashing your life. I know it's awkward that we slept together and inconvenient that I keep reminding you of... life with your wife, but I can't do anything about it! You don't have to share your deepest secrets, but I'd appreciate it if you'd stop treating me like chewing-gum on your shoe! I'll be gone as soon as I can arrange it.'

He caught her arm, stopping them both under the dim glow of a street lamp at the edge of the village. Arco tugged at his lead, but the expression on Alex's face was too wild for Jules to look away. Uncertain, he stuffed his hands into the pockets of his threadbare jeans.

'There doesn't seem to be anything in between,' he said, his voice strained.

'In between what?'

'Being complete strangers and...' He lifted a hand to her face, gritting his teeth when he gave in and grazed his fingertips over her cheek and under her chin. The touch was so light, Jules should barely have felt it, but the ripples it sent over her skin told her exactly what he was going to say. 'Between being strangers and whatever we were that first night. I'm using so much energy on *not* kissing you...' He swallowed audibly, his gaze darting to her mouth and away again.

Her breath stalled. The circle of light from the lamp and the intimate darkness, the deserted streets of an isolated village made the perfect set of circumstances to think about kissing. She had such vivid memories of the first night, standing next to the stone wall by the river as a simple goodbye kiss transformed into a joyful kind of heat and wanting.

Would he do it? Kiss her again here, tonight? What would she taste in the kiss now? His jealousy? Grief?

She understood deep in her skin what he'd meant, how much energy they'd been expending to suppress *this,* the crackle of awareness. What would happen if she just—?

20

'We should go back to the car,' he said. Grasping her hand, he took off along the narrow path of pale stones, tugging her along behind while she recovered from her surprise. He realised too late that if they weren't supposed to be kissing, they probably shouldn't hold hands either, but he was bone-tired and confused and he wanted to hold her hand, so he threaded his fingers with hers.

She held on, gripping so tightly that he had to glance at their tangled fingers to make sure he wasn't imagining it. Was she annoyed with him? She had every right to be.

As he clutched her hand and gave himself a moment to feel what he felt, without judgement, fear or guilt, he agreed that the Berengario's matchmaking scheme might have been a good idea too. He'd needed this, an hour alone with Jules somewhere outside the house to let his conflicted emotions come to a head.

The cold was seeping through his old woollen pullover by the time they returned to the car and the hand that hadn't been clasping hers was chilled. He was strangely reluctant to drive back down, even though that was the right thing to do. He gave her hand one more squeeze before letting go to climb into the driver's seat.

'Do you think Berengario interfered with the car so we'd be stranded here overnight?' she said warily after she'd settled Arco in the footwell in the back.

'I think saying that might be tempting fate.' Closing one eye as he turned the key, he shared a smile with her when the car started up without a problem.

'Phew,' she said drily.

Reaching for the old handbrake, he pressed the button and pushed and... Nothing happened. He jiggled it, but again – nothing. Frowning, he stepped on the footbrake, wrapped both hands around the lever and pushed, grunting with effort, but it wouldn't shift.

'Oh dear,' Jules said under her breath, although her tone was still dry.

'Maybe I can...' He put the car into reverse and revved, slipping in the clutch to try to jolt the wheels back a little and dislodge the brake, but the car only made a disturbing creak and then a foul smell wafted into the interior. He turned the engine off.

Jules shivered and he noted the temperature on the dashboard: eight degrees. No hypothermia, but it wouldn't be comfortable to wait in the car for long. Arco whined and barked and she settled him with a hand in his fur.

'Berengario had better answer this time,' Alex said through gritted teeth and called the old man. Of course, he didn't pick up.

'Do you think he put glue on the brake pads?'

'I don't think he wants us dead.'

'Or like one of those Korean shows: if we die at the same time, we'll be reborn on the same day and find each other in the next life.'

He turned to her fully, his elbow on the steering wheel. 'What kind of shows do you watch?'

'They're die-hard romantics apparently.'

'Yeah, *die* hard. I don't find that romantic.'

A flinch of dismay crossed her features. 'Oh God, I'm sorry. I didn't think.'

'And this is why I didn't tell you,' he replied with a deep sigh. 'I didn't want you to just see the guy whose wife died. That's what everyone else sees.'

Her nostrils flared and he could see her struggle to decide what to say next. 'You think the guy I met the first night is not who you are?'

'I think it's disturbing how easily I kept Laura a secret.' He leaned back on the headrest, feeling ambushed – by the truth about his own motives. 'I'm not resentful of you. I'm annoyed at myself for trying to keep her out of... this.' He winced, hoping she wouldn't ask what he meant by 'this' because he had no idea.

But she just said, 'You don't have to.'

'Have to what?'

'Keep her out of...'

His eyes drifted closed and his cheeks heated. 'This,' he repeated softly.

'Yeah,' she agreed hesitantly. 'This.' Then there was a weight on his shoulder and the scent of herbal shampoo and olive tree reached his nose and a strand of hair tickled his jaw and the handbrake on his emotions released until he wanted to laugh and cry at once.

He fumbled for her face, finding her forehead with his thumb because he didn't want to open his eyes yet. Even just tracing her jaw with his fingertips, he knew he wasn't even close to forgetting the heady chemistry of the day they'd met.

He nudged her face up and kissed her.

She broke off to suck in a surprised breath, but that was her only hesitation. Clenching a hand in his pullover, she kissed him back, hard enough for him to know she'd felt it every time he'd resisted doing this over the past two and a half weeks. She pushed him back in the seat and he covered her closed hand, smiling as she kissed him bossily, teaching him a lesson that he was glad to learn.

We should have been kissing all this time.

'You don't have to be jealous of Davide,' she murmured, her lips skimming his cheek, his jaw after she'd spoken the words.

'I'm not jealous of Davide right now,' he responded, searching for her mouth again and drawing out a deep kiss. 'I'm sorry I made you think I didn't want you. That first date was...'

'What was it?' She drew back with a wry smile. 'I've been trying to work that out myself.'

'A surprise,' he finished – inadequately, but the word would have to do for now.

She shivered and he noticed how cold he was himself. With a sigh, he dropped his hands from her face and looked around for his phone.

'I'll have to call the breakdown service. I have no idea how long it will take them to come out this way. Can I call you a taxi?'

She shook her head as he found the number. 'If you have to wait here, I'll wait too.'

The time estimate was three hours. 'It's a busy Saturday night,' he explained to Jules in dismay after he disconnected the call.

But her response was a shrug. 'These things happen,' she said lightly, stretching in her seat. She glanced at him. 'I thought you said this was the crossroads of Europe. Surely there should be a tow-truck on standby at all times.'

He clicked his tongue at her, but gestured her closer at the same time. 'You've had leaves in your hair all afternoon.' He picked them off and carefully untangled the twig from her pony-tail, trying not to think of Berengario's words about wanting to take care of her. It was his character, that was all.

She might know a little about his situation now, but they'd still promised each other no expectations – especially not the expectation that she might stay longer than necessary.

'Your passport will be on its way soon, yes?' he forced himself to ask.

She nodded. 'I had an email from the Italian passport office saying the application had been approved. That one might be another week. My new Australian one should be on its way too, according to the processing times.'

'Mmph,' was all he managed to say in response.

'Do you think... we'll keep kissing for that time? More?' She peered at him guardedly.

'I want to,' he answered, a little dismayed that she'd been reckless – brave – enough to ask.

'But?'

Had he implied a 'but'? Perhaps there was always a 'but' with him: he was single *but* he'd been married and his wife had died; he liked her a lot *but* he'd belonged to someone else first; they were good together in bed *but* she would never have a chance to get to know him properly in such a short time.

'Well, I don't sleep well. I told you that.'

'Is that since she died?'

He nodded, the feelings rising in his throat.

She studied him and apprehension tightened in his chest again, wondering what she saw, what the damage was three years after the worst had happened.

Glancing away as though she'd seen enough, she gave his

hand a brief squeeze then snatched hers back. 'Your hands are *freezing*! How are we going to manage three hours of this?'

Peering back at the rustic restaurant, shuttered and empty, he said, 'Maybe Gabriella leaves a key out.'

* * *

Arco was the first to zip inside after Alex jiggled the back door of the restaurant open. Maddalena had called her friend to ask about a key, so thankfully they weren't breaking and entering. Apparently Gabriella was in Udine for the evening and wouldn't be back until tomorrow.

Alex had to duck under the lintel as he followed Jules into the lingering warmth of the kitchen and switched on the light. She still felt a glow under her skin when she looked at him, fired up again by the kisses in the car. She wasn't looking for everlasting love, happily-ever-after any more, like the foolish twenty-five-year-old Jules who'd fallen for Luca and turned her life upside down. But whatever 'this' was between them, she was pleasantly tipsy on it.

Following Arco through the archway and into the dining room, Jules sighed with relief to find the air still warm. Alex gestured to an old stove in the corner and she approached happily, pressing her palms to the pink glazed tiles that still held heat from the fire.

Arco turned in a circle and squeezed into the space between the stove and the table beside it, while Jules slipped into the bench seat to admire the heavy old beams in the ceiling and the rusty ironwork nailed into the exposed stone walls. In the middle of the room was a fireplace, open on all sides, with an enormous decorative flue hanging from the ceiling above, plastered and edged with red and white fabric.

'*That*,' Alex said, following her gaze, 'is a lovely fogolâr.'

'It's a real fire hazard,' she responded.

He lifted his hands in a shrug. 'That too. Gabriella said there was some jota left in the fridge that we can have. I'll put it on to warm.'

Jules rummaged in her backpack for the foil tray of dog food she'd packed that morning and set it in front of Arco. He was so tired, he just stuck his nose against the packaging at first, before hauling himself to his feet and swallowing down the wet food seemingly without chewing.

'Did he just burp?' Alex asked, appearing in the room again with two glasses of water and a puzzled smile.

'He burps a lot. Doesn't Attila do that?' Her own smile wobbled as she remembered that Attila was Laura's pet and that was why Alex had stumbled over his admission the first night that he hadn't named the cat. She certainly couldn't fault him for keeping the truth from her when she now seemed to put her foot in it with every sentence she uttered.

But he didn't get that haunted look in his eyes, he just said, 'Attila would never burp with an audience, so if he does, I'll never hear it.'

'He should teach Arco some manners while we're here.'

'Did you say you've only had Arco just over a year? How did that happen?' he asked as he opened the door of the tiled stove and peered in.

'God, you want to hear all about my stupid mistakes? Now I finally understand a little what you've been through, I feel bad for complaining about a break-up.'

'Jules,' he said carefully, his voice deep. 'We don't compare heartache. It doesn't help anyone, including me. I have enough pity from myself.' He rubbed a hand over his eyes.

'You're right,' she agreed.

Satisfied with her answer, Alex turned away again to stuff some newspaper and three pieces of wood into the stove, adding a rolled-up firelighter and setting it all expertly alight with a single match, allowing them to burn with the door open for a few moments. Staring into the flames, it seemed easier for her to talk.

'Arco is a symptom of my stubbornness. I jumped into the relationship with Luca too fast and I stayed to salvage my pride. Maybe I sensed him drawing away and I thought a pet might keep us together, but it only gave us something else to argue about after we broke up.'

'Is that why you didn't want to stay with me? Did it trigger your feelings, moving in with someone you... well, you know.'

'I didn't really think of it like that,' she reassured him. 'That one time with you was very different from the two years with Luca. And my main worry was keeping my hands off you.'

'That challenge I am familiar with,' he said earnestly, turning around again, but when he pressed his lips together, she could make out the smile he was stifling. 'Luca, is it?' he asked. 'The guy I'm supposed to beat up? What? The beating up was your idea.'

'It was not. I prefer non-violence.'

'So you want me to beat him up in a figurative sense?'

'Do you have a special book of Furlan insults or something?'

His smile broke out and it felt like she'd won a prize. 'We save those for the people of Trieste.'

'You weirdos,' she teased.

'"Va' a vore." That's what a Furlan would tell your Luca.' He stood and disappeared back into the kitchen.

'What does it mean?' she called after him, scooting to the end of the bench so she could see him stirring something over the gas stove.

'"Go to work",' he translated. 'He sounds a bit useless.'

Jules snorted water up her nose. Alex peered around the

doorway in concern, but she waved him back into the kitchen, pressing a hand to her chest. 'I'm okay,' she croaked. 'But how do you say it again? I love that. He always had big plans for the future, but getting his hands dirty in the here and now was not his style.'

'Whereas you've been a lifesaver for Maddalena. No wonder Berengario insists you have Friulian roots.' He set two bowls of thick stew with beans and chunks of something unidentifiable onto the table and collapsed into the chair opposite Jules with a tired sigh. The dish would have looked less than appetising if it weren't for the scent of garlic and smoked meat rising off it. 'Va' a vore,' he repeated. 'That's the phrase.'

'Mandi, va' a vore!' she said, grinning when he chuckled. 'Bon pitìc,' she added, gesturing to the bowls.

'You remembered the Furlan for "buon appetito"?' He looked impressed and she wished she could take credit for being amazing at languages.

But in this case, there was a simple explanation that didn't involve much effort on her part. 'It's painted on one of your ceramic bowls,' she reminded him.

'It's still appreciated, when you try to learn the language.'

If he kept giving her those smiles, she'd have all the incentive she needed to learn Furlan.

'What's this dish, then?' she asked.

To her surprise, Alex laughed again. 'Jota,' he supplied. 'The original meaning of the term is a bit lost, but it probably means the food that the pigs eat? You know what I mean?'

She peered at her bowl. 'And this pig slop is a local delicacy? Maybe I should have foraged for chestnuts instead.'

Alex drizzled olive oil over his swill and tucked in, ignoring her, so she did the same, grasping her spoon and scooping up a mouthful of the beige stew. The pork, potato and garlic in the warm, lightly salty broth gave her the comfort of an imminent full stomach, but there was a tang to it as well, a hint of Eastern Europe, she guessed.

'Is that cabbage? This really is peasant food.'

'Peasant food is a compliment in Friûl,' he quipped, pointing his spoon at her. 'It's crauti – sauerkraut. This is a dish from the Trieste region and Trieste has half a foot in Slovenia and is a bit stuck in its days of Hapsburg greatness, hence the sauerkraut.'

'I thought you only liked to insult people from Trieste, but here you are enjoying their food.'

His lips formed that little pout she remembered from their first date. 'As we say, the bell-tower of your home town is always the tallest.'

'And you wonder why the region is so scarred when you offer to beat people up and have fights with your neighbours.'

'It's not all our fault. It's the earthquakes as well.'

'Earthquakes! What woes have not befallen Friûl in its history?' she teased.

He didn't respond and Jules wondered whether he was thinking about his own woes, rather than those of his home. If he didn't want to talk about his wife, she respected that, but she couldn't think of anything else to say, her mind was so full of questions.

Alex sighed, hanging his head. 'Ask me,' he muttered. 'I can see you want to.'

'Ask you what?'

'Something. About her. I should have told you. I don't need pity, and sympathy is even worse. So ask me what you want to know and anything you don't ask me at least won't upset you.'

Her skin prickled at the thought that he was worried about upsetting *her*. Taking a deep breath, she dived straight in. 'How did she die?'

Her throat clogged, realising too late how the question reduced this unknown woman's life to her last moments. How much must Alex hate that! She wished they didn't have this hurdle to overcome before their relationship – *friendship* – could return to even ground. She considered rescinding the question, but with a flick of his brow he drew a breath to answer.

'A car accident.' His mouth was thin, pulled tight. 'That was the cause anyway.'

'How old was she?'

'Twenty-eight.'

She didn't have to say it to know he was thinking the same thing: her own twenty-eighth birthday was two weeks away. The unwanted sympathy rushed at her again.

'I know I'm wearing her jacket. Is it her house too? Did you inherit it from her?'

'Yes, it belonged to her grandmother, Gigi. It was closed up for a long time before I came home and... needed it again.'

'She didn't die here?'

He shook his head. 'In London. Guy's Hospital.'

'Did you move to London with her?'

'Mmhmm. She was a corporate lawyer – something to do with mergers and acquisitions.'

'Wow,' Jules said, hoping he didn't catch the tickle of her own inadequacy in her tone. How sad was it to compare herself to a dead woman? Glancing warily at Alex, she found him staring blankly at the stove. It struck her, how different that first date would have been, if he'd told her he'd lost his wife. She understood why he hadn't wanted to be that person, just for one evening.

But there was no solution to the death of a loved one. He couldn't just leave, the way she'd left Luca. She almost wished she didn't understand how complicated it was for him to be attracted to someone else.

He sighed and stifled a yawn and Jules felt the same lethargy creep into her skin, now her stomach was full of pork and potatoes and sauerkraut, and the warmth from the stove had grown fuggy and thick. Alex stood to wash the bowls, but she took them from him and ushered him to the bench seat.

'You rest,' she instructed him firmly.

When she'd finished the dishes, she returned to the dining room to find him slumped against the wall, his head lolling. But he blinked and then gave her a groggy smile. She wondered how much he usually slept, how he managed to function. The hollows under his eyes were a deep grey, the skin puckered, but as he blinked at her, she caught glimpses of the vivid blue of his irises.

She didn't want to be curious or hear a sob story that would no doubt upset her, but she couldn't help but *wonder*. What had they looked like together, Alex and Laura? Had they bantered and joked the way she and Alex did?

How much he must have loved her. She knew him well enough for that thought to kick her in the stomach and that served as a warning. Perhaps he should have told Jules he was a widower, but she hadn't really wanted the heartache of imagining what he'd gone through – what he *was going* through, she realised with dismay.

Even if she should have learned her lesson by now, she still scooted over to him on the bench and tucked herself into his side. He lifted his arm, draping it heavily around her back, and she sank into him and ignored the pricking of tears now she understood why he'd been so conflicted these past two weeks.

The platonic housemate thing had been a bad idea, when they could have been holding each other like this.

'Do we need to talk about... this?' he mumbled sleepily,

pressing a clumsy kiss to her hairline and then his eyelids drooped and closed.

This, between them, whatever it was, she didn't want to question it yet.

'We don't have to talk right now,' she comforted him softly.

'Good,' he murmured. 'I like this – you. But there were things about Laura's death that I struggled with.'

'I understand,' she said, muffling the words in his old pullover when her nose began to sting with the urge to cry.

'You don't,' he insisted with a sigh.

Settling her palm over his chest as though she were stemming the bleeding of his heart, she said, 'Shh. I can tell it was traumatic. That's enough. I don't need the whole story.'

He took a breath as though he were going to say something, but stalled. 'I suppose it's enough for now – for you. That's good,' he finally said, his voice rough.

'Keep your secrets,' Jules whispered when his breathing evened out. He was more passed out than peacefully asleep, but even that must have been some relief for him. 'I don't think I can hear it.'

21

Jules was jolted awake by the tinkle of Alex's phone, where it sat on the table. She lay awkwardly sprawled on him, nearly falling off the bench now he'd slumped further.

He grumbled something unintelligible and was so groggy she would have mistaken him for drunk if she hadn't known it was just the long day and his erratic sleep. Snatching his phone, she silenced the ringtone and extricated herself as carefully as she could, slipping into the kitchen to answer.

'Pronto,' she said. At least she'd trained herself to confidently answer the phone in Italian over the past three years. The person on the line had a thick accent that she struggled with, so she asked him to speak more slowly, eventually understanding that the breakdown service had arrived. 'Arrivando! Un minuto,' she assured the man that she was coming, fetching her jacket and ending the call.

Glancing at Alex, she quickly collected a few more seat cushions and propped his head up, tugging his feet onto the bench seat with a silent apology to Gabriella. But his sleep was worth the bad manners. Finding Alex's keys in the kitchen, she headed outside to deal with the car.

It seemed to be an easy fix, once the mechanic towed the Fiat down onto the flat and crawled underneath, and the car didn't need to be repaired in the shop. When the flashing lights of the truck disappeared again down the mountain, the night was cool and still and dark. Glancing at her phone, Jules saw it was past ten o'clock.

There was no way she'd wake Alex to drive down the mountain now.

Instead, she locked the car and slipped back inside, sighing when the warmth embraced her. She opened the stove and carefully added another two pieces of wood. Tiptoeing to the bench, she checked that Alex was still sleeping, allowing satisfaction to creep over her when she observed his even breaths and the relaxed lines of his face.

She wanted to slip back onto the bench with him, but there wasn't room now he was stretched out on it, so she fashioned her own bed on a row of chairs, turned off the light and tried to sleep despite her spiralling thoughts.

Now she knew about Laura, it was as though the stopper on his personality had been popped and the man from their first date had appeared in front of her again. Except now she knew he was also a stubborn, grieving husband, and that part didn't just disappear. She didn't want it to disappear, even though tearing her heart out over a man was not a sensible next step in working out her life.

Everything in Friuli had been more than she'd bargained for, but as long as she left at the end, these few weeks could be a seminal period of learning and change in her life, not another poor decision like moving to Italy for Luca.

When she opened her eyes, there was light creeping around

the shutters. Awkwardly pushing herself up from the narrow chairs, her back twinged and her shoulder ached. She must have slept for longer than she'd thought, if the crick in her neck was anything to go by.

'There's no hurry.' Alex crouched in front of her with a half-smile on his lips. His hair was mussed and his beard a little fuzzy, but his eyes were bright and it was lovely to see his face first thing in the morning.

Arco bustled up to her, nuzzling her knee firmly until she gave him a rub. Alex had his coat on and she realised he must have taken the dog outside and let her sleep.

'Don't we have to get back?'

'The clocks changed overnight, so it's only six thirty.'

'Well in that case...' She stroked a thumb over his cheek, her fingers drifting into his hair. His smile faded, but he didn't pull away. Still not sure if she was supposed to do it, she pressed a feathery kiss to his lips and pulled back again, but he followed, dropping his knees to the floor for stability so he could take her face in both of his hands and kiss her properly. A zing of gratification – and well-being and comfort – shivered through her as his fingers tangled in her hair.

'Good morning,' he murmured as he drew back and peered at her, his voice rough. 'Did you deal with the car in the middle of the night?'

She nodded. 'It's all fixed. You were sleeping so...'

'Thanks.' He pressed another hard kiss to her mouth.

'Did you sleep okay after that?'

He gave an eloquent toss of his head. 'Not too bad. How's your neck? You didn't look comfortable.'

Her cheeks heated at the thought that he'd watched her while she'd slept, but she'd done the same to him last night. 'It hurts a bit.' He dropped his warm fingers to the back of her neck. 'Ohh, that's better,' she rasped as his fingertips dug in and massaged.

'I took Arco out already, but maybe you want to see the place in the daylight?'

She grinned. 'Definitely. I wished last night that Berengario had found a way to send us on this fool's errand in the light.'

'An oversight, for sure,' he said with a chuckle. 'Come on.' Grasping her hand, he tugged her to her feet.

Outside, it was still cold even though she was wrapped up. The mist had cleared and the sight that greeted Jules as she came around to the front of the building made her come to a sudden halt. Wild forested hills stretched before her, with the hazy grey mountains in the distance, topped with white. Trees welcomed the morning light in every shade from deep green to glowing orange and red. The only signs of human settlement were the occasional tiny hamlets of clay-roofed houses with thin ribbons of smoke emerging from the chimneys.

She was looking down on a secret valley. The forest didn't judge her – and had seen much worse than a woman who had fancied herself in love with someone who didn't love her back. The landscape hinted at a bigger picture – a future that would wind its path no matter how many mistakes Jules made.

When Alex's arms came around her and she leant back into him, she wondered whether perhaps her next mistake was currently keeping her warm against the chill. Now though, she was looking forward to making it, no matter the consequences.

* * *

The Fiat made it back down the mountain, although she could tell Alex was nervous. The roads grew wider and the more frequent houses, businesses and workshops were evidence of returning to civilisation.

She knew the river was coming and pressed her face to the window to catch a glimpse of the ravine and the rushing green water. When she turned back, Alex was smiling indulgently at her.

'There's something about that river. It's not wide or grand, but it feels like... this place. A hidden gem.'

'When you leave, we'll have to swear you to silence.'

She laughed, leaning back against the headrest. Although thoughts of her departure were a little mixed, especially when she glanced at a particular square jaw and a figure that didn't quite fit in the driver's seat of the little car, that prospect was somewhere in the hazy future and not today.

She recognised the outskirts of Cividale, the newer houses that still had clay roof tiles like the ancient buildings within the city walls. A white sign announced they were entering Cividale del Friuli, with 'Cividât' in Furlan added beneath, but they had left the area where the names were repeated in Slovene.

Navigating back streets until they reached the city wall, Alex drove through the narrow gate and then they were in the old town of colourful buildings with painted shutters, brick bell-towers and ancient stone walls. Passing carefully under the crumbling arch into the courtyard in front of Alex's house, they pulled into the parking space behind.

Alex hopped out before Jules had decided whether or not she was going to grab him for a kiss and she was rather grumpy about that until he wrenched open her door and hauled her out – and against him. His arm tight around her back, he lifted a hand to her face and rested his cheek against hers for a moment, before pressing a light, restrained kiss to her lips.

'I hope you're okay with...'

'This?' she asked, gratified when her joke coaxed out his smile. God, she'd missed that smile. She kissed him back. The hand on her face stiffened and he deepened the kiss, making her skin tingle right to her toes. When he drew back, she looked him in the eye and reassured him. 'But I know it's not... we're not...'

'"This",' he began with another little kiss, as though he couldn't help himself, 'is what it is, hmm? Just keep talking to me.'

'You too,' she warned, giving him a playful shove, 'Mr Strong-Silent-Type.' After she'd attached Arco's lead and let him out of the car, Alex laced his fingers with hers as they headed for the front door.

But as soon as they passed into the courtyard, Alex stiffened and shook off her hand. The sting of the action caught her by surprise and she was about to ask what was wrong with him when she saw the reason he'd panicked. Walking across the courtyard from Elena's apartment was Berengario, dressed for another day of olive harvesting.

'Eccovi!' he exclaimed at their appearance, gesticulating with his wrinkled cap. He drawled something else that sounded like a question.

Alex threw up his arm as well. '*What happened*?' he repeated in a raised voice. 'Exactly what you wanted to happen.' He slipped into his native language as the two sparred, Alex agitated and Berengario puffing up his chest and sneering to hide the defensive glint in his eye.

'That old car is a piece of shit,' he said suddenly, in careful English. 'I told you to buy a new one two years ago.'

'And you told me to take Jules sightseeing in the dark!'

'Jules, hmm? You are friends again I see. It worked out well, didn't it?' Berengario asked, his chin in the air. Jules wasn't sure if she imagined his gaze dipping to their hands – or the emphasis on the word 'friends'. 'But you can go and wash.' She wasn't imagining the wrinkle of his nose. 'I'll see you at Due Pini later.'

She followed Alex to his door, where he fumbled with his keys before heaving it open with a little too much force. When she'd closed it carefully behind her, he leaned on the wall by the stairs, his head falling back.

'I'm sorry.' The apology – and the strain in his jaw told her he was as mixed-up as she was – went a long way to settling her resentment. 'I reacted without thinking, but I still have to live here after you go – live with their concern. I thought I could just go with it, but that's harder than I thought.'

The tension drained from her, replaced by a bleak kind of acceptance. 'You still have to hide from your interfering Italian family and your zombie neighbours,' she said with a nod, her voice trailing off. 'And I won't always be here to protect you.'

With a chuckle that was almost a sigh, he snagged the waist-band of her jeans and tugged until she bumped up against him again. 'Just remember,' he said, giving her a squeeze and a breathy kiss to her cheek before straightening and setting her away from him again, 'I never *don't* want to kiss you.'

22

Alex wasn't sure how much Berengario knew, but whatever he'd seen that morning had been enough for him to step up his interference to excruciating levels. Maddalena was at the mill supervising the pressing, leaving Berengario to throw them together at every chance.

He shooed Davide away whenever he came near Jules – not that it stopped Alex asking her if she'd told his cousin-in-law to call her Jules as well. The twinkle in her eyes when she'd realised he was still jealous had been worth it, especially since it temporarily banished the shadow of caution she'd been wearing in her expression since they were nearly caught holding hands.

Berengario sent them alone to the farthest tree and instructed Alex to hold the ladder for her as she stretched for the high berries. Alex couldn't quite resist a crooked smile at the view from below.

After pausing at lunchtime for blecs – rustic buckwheat pasta with butter and cheese – they were headed into town to the mill – together, at Berengario's instruction – with the next load of berries and firm instructions to give Jules a taste of the new oil.

Arco was frolicking with Chanel, so Marisa promised to keep an eye on him.

'I'm not the best tour guide,' Alex pointed out to Berengario as they closed the tray on the truck in preparation for the drive back to Cividale.

'That's certainly true,' his friend muttered. 'But for God's sake you can be a bit more hospitable? She likes you,' he added out of the side of his mouth.

'We're not primary school children,' Alex responded, annoyed by the complex subtext of truth and obfuscation in the conversation.

'No?' Giving Alex another slap on the back of the head, Berengario stomped off.

'I still like him better than Luca's mother,' Jules commented as she fastened her seat belt.

'Mothers-in-law are always problematic – Italian ones doubly so,' he said lightly, starting the engine of the old pickup.

'You know, for all the stupid mistakes I made, there's one thing I did right: choosing Italian bureaucracy over marriage.'

'That's an interesting way to express it.' Questions flooded his mind, now his self-preservation instincts were in retreat and his curiosity could come to the fore.

'It seemed the sensible thing at the time – which makes me laugh because moving to another country for a two-month relationship is not sensible, no matter how you look at it. But anyway, I knew I was theoretically eligible for Italian citizenship, so I applied for that instead of getting married like we'd discussed.'

He tried to respond, but choking out *You nearly got married after two months?!* didn't feel like the right thing to say.

'Urgh, imagine going through a divorce on top of everything right now – it was definitely a close call. I was way too young to get married anyway, regardless of how long we'd been together.'

She glanced at him suddenly. 'Uh, I don't mean to imply anything if you got married young.'

He gave an awkward shrug. 'We *were* young. Twenty-four.'

'Bloody hell!'

He didn't always notice her accent, but in that expression he picked up on the broader vowels than he'd been used to in British English – and her emphatic tone made him smile.

'But we met when we were teenagers and got together when we were nineteen.'

'Wow, really? At nineteen I was still getting drunk on pre-mixed vodka drinks.'

He shuddered involuntarily.

'Yeah, I know. I was not classy at nineteen. I bet you started drinking wine at the table with your parents in a civilised, Italian manner.'

'We joke that Furlans are alcoholics who started drinking wine at six years old, but at least as teenagers we mix our *own* rum and coke.' He glanced sideways to find her gawping at him and gave her a wink.

'How old are you? With the tired eyes, it's hard to tell.' *Tired eyes.* Strangely, he didn't mind the observation, especially not in her matter-of-fact tone.

'Younger than I look. I'm thirty-one.'

'You lost her before you were even thirty?'

He nodded, checking his blind spot before overtaking a puttering tractor. 'And you avoided being married and divorced by thirty.'

'I'm sorry if I'm talking about her too much – if that's weird.'

He shook his head. 'As long as you don't ask how it felt the moment she took her last breath, I'll manage.' When he glanced at her this time, it was to find her expression unexpectedly warm.

'I'm glad there are Italian husbands out there like you,' she said quietly, playfully, but it still caught him in the chest. 'I can't imagine your mother-in-law disapproved of you.'

'She got used to me after the first couple of years.'

'So let me get this straight finally: Maddalena is Laura's aunt,' she said, 'and Berengario is her grandfather?'

Alex nodded. 'Berengario is how Laura and I met. He was my accordion teacher.'

'Is it difficult now, seeing them so often?'

'That problem has got better with time,' he admitted. 'Laura's parents moved away after it happened – left everything behind, especially me. I understand that.'

'That explains why Maddalena made that comment about her sister not coming back for Laura's jacket. You weren't tempted to do the same? Run away?'

'A few times, but I needed home. If I'd left, I would have been pretending it hadn't happened and I couldn't allow that either.'

'I have seen how grumpy you get when you're pretending.'

'I'm honestly amazed that you're still putting up with me.' She didn't respond immediately, so he groped for her hand, missed, and ended up squeezing her forearm because that's all he could reach while concentrating on the road.

'To be honest,' she said, her voice husky, 'I'm kind of hoping to sleep with you again.'

Of the gamut of responses he felt to that statement, the one that won was a deep laugh. 'That can be arranged.'

'I like you for your body as well as those sad blue eyes.'

'What do I say to that? I like you for your body as well? You already know what I think about your eyes.'

He gave her a smile over the centre console and she smiled back and he nearly missed the turning for the olive mill.

* * *

'But I haven't finished unpacking the truck!' Jules protested weakly, when Maddalena took her arm in a firm grip and dragged her past the thrumming, chugging machinery to a stainless steel vat. Her host-slash-employer was brimming with energy today, wearing trousers for once, although her habitual apron was still in place.

'Alex will finish. You need to taste the oil, learn why you have been working hard!'

'I know why I've been working hard: to help *you*,' Jules insisted. 'It's not fair to make Alex do all the work.' He was hefting the crates of green-to-purple olives, with a scattering of leaves, into the sorting machine.

Maddalena raised her voice. 'Alex will agree with me!'

He glanced up, still with a small smile on his lips. Jules wondered if there was any chance Maddalena *hadn't* noticed that something had changed between them. 'I agree with Madda! This weekend is the most important date on her calendar and you need to understand why.'

She frowned, puzzled. 'I have tasted olive oil before – almost every day since I've lived in Italy. I've even tasted *your* olive oil,' she pointed out to Maddalena.

Waving a hand dismissively, she said, 'You've tasted last year's. It's too old now. You need the bite of the young oil.'

'I'm really not sure I'll be able to tell the difference,' Jules said apologetically, trying not to think of the horribly bitter fresh olive she'd tried. 'I'm not a connoisseur.'

Maddalena stilled, studying her, and Jules wondered what she saw that was so interesting. 'Do you think I am? A connoisseur?'

Jules thought of Due Pini, the rusty equipment pushed to one side – and not in a decorative way – the wandering animals and the wild olives that grew whichever way they wanted. The lunches were rustic and hearty and presented with care, but the ingredients were simple and local, not numerous and not, she guessed, very expensive.

The Agriturismo Azienda Agricola Biologica Due Pini was not a place that aimed for exclusive quality. This was Friuli after all, where bitterness was honoured, hard work was prized and there were cold winds and scars of history and self-deprecating jokes. Friulian and epicurean were two words that rarely went together.

'I suppose not,' Jules admitted. 'But why is the finest oil so important to you then?'

'The taste is an expression of the land. Young oil is unique. I would almost say it's a different substance to oil that has been bottled one month or more ago. Because of that, it is only in autumn, only in the countryside that you find this taste. If I could preserve it, I would be rich – that's for certain. But sometimes the best things in life no money can buy – like oil straight from the mill.'

Jules was speechless as she studied her hard-working host. The simple wisdom of Maddalena's words touched her deeply. The tasting was offered not out of a sense of superiority – as Luca's mother had tried to educate her palate – but as a gesture of gratefulness and pride in the land, land she had worked too.

'Here, you need to taste,' Maddalena said with an approving smile, fetching two small glasses from a shelf.

Hanging over the vat was a steel tube, dribbling thick, green liquid. It was slightly cloudy and looked nothing like the product on the supermarket shelves.

'You can taste oil like wine, with the nose and eyes first, but our oil is special enough that you can just sip it and you'll understand.' She held the squat, bulbous glasses briefly under the flow of oil and handed one to Jules.

'Will I turn into some kind of superhero if I drink this?' she joked, but she did rather have the impression that being here had already done her good – even when she tried to take Alex out of the equation.

'Or a zombie,' Alex called out with a wink.

She gave him a dry look. 'I could be even more help on the farm with superhuman strength.'

'You've been super as a human anyway. Now taste the fruits of our hard work,' Maddalena said, giving her a nudge.

'All right, all right!'

Maddalena observed her intently and Jules felt Alex's gaze on her as well, where he'd paused his work to watch. What did they expect to happen? She wasn't the biggest fan of olive oil, even – or especially – after spending two days with the things falling on her head. She only hoped she didn't gag after sipping the stuff neat.

She lifted the glass to her lips. As soon as the scent touched her nose, the zesty scent of tomato plants and grass with a nutty, bitter tang, she had the first inkling of what Maddalena had been talking about. She took a big sip.

23

Jules coughed and spluttered and her hand flew to her chest as peppery spice hit the back of her throat. 'Phew! Holy hell!' she muttered, peering into the glass. The smooth, elastic texture of the oil lingered in her mouth with an aftertaste that was almost like... sour apples?

Alex appeared at her side to give her a hearty thump on her back, his deep laughter ringing in her ears.

'Hey! Careful! I'll spill it!' She brandished her glass at him, still licking her lips as the fruity finish and the spice mixed on her tongue. Peering at the innocuous-looking liquid, she marvelled that Maddalena had not been exaggerating. The fresh oil was like nothing she'd ever tasted.

'Well?' her host prompted.

Before she answered, she took another sip. Prepared for the flames and the bitterness this time, she picked up the intensely savoury flavour on the front of her tongue – as comforting as a fire in the kitchen stove.

'I could almost drink this.' She eyed Maddalena and Alex. 'But you could have warned me about the spice.'

'I think we did,' Alex pointed out.

'It packs a punch,' she said emphatically.

'But you have a taste for it,' Maddalena pointed out.

Taking another sip, letting the kick of spice warm her from the inside, she had to agree. 'It appears I do.'

* * *

That evening as the sun set behind the hills terraced with vineyards, the tired, dusty group of olive pickers brushed the leaves out of their hair and gathered in front of the farmhouse to grill steak and fish and drink the dry white Friulano wine that the locals still called tocai.

Jules and Alex had brought a metal flask of fresh oil back from the mill that afternoon, which was drizzled liberally on bread toasted on the grill.

'To your first harvest,' Alex said, tapping his tumbler of wine against hers as they perched on the wooden rails of a broken fence.

She sipped the wine, watching the distant horizon flare with colour, as pink as the farmhouse. 'My first? How many more will there be?'

He followed her gaze, his smile slipping. 'The wrong words, I suppose. For me, it's something to look forward to every year, a ritual. Something that keeps you going when you're not sure how.'

Jules didn't know what to say, but she was beginning to understand how deeply – how completely – the loss of Laura had reshaped his life. She was glad he'd had Berengario and Maddalena, even if the old man was nosy and interfering – and a menace with the wine, constantly refilling their glasses.

Maddalena returned from the mill after dark and the helpers

who didn't trudge home in exhaustion moved inside to the fire. She was efficient and down-to-earth as always, but Jules imagined she must be ready to drop after the weeks of preparations.

Alex had found himself drawn into a conversation about music, so Jules drifted to where Maddalena was stoking the fire on the big hearth.

'Can I help with anything?'

'Ah, bless you, dear,' her host said with a warm smile. 'But you go enjoy yourself.'

'I don't know anyone and I don't speak Italian well enough to hold a long conversation – and certainly not in Furlan.' She didn't want any more flashbacks to the awkward meals with Luca and his friends when the conversation had swirled around her until she'd felt slow and stupid.

'Go and talk to Alex, then. He smiles more with you.'

Jules swallowed, trying to keep her game face on. She wouldn't cause any trouble for Alex. 'He seems happy right now,' she pointed out.

As if on cue, the group of men he was sitting with broke into laughter and raised their glasses. Alex was the only one without any grey hair. The barman from their first date was in the group and Jules was forced to think of Alex's nervousness that night in a different light. Everyone was a friend and a neighbour and they all knew he'd lost his wife in tragic circumstances and struggled to get past it.

Berengario declared something with a slap on the table and then started singing in a rowdy voice. The other men joined in with the jaunty song that seemed to match the felt hats that some of them wore.

Jules expected a kind of landlubbing sea shanty, but the song soon became an a cappella masterpiece in four-part harmony and she stared, her jaw dropping when Alex joined in with a sturdy bass part. They knew all the words by heart; their voices blended until the room seemed to be transported back in time.

After holding the last note, a nod from Berengario was enough for the song to dissolve into cheering and lifted hats – and more wine sloshed into tumblers. The rest of the pickers applauded and raised their glasses.

Maddalena smiled indulgently. 'Papà was only in the army for two years, but he's stayed an Alpino at heart all his life.'

'That was an old army song?'

She nodded. 'He directs the local Coro Alpino, the charity choir for veterans and supporters – and he's made Alex come along since he was a teenager, the poor boy.'

'It's good that he's had you two. Where are his own parents?'

'It was always just his mum when he was growing up and she moved to Verona when he and Laura got married. She has a new partner. Alex would never let her come back and look after him, but I keep her updated.' Maddalena gave Jules a conspiratorial smile.

Jules was faintly disturbed that those updates might have included her. Surely not. She hadn't been here long and would be gone again soon – not worth a news report in Alex's life.

'I think,' Maddalena began again, studying the table of old men – and Alex, 'he might have had a little too much to drink.'

He blinked lazily and leaned on his hand, his cheek bunched and his lips pouting. When the older men broke out in laughter again, he grinned sluggishly, but he looked ready to melt into the floor.

'He must have been so tired,' Jules commented.

'He still sleeps badly?' Maddalena asked, her eyes suddenly as haunted as Alex's. 'I thought that had improved. It hasn't improved since you moved in?'

Jules flushed and dropped her gaze, her stomach swimming.

'We're not... Really, it's not helpful for anyone to think I'm going to make his life better or make up for the loss of Laura. I'm here to work for a couple of weeks, not to cure his insomnia.'

Maddalena squeezed her arm and when Jules looked up, the older woman's expression was grave and contrite. 'You're right, of course. You need to follow your own path and he believes his is set. But I can see he enjoys your company and, well, I can't stop that small sign from giving me hope.'

'I don't want to disappoint you, if you get your hopes up on my account. To be honest, I don't think he *wants* to improve and there's nothing I can do about that.'

'It's okay,' Maddalena assured Jules with a firm nod. 'And don't worry about disappointing me. I'm lucky you're here! I don't know what I would have done without you.'

Jules quietly fell apart at those words, holding her head up only out of stubbornness. Despite her poor Italian, her tired emotions and her plans to leave in a hurry, she felt lucky to be where she was too.

At the table on the far side of the room, Alex's eyes drooped and he pitched forward, before catching himself and propping himself up on the table with one big hand that was covered in scratches from the harvest. Berengario slung an arm around him, disguising what was obvious to Jules as concern in boisterous affection. He said something gruff that made the others laugh and squeezed Alex to him.

Jules turned briefly to Maddalena. 'I'd better take him home. I managed to avoid the worst of Berengario's refills, so I'm okay to drive.'

Alex managed to stand and trail Jules to the door without stumbling, but she snaked an arm around him as soon as they were out of sight of the others, glad Arco bounded straight for the car rather than tearing off into the darkness. Alex swayed a little, but thankfully remained upright as far as the Fiat, since there was no way Jules could support his weight.

'In you go,' she said with a faint smile after opening the passenger door. Steadying him with both arms around his waist, she helped him drop into the seat, chuckling when she nearly tumbled into his lap in the process. 'This car is not big enough for this,' she mumbled.

His hand came up, tucking a strand of hair behind her ear and settling on her cheek. Jules froze, her face inches from his. 'The car is big enough for *this*,' he said with a sigh, resting his forehead against her jaw. 'Jules,' he murmured, his voice rumbly. 'I'm sorry.'

'Shh,' she said, trying to give him a soothing stroke that wasn't too intimate. But the instant her fingertips found his rough cheek, she was thinking of the kisses in the car last night – the kisses by the city wall. 'You don't have to apologise.'

'I wanted to spend time with you tonight. But I had too much wine,' he said, blinking as he made an attempt to speak seriously, only to be undermined by his slurred speech.

'It's okay,' she assured him. She drew back slowly, patting his cheek as she straightened and then closed the passenger door. Arco jumped into his spot in the footwell in the back.

When she came around to the driver's side and plonked herself into the seat, Alex said, 'It's not okay.' This time his voice was steady. 'I'm scared of... anything with you. Maybe I got drunk on purpose.'

Her chest tightened and she ignored everything – his words, her emotions – while she fastened her seat belt and started the car. 'At least you're honest,' she muttered.

'I haven't slept with anyone *twice* since Laura. I haven't wanted to.'

'I get it,' she said softly as she started the engine and eased the car out of its spot.

'No,' he said, shaking his head floppily against the seat. 'I haven't wanted anyone except her. But I want you.'

Goosebumps whooshed up her chest and her foot on the accelerator faltered. Gulping, she kept her gaze firmly on the road ahead. 'It's nice to know we were that good together,' she joked.

His deep sigh suggested he hadn't been fooled by her tone. 'If you weren't leaving...'

Her heart seized up again. 'Don't even go there,' she ordered in a panic. 'I don't live here and I can't live here, especially not with you.'

He was silent and she glanced over to find his eyes closed, but his jaw moved and his Adam's apple bobbed as he swallowed. 'Because Luca made you feel inadequate.'

'Don't make it sound so trivial. I literally have nothing because of him and the choices I made in that relationship. It's a risk I can't take again.'

'Especially not for me,' he mumbled with a shaky nod.

She opened her mouth to correct his misconception, to tell him she was worried he was the only one who could make her doubt her convictions, even a little, but then she realised he was probably talking about Laura and how much he still longed for her.

In that regard, he was right. She couldn't take a risk with her life – again – for someone who wasn't ready to commit to someone new.

Reaching the outskirts of Cividale, she slowed the car, pulling to a stop at the lights before the Ponte del Diavolo to allow the oncoming traffic over the narrow bridge first. The bell-tower of the cathedral was illuminated gold against the navy sky. The view of buildings clinging to the edge of the ravine was a sight that struck her with familiarity – and the little square where she'd first met Alex seemed to call to her gaze as the car idled and she waited for her turn to cross.

After a few tight corners in the narrow streets of the old town, she was peering up at the low archway and pulling the car carefully into its parking space by the unkempt gardens at the back of the Alex's building. The spindly plants were browning off and wilting as the nights grew colder, the last few green tomatoes never to ripen.

Alex wasn't quite asleep when she opened the passenger door. Gripping the roof of the Fiat, he hauled himself upright with a groan. Letting Arco out and locking the car, she wrapped her arm around Alex's waist once more to shepherd him to the apartment door.

'What I meant before...'

She wanted to stop him talking, but she didn't have the heart to. Instead, she just cocked her head and waited.

'...about you leaving. I would feel worse if you weren't leaving. I'd be upset with myself for getting involved with you when Laura came first. At least this way, you'll walk away from me. You deserve first love with a whole heart. But I just think sometimes that even I could love you better than Luca did. It's not fair.'

'Oh shit,' she whispered to herself as her eyes stung with tears. Pressing the ball of her hand to her forehead to stem the urge to cry, her mind raced. 'Of course you could,' she said tightly. 'But you won't. You're too stubborn for that.'

'And you're too stubborn to let me.' He pressed a kiss to her hair and she was worried about her own balance.

'And so, here we are,' she said softly. 'Not lovers, not friends – not anything. Future memories.'

'Good ones?' he asked, peering at her from under raised eyebrows.

She gave him a teasing shove. 'Yes, good ones.' *The best ones from all of Italy.*

As she dropped him off at his bedroom door, ignoring the lingering look he gave her as he propped himself against the doorframe, she knew she was just as afraid as he was.

Alessandro Mattelig, you would break my heart if I gave you the chance.

24

Alcohol and insomnia did not mix. Alex knew this, but it still hit him hard when he spent a couple of hours exhausted and slowly sobering up, but unable to sleep. He dozed off in the early hours of the morning – he tried to convince himself he always would eventually – but woke again a little before six with the words *ten days* ringing in his head. How many had it been now since her appointment? Five of those days were already gone.

He got up and dressed and set the fire in the kitchen stove before heading out to his disorganised shed to put the final touches to his latest project. Attila followed him out, watching disdainfully as he gave it one last check and grease before rolling it into the courtyard and leaning it against the persimmon tree.

'I thought you'd like this, because it will get the dog out of the house,' he mumbled to the cat who responded with a flick of his tail and a doubtful look. 'But don't you think it's going to be strange to go back to just the two of us?'

He realised with a grim frown that it had never just been the two of them. With Attila, they'd always been *three*. Laura had just been absent.

When he went back inside, he heard muffled footsteps upstairs and his heart beat uncomfortably, anticipating showing her his solution to the one pressing problem he could solve – and seeing her face after last night. The platonic housemate plan was in tatters after everything they'd shared. He'd lost his bearings and he wasn't sure what she would think of him this morning.

He poked his head out of the kitchen as she emerged at the bottom of the stairs and his loopy heartbeat became an ache. Her untidy ponytail and the thick socks she wore over her normal ones at home made an intimate picture. The baggy woollen cardigan she'd barely taken off since she bought it completed a picture he wanted to keep for longer than the next week or so. But when he lifted his gaze to her face, her eyes were set in dark circles as though she hadn't slept well either.

'Hey,' she said, padding down the hallway.

They drank their coffee in silence, until he accepted the fact that he was going to have to say something.

'I'm sorry – about last night.'

She gave a half-hearted laugh. 'What about specifically? Getting drunk? Or not sleeping with me? It's okay, Alex,' she reassured him. 'I'm leaving soon and you're... whatever you are. Still grieving. I'm not angry at you. It's just difficult to judge how close we should get, when we don't want to hurt each other at the end. Living in the same house...'

He glided his fingertips over the back of her hand. 'Exactly,' he said, when she trailed off. He wasn't sure what she'd meant by 'still grieving' as he'd always be grieving in some way – but those ways changed, sometimes without him even realising it. He liked touching her hand. That was a new stage of grieving that made his stomach flip when he acknowledged it.

She set her espresso cup on to the saucer and stood. 'I should go and see if Berengario is... Oh, he's not working on the farm this week. I should—'

'About that,' he said, unexpectedly nervous, 'let me show you something.'

Taking her hand to lead her to the door, he noticed what he'd done and panicked, but made the possibly poor decision to keep holding on.

'Do I need to close my eyes or something?' she asked as she slipped into her shoes and grabbed Arco's harness and lead from the hook.

He smiled at that dry tone he knew well. 'No, you'll see it as soon as I open the door.' He hesitated one final time. 'If you don't want to use it, that's fine—'

'Just show me, Mr Mattelig.'

He did as she asked, watching her carefully. When she caught sight of the white-framed bicycle with its two wicker baskets and gleaming – if he said so himself – chain and gear cassette, she grinned and he finally released his breath.

'That is just perfect, Alex.'

'It's an old bike I've been meaning to repair for a long time,' he explained, ignoring the heat in his cheeks. 'The rear basket should be big enough for Arco. I asked Marisa and she said dogs prefer baskets like this to be quite small so they feel secure, but he might take a little while to get used to it so...'

Her fingertips brushed over the wire cage he'd fashioned to attach to the basket with two old belts.

'I cannot wait to try this out.'

'Want to do a circle around the courtyard? I need to see if the saddle is the right height anyway.'

She hopped up onto the seat with a bit of a wobble, but after her first loop over the flagstones, she was pedalling confidently – but perhaps not quite comfortably.

'Stop!' He said, waving her over. 'Let me raise the seat. I knew you were tall, but I underestimated how long your legs are.' Her legs looked even longer when she was up on a bike. Her height was something that she wore so well, as much as part of her as her strong chin. She had such a lovely fig—

'Are you checking me out?'

He snapped his gaze up to hers. 'Sorry.' He gave himself a shake and took the bike from her to loosen the stem and lift the seat – to accommodate her lovely, long legs. Clearing his throat, he said, 'I'll ride with you the first time, in case Arco panics.' The look she gave him – soft and a little wobbly – made him want to give her bicycles every day.

When they were ready to go, he produced an extra helmet and held the bike steady for her to lift Arco into the basket. It took her a few attempts with the rather reluctant Lagotto, who barked and wriggled and eventually drew the neighbours to their windows in curiosity. Alex waved at each figure that appeared when the shutters were flung open.

'Give the dog a bone!' called Siore Cudrig.

'No, he might choke!' Siôr Mauri disagreed from the floor below. 'Let him run beside the bici! Why put him in a stupid basket? Dogs need to run.'

'He will be run over! The boy has crafted a good solution. He's so good with his hands.'

'If he's so good, why is the postbox by the gate still hanging by one screw? And there's a paver missing. He's too busy doing *something else* with his hands.'

'And *you're* busy doing nothing at all with your hands! I hear your TV all day.'

'I hear your washing machine every day!'

'Are they talking about us?' Jules asked out of the side of her mouth. 'I only understood something about a washing machine and a TV.'

'Always assume they are talking about us.'

'What are they saying?'

'Aside from speculating about what we do to each other with our hands? Not much.'

He expected a splutter or an outraged choke, but she chuckled, rubbing a hand over her eyes. 'How often do you think the subjects of gossip are actually doing *less* than everyone assumes? Do you think they'd be disappointed to know?'

'Definitely,' he said with a wink as he unlocked the chain on his own mountain bike. Her hand landed on his shoulder and she leaned over until her cheek was a breath from his, then she paused. 'What are you doing?' he whispered.

'They like to gossip, don't they?'

'It's one of their five-a-day.'

'I'm feeding them, then,' she said with a smile. 'And I'm saying thank you for the bike.' Her lips landed on his cheek, lingering, warm and a little clumsy.

He hopped on his bike with his face flaming, but a lightness in him he wasn't sure he deserved. Siore Cudrig and Siôr Mauri were talking about him, but something entirely unrelated to Laura. It felt better than he would have expected.

Arco barked sharply all through town, even when Jules shushed him with a soothing voice and slipped him a chewy treat. Alex rode in front, directing her onto the little strips of concrete allowing them to cycle more easily over the bumpy cobbles.

'Is he all right? Do you want to stop?' he called back.

'I think it's okay. He's barking, but he's not panicking. Hopefully he'll stop soon.'

When they reached the open road, with the wind in his face,

Arco's barking became more sporadic – and there were fewer people to disturb.

'This is so much fun!' Jules exclaimed, and Alex peered over his shoulder to see a broad smile lighting her face. 'I liked the walk, but the bike ride is heaven. I think autumn is my favourite season.'

'You haven't seen the other three here.'

'True,' she said wistfully. 'And there isn't really an autumn at — Where I— In Brisbane,' she finished.

'You'll have to enjoy it while you can.'

He glanced back to find her watching him. 'I will.'

'The mountain biking is fantastic around here,' he said over his shoulder.

'I heard you were the local champion,' she responded with amusement in her voice.

He didn't acknowledge her comment, even as his cheeks heated again. 'Since you like the forest so much, you should try it. Stop and collect some chestnuts when you take a break. That bike's a hybrid, but if you stick to the flatter trails, it would be okay.'

She didn't respond and then a tractor puttered past, drowning out anything she tried to say. Eventually, he heard her mumble, 'Maybe I'll try it, if I have time,' in a half-hearted tone.

They turned off the main road and juddered over the stony track to Due Pini, which set Arco off again. Pulling up in front of the farmhouse, Alex tugged off his helmet and looked back to see Jules step off her bike, her cheeks pink from the cool air. She opened the basket and lifted Arco down, letting the dog run free now he'd made peace with the goats and knew his way around the farm.

'Thank you,' she said, her eyes bright.

'I could thank *you*,' he said thoughtfully. 'It felt good to get out on the bike in the morning.'

Her smile slipped. 'Did you sleep okay, after last night?'

'Not really. I shouldn't get drunk, but sometimes...'

'I've made your sleep worse, haven't I?' she asked, her eyes pinning him where he was.

He gave an ambiguous shrug.

'Is that why you didn't want me as a housemate?'

'Partly,' he admitted. 'But it's not your fault. Sometimes I sleep okay. It's unpredictable.'

She took a step closer, chewing on her lip. 'But you think if I... slept in your bed, it wouldn't help?' She squeezed one eye shut as she mumbled the question.

Even as his heart banged against his chest alarmingly, he smiled at her, the charmingly loopy expression on her face that perfectly expressed his feelings as well – this situation they found themselves in where the attraction only seemed to grow, but so did the complications.

'You have a bed upstairs.'

'You wouldn't sleep worse than usual, would you?'

'*You* would,' he pointed out, although the sudden thought of her pressed into his side as she snuffled softly filled his mind and wouldn't leave.

'Alex, I slept on a row of chairs in a restaurant on Saturday night and I didn't notice you getting up at the crack of dawn.'

'You were fast asleep,' he agreed with a lift of his eyebrows.

'It's worth a try, surely. It's really cold in that room upstairs.'

'I can fix the—'

'God, Alex, you're trying really hard to stop this happening. Do you want me to stop asking? We're going to leave things as they are?'

He licked his lips, staring at her as she drew closer, her face lifting to his. He didn't want to leave things as they were, but giving in and kissing her, holding her, letting things happen, could trigger a host of responses he couldn't predict.

Still, he replied, 'No,' his voice barely above a whisper. 'I don't think we're going to leave things as they are.' Her mouth opened on a slow breath. She set off so many fireworks in him, but he couldn't pretend he didn't like the explosions. 'Jules,' he said – a question, a statement, he had no idea.

He heard Maddalena calling out a greeting and jerked back, turning away and lifting a hand to his hair in a nervous move to cover the irregularity of his breath.

'Mandi,' he rasped, clearing his throat as he bent down to press a kiss to Maddalena's cheeks when she approached. Laura's aunt was wearing one of her usual long skirts, her hair tied back in a scarf.

'What a wonderful idea to come on a bike!' she exclaimed. 'Dear, you're a treasure for coming again so early after last night.' She pressed kisses to both of Jules's cheeks.

'I'll, uhm... I've got to—' He gestured back in the direction of Cividale. 'I'll see you tomorrow night for the gnot dai muarts,' he said to Maddalena.

25

Now that the clocks had changed, darkness fell swiftly over the clay roofs of Cividale. The last rays of the sun were reaching over the mountains as Jules cycled across the Ponte del Diavolo on the evening of Halloween after a day of pruning grapevines.

Pumpkins and withered ears of corn had appeared on the windowsills and the yellows in the trees had turned towards orange or red. The bite in the air had returned and Jules was wrapped up in both her thick cardigan and Laura's jacket.

Although the pumpkins and scarecrows had brought to her mind excited children with buckets knocking on doors, Maddalena had explained that the gnot dai muarts – the night of the dead in Furlan – was an ancient tradition of honouring spirits who were said to parade through the town at midnight.

The celebration was also to mark the end of the harvest season and the coming of winter, which only made Jules conscious that her time here was ticking, even as she struggled to imagine a life where she didn't go to Due Pini every day and come home to the white courtyard with the laden persimmon tree every evening.

Hurrying inside when she got home, she called out, 'Sorry I'm late! Are you ready to go?'

Alex appeared in the kitchen door, licking his finger. 'Yes, let me turn this off and I'll put my coat on.'

She drifted to the kitchen, drawn as usual by the thick warmth of the stove and the scent of garlic and herbs. Attila sat on the windowsill, his tail flicking as he disparagingly observed his human's activities. When Arco followed Jules in, Attila shot to his feet, back arching, and fluffed up into an angry white ball. Alex gave the cat a withering look and stroked his hand down Attila's back.

'That smells amazing,' Jules commented. 'Do we really have to wander around town looking for spirits when we could just eat that straight away? And I could have a shower,' she said, looking down at herself thoughtfully and wrinkling her nose.

He gave her a tolerant smile as he moved the saucepan off the stove and padded into the hallway to slip into his shoes and coat. 'Berengario will never forgive you if you don't come.'

Picking up Arco's lead, she frowned at Alex as he hefted his accordion case and locked up. Passing under the old archway, they hurried along the narrow lane to the main piazza where a small crowd had gathered. Alex left his accordion by a group of old men who were enjoying tiny glasses of schnapps. The jumbled buildings on the square were lit by the wavering flames of lanterns, and next to the fountain with the lion heads stood Berengario in his felt hat and a dark wool cape, holding a flaming torch.

'It's a bit dramatic, isn't it?' she whispered to Alex. The sky had darkened to slate and with the lights of the square switched off and all the lanterns, the effect was decidedly creepy.

'Do you need to hold my hand?'

She was glad to hear him joking. Apparently she was the only one thinking about his wife on the night of the dead. 'Are you sure? Everyone's watching.'

Leaning down to speak into her ear, he said, 'They already think we're sleeping together.' He took her hand, slipping his fingers through hers, and between the shivers from his breath on her skin and the firmness of his grip, it took Jules a moment to be able to respond.

'With that logic, there are a few other things we could be doing,' she mumbled, but she didn't let go of his hand.

Berengario called out to get the crowd's attention and then spoke a brief introduction in Italian, repeating himself in English. 'Here in Friûl, we remember our Celtic roots from pre-Roman times, lingering in the striis and sbilfs and particularly our abundant aganis – our witches and elves and the spirits of the waters. Around this time, too, in our tradition, we remember the souls of the people who have died, by sharing bread with our friends and neighbours.'

Jules didn't think she'd imagined Berengario's gaze flicking to Alex. He didn't react, but she was glad her hand already held tightly to his.

'Tonight you will see the magic of Cividât, our ancient city of Celts and Romans and Lombards. Follow me!'

In the darkness, the contemporary touches faded and Jules could almost imagine the centuries of past inhabitants joining them on the leisurely walk under the archways of the city. They passed the mediaeval red-brick house Jules remembered from her first night – with Alex – and he squeezed her hand as they passed the spot where they'd first kissed.

Berengario produced a key and the group shuffled through the back gate of the historic convent tucked along the river. Ducking through a small wooden door in a humble brick wall, they soon discovered the treasure inside, as they spilled into the chapel that was the pride of Cividale, a rare example of pre-medi-aeval architecture with stuccoed floral patterns and reliefs of saints in ornate detail.

The light of Berengario's torch flickered on the walls and the high-relief images appeared to move, looking down on the gawking visitors from their positions several metres higher – and fourteen centuries in the past

'Who were these "Longobardi" he keeps talking about? It sounds like long beards. Or would that be *barbo*.'

'Barb*a*,' he corrected. 'But it does come from a Germanic word for long beards. They invaded this region in the sixth century after the retreat of Roman influence. They were a little like the Vikings, as I understand it – a northern tribe.'

'Ah, okay. So what about the short beards? Would they be the "Cortobardi"?' she asked, stroking his chin.

He snatched her hand away with a chuckle.

Berengario led them to a lookout over the river, where a persimmon tree stood guard. Like the one in Alex's courtyard, it was heavy with plump orange fruit, but almost entirely bare of leaves in its exposed position. Then the walk continued to another strange little door in an inconspicuous wall in one of the many narrow lanes of the town.

The sign above the door read 'Camera funeraria dell' ipogeo celtico,' which made Jules frown doubtfully. She wasn't sure about 'ipogeo', but the first part sounded like a funeral room.

'Here is the real Celtic history of Cividât,' Berengario said. 'These underground tunnels have had many uses over the centuries, although their original purpose is unknown. Stay close. It will be very dark inside. And watch your step.'

'Watch your head, more like it,' Jules said with a grimace as she ducked low under the door. Alex had to bend nearly in half. Inside, the tunnels were claustrophobic, carved into the rock by the hands of people and not machines, with crooked walls and uneven ceilings. As Berengario gathered his charges around the rough-hewn image of a face in the rock, he ushered Alex and Jules back into a corner to make room.

'I know you two have the height of the northern Lombards and not the ancient Celts, but if you stand back, there will be room for everyone. Further back. Pull Arco with you.'

When she found herself stuffed into a tiny stone niche with Alex at her back, Jules eyed Berengario and suspected he was stifling a smile at their predicament. When Alex's hand crept around her waist and his chin settled on her shoulder, she didn't begrudge the old man his scheming.

After Berengario's dramatic tour of the Celtic tunnels, the group wandered back to the main piazza, where music was playing and a contemporary dance troupe swirled and leaped in black capes while an ensemble of drummers kept time. The scent of roasting chestnuts reached Jules's nose and she noticed a woman in a scarf standing behind a roasting drum, a little tower of paper cones next to her.

'I have to—' Alex gestured over his shoulder to where Berengario was beckoning to him. 'The choir is singing.'

'Oh,' Jules said, finally putting together Alex's 'rehearsals' and the atmospheric harmonies from Sunday night. 'Okay. I'll get some chestnuts and come and listen.'

He scrunched up his nose. 'I hope you like old army songs.'

As he walked away, he pulled a crushed felt hat out of his jacket and shoved it on his head as he joined the semicircle of older men gathered around Berengario. One of the drummers stood ready to accompany them.

Armed with her warm parcel of chestnuts, Jules found a position directly in front of the choir and enjoyed Alex's discomfort as she watched him intently. He tugged at the collar of his shirt as they picked their starting notes and then Berengario launched them into song.

Jules couldn't help but grin. The song was a jaunty a cappella number, complete with 'pum-pa-tum-pums' and lively bass ringing out from Alex's deep voice. There weren't many members under fifty and she imagined Alex might never have joined the choir if it hadn't been for Berengario. But he seemed to be enjoying himself and his rich voice, a firm foundation for the harmonies above, would definitely have been missed while he was away in London.

For the next song, Alex accompanied the choir on the accordion as well as singing, his fingers lively on the keys as he finessed the bellows to match the dynamics of the voices. Jules studied his instrument – the same one he'd been playing the day they'd met. The brand name in silver letters near the keyboard read 'Victoria'. She wondered how old the instrument was and wished she could have seen him play in London.

They sang four songs to raucous applause and some audience participation and then the low-key celebration came to an end, people drifting through the Venetian arcade on the square to find dinner at an osteria, or heading home along the lanes.

Jules snatched Alex's hat before he could stow it back in his coat. Tugging it over her ears, she grinned at him.

'You have a lovely voice.'

'And *you* didn't save me any chestnuts,' he said with mock censure. When he grasped her around the waist and pressed a soft kiss to her mouth, she forgot anything she might have quipped in return.

'Are we really doing this now? Kissing in public?'

'It would appear so,' he said with half a smile. 'Come on, let's eat dinner.'

* * *

Bolstered by creamy pumpkin soup and a glass of wine and lulled by the fire in the stove half an hour later, Jules leaned her elbow on the table and asked, 'What's the story with the choir? Is it connected to Berengario's accordion classes?'

He shook his head. 'It's our local coro alpino, the choir of the voluntary association of the Alpini, the alpine troops. It's a very traditional repertoire. I could sing these songs at the Fogolâr Furlan – the Friulian club – in every city I visit. I even sang them in a pizza restaurant in London a few times. But they're well-known in Veneto as well, and all across the north.'

'So it is an army thing?'

'Yeah, the motto of the association is "Onorare i morti aiutando i vivi." Honour the dead by helping the living. I'm not involved so much with the association, but it's a cultural institution around here and the veterans and volunteers do all kinds of work.'

'Did it...' Jules began, not sure if she should ask the question or not. 'It doesn't bother you when people talk about those who've died? There's a lot of remembering going on in this place. Earthquakes, wars, famines...'

She waited to see if he'd withdraw, but it seemed he'd given up on that since Saturday. But he did stare pensively into his soup for a few moments before answering. 'You're right about remembering. It's a culture. But it's not the same as the way I remember Laura.'

'How is it different?'

He glanced at her, as though measuring how much she truly wanted the answer. 'The acts of remembering are planned and scheduled and carried out with tradition. But I don't have to *make* myself remember her. I just do. Maybe other people make themselves remember her, but I can't help it.'

'I suppose that's where nights like this gnot dai muarts come from,' she mused. 'Because it feels like people we love can't really be gone.'

Alex's response was a dark laugh that suggested she'd said the wrong thing. 'Laura is gone. She doesn't whisper to me in the shadows or come to me in dreams. She's very gone.' He leaned on the table and hung his head, rubbing his hand over the back. 'Sorry about this.'

'I brought it up, Alex,' she said gently.

Lifting his head, he pinned her with an unexpectedly penetrating look. 'Do you think if I'd told you all of this that night at Salvino's bar, we would still have slept together?'

Memories of that night surfaced and twisted together with this broken Alex, who'd tried to spare her what he'd been through. There was so much behind his question: guilt, a little desperation, a need for vindication. But after the past few days of honesty and casual affection that felt anything but casual, her answer could determine what happened next, how far they were willing to bend towards each other. A reckless answer now with the truth of all the feelings that bubbled up in her when she looked at him could bend her so far she might break.

Recklessness had always been her weakness.

26

Sitting in his own kitchen had never felt like a roller coaster before, but waiting for an answer to his question had Alex's stomach lifting and dropping out of his control. Jules looked at him straight on without flinching, seeing all the feelings behind his question but not shying away from the difficult truth.

Still, he didn't want to imagine how she'd react if she knew about Laura's last days, as much as he wanted to explain himself. Perhaps if she just accepted his grief the way she seemed to, he wouldn't have to tell her. Like that first night, when she'd accepted his inarticulate explanation about why he wasn't looking for love.

She took a deep breath and leaned close, almost conspiratorially, and the impression of being on her team prickled over him far too pleasantly. 'I don't think the answer matters as much as you think it does. I liked you then... and I like you now. If you want—'

That half an answer was enough of a miracle. He grasped her face in both hands, closed the distance between them and kissed her, lingering, testing – her and himself. With the conversation about Laura in the room like a real ghost, he kissed her with the weeks of wanting he'd stuffed down inside.

Her hand closed in his pullover in a firm grip. Reservations flying from his mind, he grasped her waist and hauled her into his lap. She smiled against his lips, her kisses growing clumsy as he felt her chuckle under his hands.

'I love how you go a little wild when we do this,' she murmured, her lips moving to his jaw, lower, sending goose-bumps up his chest.

Lifting her head back up, he kissed her harder, losing his fingers in her hair. 'It's you,' he groaned. 'It's this—'

Arco gave a sharp bark and jumped at them, hopping and pawing at Jules as though he thought she and Alex were wrestling.

'Shh, boy,' she crooned to the dog. 'It's okay.' He barked again and Jules grimaced.

'How about we put him to bed in here. He's got a blanket by the fire. Maybe he'll get the message that he can relax.'

'And we continue this... in your bed?'

He pressed a quick kiss to her lips. 'I don't think we'll fit in yours and I hear it's cold up there.'

'I won't stay the night,' she said solemnly, and he almost wished he'd never mentioned that worry to her.

He sighed. 'It's not that I don't want you there.'

'I suggested it. This isn't quite a one-night stand any more, but I'm still leaving the country soon. "No expectations" still stands. You're not breaking any rules.'

'It's not rules I'm worried about breaking.' He wished they didn't have to have this conversation. He wished it could be as easy as falling into bed together like that first night, but there was too much between them now.

Expecting her to pull away, he was surprised when she brought her hand to his cheek and drew close. 'I'm a big girl, Alex. I survived my relationship with Luca. You don't have to worry about me.'

Her comment didn't make him happy. He turned away when she tried to kiss him. 'You deserve better,' he said hotly. 'But it wasn't *your* heart I was talking about anyway. *I* don't particularly want to be left behind again.'

If he'd expected her to be shocked by that statement, he was disappointed. She pressed her forehead to his and smiled, an amused glint in her eyes. 'You're so sweet, Alessandro Mattelig,' she said softly, pressing kisses to his cheek and up to his temple.

'I've been bad-tempered and a terrible host,' he pointed out, but lifted his chin in invitation.

'You'll be all right,' she said, running her hands through his hair and pressing a kiss to his proffered lips. 'You haven't known me long.'

Nudging her back with hands on her hips, he gazed at her until he knew she was paying attention. 'I am going to miss you when you go.'

That finally brought a solemn expression to her face. 'I suppose I have to believe you, because I'm going to miss you too.'

'If that's clear, then let's put Arco to bed and... have a second-night stand,' he said, peering sheepishly up into her eyes.

The dog thankfully settled down when the light was off and they closed the kitchen door behind them. There was no sign of Attila, but with a wall between the two animals, they should be safe from unexpected crashes this time.

Taking her hand, he drew her into his room for only the second time, despite the three weeks they'd been housemates. Maybe it wasn't fair to either of them to get more involved, but he still wanted to show her what she was worth, how stunning and

wonderful she was, how she made him feel intensely human –
alive, as much as that thought pinched.

She was right, they weren't breaking any rules being together
like this, her skin under his hands and his body fitting to hers.
Such a thick haze of gratification settled over him when he
opened his mouth on her neck and made her gasp and squirm.

Her smile was familiar when she tugged him onto the bed
with her – playful, bright and a little provoking. Stroking his
hand along her leg, slowly, thoroughly, from ankle to thigh, he
was only more fascinated now he'd seen her every day. Exploring
her stubborn jaw with his lips was headier; the way she
welcomed him to her was more touching; all the sensations were
sharper for the three weeks they'd spent together but not
together.

The first time had been so intense it had muddled his
thoughts. The second time washed over him with an ache.

In the back of his mind, the better it felt to be close to her, the
more he worried he was failing Laura – and Laura's family and
even Jules herself. But it wasn't enough for him to stop and she
held him too tight for his reservations to surface. Her hands
roving frantically into his hair, over his shoulders and across his
back, she clutched at him, breathed his name and he sank heavily, feeling a little drunk, and then completely overcome.

* * *

As Jules struggled to get her breath back, her oversensitive fingers
stroked tiny circles on the skin of his shoulder blades, cata-
loguing the little bumps and indentations. Her mind was soft and
sluggish. The world appeared to be in slightly different colours
and Alex felt immeasurably precious.

He'd loved his wife with everything in him, struggled to accept the warmth between them now, but that was all part of the miracle of him in her arms. Pressing a kiss to his temple, where he'd dropped his head to her neck, she ran her fingers through his hair, dragging a deep sigh from him.

'You okay?' she asked.

'Yeah,' he mumbled against her shoulder. 'At least I think so. I can't seem to move.' He managed to flop down next to her, peering at her from beneath half-closed eyelids.

That wasn't quite what she'd meant with her question, but she hesitated for a moment, wondering if he even wanted to talk about that shadow that came into his eyes sometimes when they were intimate. He probably didn't want to know that the shadow hadn't been there the first time. He'd managed to do more than just not mention his wife that night.

She propped herself up on an elbow and ran her eyes down his torso with a small smile, following a moment later with her fingers. Brushing over a sensitive spot at his side, he flinched and snatched her hand away with half a smile.

'Just wait until I can move again and I'll get you back,' he threatened – completely ineffectually in a breathy, exhausted tone.

Noticing the tattoo around his biceps, she lifted herself higher to peer at it. Outlined in black ink were two small leaves with jagged edges and veins drawn in lighter ink work. The image was simple and striking. 'Bay leaves, right? Does it mean something? It's the only tattoo you have.'

He nodded, his jaw tight. 'I had it done when Laura and I got engaged. She didn't want her name stamped onto my skin, so I got these – alloro, bay leaves. The scientific name is laurus nobilis.'

'She didn't mind the symbol instead of her name?'

'She told me I didn't have anything to prove,' he said, his expression distant.

'Wise woman.' She meant the words wholeheartedly, but had to swallow a spike of unexpected discomfort as she said them. The woman was dead and Jules was *jealous*? Urgh.

'Very wise,' Alex agreed, oblivious to her silent struggle. 'But it wasn't about that. I got it for me, as a kind of outward sign of something that had changed in me. To celebrate it, make it real. She was happy with that.'

'You were envious that she got to wear a ring? I'm not sure diamonds would suit you.'

His only response was a narrow look that she completely deserved – for more reasons than he realised.

She gave his shoulder an absent poke to distract herself from what she was about to say. 'When I asked if you were okay, I kind of meant are you okay with what just happened between us?'

He looked away, rolling his head so he could stare at the ceiling for a few breaths. 'More okay with it than I probably should be,' he said flatly.

'Ah, well that answers my other question.'

'Other question?'

She bit her lip. He was so adorably earnest with his brow low. 'About the guilt. It's strong and healthy.' Lying down on her side with her head facing him on the pillow, she dared to ask, 'Does it feel like you were unfaithful just then?'

'No!' His eyes fluttered with panic. 'No, of course not. Why would you even—?'

'It does a little?'

His Adam's apple bobbed as he considered his answer. 'Yes.'

As she pressed a light kiss to his shoulder, he grimaced as though the gesture were difficult to bear. 'I just wanted you to know it's okay if you feel that. I've never lost anyone that close, but I know you.' She trailed off, stumbling over the truth of that statement.

'It's not rational, I know. She's gone and she wouldn't have wanted me to become a monk, but...'

'You want to be faithful. Alex, I admire that.' Truly, she did, even if it made her throat clog up with something stupid like self-pity and he'd known this would happen, the sensitive, thoughtful bastard. She hoped none of this stuff showed on her face.

He glanced at her doubtfully. 'I'm worried it's more than that. I like to think that I keep her alive. If she's still the only one for me, for the rest of my life, then she's still there – in me. When I feel something good with you—' He swallowed, hard. 'A little place inside me writes over her memory and I can't...'

Her hand gripped more tightly. 'Nobody's writing over anything!' she objected. 'You told me tonight that you don't need any special rituals or anniversaries to make you remember. You'll always love her and that...' She ran out of words.

'That makes you feel rejected. Right? We end up here again.'

Her eyes stung. She wished she could deny it, but this second-night stand had tipped her over into feelings she didn't know what to do with and she only had herself to blame.

'If it helps, I'm still glad we did it – again.'

'I think I am too,' he agreed faintly.

A sudden cry from right outside the window made Jules bolt upright. The shutters on the bedroom window were closed, but the cry sounded again – very close – a howling, plaintive sound. Alex sat up and placed a soothing hand on her arm. 'It's just Attila wanting to come in. I must have locked the cat flap.'

'He has impeccable timing,' Jules mumbled. 'I'd better...' She pulled on her underwear and tracksuit bottoms in a hurry, slipping her shirt over her head as Alex headed for the door in his boxers.

Standing in the hallway behind Alex as he opened the door for the cat, she caught a glimpse of movement in the courtyard, someone near the persimmon tree. 'Confirming the neighbours' suspicions about us?' she joked as she let Arco out of the kitchen. Attila hissed and escaped into Alex's workshop.

What he said next knocked the breath out of her. 'You made so much noise, I don't think any doubt remained.'

'I—I—' she scoffed. '*You* were the one who—'

'Shh,' he said with a smile, grasping her shirt and pulling her closer. 'I'm joking.' He kissed her, soft and slow, and all the words they'd exchanged, the mixed-up thoughts and feelings fused and grew into something bright.

Her arms wrapped around his neck and she could happily have wound up for another go, but instead of diving into the warm covers and heady company in Alex's bed, she dragged her feet up the stairs to her own, shivering when she sat on the cold sheets. As she set her phone on the night table, the date on the display seemed to stare back at her.

It had been seven days since her appointment in Parma. The trees had dropped more leaves; there were no more olives ripening to purple, only tangy oil, and her brusque and distant housemate had finally allowed her to see him again in vivid focus.

But the time had also elapsed in a blink. Any day now, the postman could deliver her passports, that she'd hoped would open the door to the next stage of her life – leaving Italy behind. Suddenly, she wasn't ready.

When she eventually drifted off to sleep, it was to the distant croon of an accordion – a little wonky and out of tune. He must have fixed the bellows on the tattered old instrument from the market. A hot tear dripped onto her pillow when she reflected on his late-night accordion surgery. He tinkered and tweaked and brought life back into instruments others had long given up on – perhaps because he thought he himself was beyond repair.

She wanted something more with him. It wouldn't help to deny it. But only a fool would stay to have her heart broken twice.

27

The festival honouring the dead continued the following day. All Saints' Day was a holiday and Alex disappeared with Berengario and his accordion to sing at various events while Jules found herself back at Due Pini to keep busy, slowly improving her wood-chopping technique. When she returned in the afternoon, Alex's neighbours took turns to ring the doorbell and brusquely hand over small, wrapped packages – biscuits, some kind of sweet bread made with dark flour and a paper bag of beans.

When Alex got home and caught sight of them he sighed, explaining in a clipped tone that it was the night to pray for the dead.

'Which everyone seems to think is my special holiday,' he mumbled, before taking himself off to the shower.

Afterwards, he obviously didn't want to talk about it and Jules didn't judge when he kissed her instead and tugged her into his room. But she was careful to leave again before she fell asleep, one last protection against feelings she wouldn't be able to take back.

On Thursday and Friday, Maddalena insisted she go home after lunch and Jules made use of her newly-acquired freedom of the Friulian plain – her bicycle – to explore further along the emerald river, parking her bike in a village and walking in the hills with Arco before stopping to taste the most famous speciality of the valley, the spiced bread with nuts and grappa called gubana.

Although she spent all morning out in the vines or repairing the chicken coop with wire-cutters and her bare hands, or clearing the tomato plants that had died off in the polytunnel, she had no desire to go inside to the stove until the first chill of the evening chased away the sun. The bright-eyed, rough-skinned woman who stared back at her in the mirror in the evening would have been a stranger three weeks ago.

A stranger, too, was the rumpled woman who dragged herself out of Alex's bed every night just before she went to sleep, despite the big, warm hand that sometimes fumbled to stop her. On Friday evening, he fell asleep before she did, his lashes casting shadows over the hollows of his eyes. It was even harder to leave with him so peaceful beside her. But on Saturday morning Alex looked even more wrecked than usual, his hair standing up on one side and refusing to be tamed, even after he emerged from the bathroom ready for work.

'Did you sleep at all?' she asked warily, worried that his early night yesterday evening had led to a worse night's sleep.

He shook his head and said in a gravelly voice, 'Slept through.'

'Really?'

He eyed her. 'Sometimes it happens.'

'But you look like shit.'

He smiled then and ruffled her hair. 'I feel like I've slept for three weeks.' With a dismayed glance at her, he added, 'Except that you're still here, which suggests it hasn't been that long since yesterday.'

Maddalena had insisted she take Saturday off with a strong hint that she should spend time with Alex. Jules hadn't had the heart to tell the older woman that he was working anyway – although she'd also developed a few plans for his long lunch break – so she farewelled him at the door, feeling a little forlorn.

At the last minute, he turned back and pressed a quick kiss to her lips that left her stunned. Coming back to herself, her gaze flickered around the courtyard, wondering which of the neighbours might have witnessed that and trying not to be touched that Alex had done it anyway.

Jules was so uncertain about what was going on between her and Alex – and scared to upset the delicate balance they'd created – that her phone call to her mum was tongue-tied as she tried to avoid mentioning her housemate at all. If Brenda noticed, she thankfully didn't say anything.

Her long walk with Arco started out wet and ended soaking, too muddy even to collect chestnuts. By the time she cycled home from where she'd left her bike, even Davide's solid shoes were drenched and the dark clouds rolling in made it feel like four o'clock and not midday.

As she hurried for the door, the top branches of the persimmon tree whipped in the wind, even though it was protected on all sides in the little courtyard. Siore Cudrig's pumpkin decoration was nowhere to be seen and the lanterns under the tree had fallen on their sides.

Jules closed the door behind her with a sigh of relief, but her stomach didn't settle. Texting Maddalena, she asked if everything was all right at Due Pini. They probably hadn't had many lunch customers in the downpour.

Even when Maddalena replied that she'd weathered worse

before and everything was all right, the sense of unease still plagued Jules. She showered and then blow-dried Arco with an amused smile. She needed to take him to Marisa to be clipped. He couldn't have all this fur in Brisbane, where temperatures were over thirty degrees already.

Brisbane was as abstract a thought as thirty degrees when it was about eight outside and the sky was thick with cloud. Despite the storm and the worry cramps, Jules was satisfied to keep it that way.

She was just thinking about cooking something for lunch when she noticed Attila's food bowl on the windowsill was still full.

'He's probably fine,' she muttered to herself and tried to swallow the panic in her throat. But she abandoned her own plans for food to look for him. He wasn't in Alex's living room, on the tatty sofa with the throw blanket on it, where they'd watched an old thriller and fooled around last night. The only things in the workshop were Alex's neatly packed tools and the carcass of the poor red accordion. She even checked under the table and behind the curtains.

Alex's room was similarly empty and although she felt justified in checking in his cupboard, she immediately regretted intruding when she found a framed photo of a smiling woman with dark eyes and olive skin, giving the camera a scrunched-up smile that couldn't hide how beautiful she was – dainty and good-tempered.

The photo was stacked on top of a moving box, lying carelessly face up, as though he'd stashed it in the cupboard in a hurry – because Jules was now spending time in his room?

Placing the photo of Laura carefully back where she'd found it, she returned to the immediate problem of weather plus missing cat. She'd bet that Attila had found a cosy fireplace somewhere in a luxury hotel to see out the storm, except that she hadn't seen any luxury hotels anywhere around here and even that diabolical cat couldn't drive.

When she went to the front door and peered out, keeping a hand on Arco's back to communicate that he should stay inside with her, the rain was falling in sheets and the occasional crack could be heard in the courtyard. It wasn't thunder. It sounded like two stones clapping together.

Peering hopefully around the courtyard, Jules called for the cat, not sure if he would come for her anyway. 'Attila! Here, puss! Micio!' she called, trying the pet name that Alex called him and making kissy noises.

Another crack sounded and this time Jules saw where it came from. A chunk of ice the size of a chestnut had slammed into the ground in front of her. As she watched, smaller balls landed beside it, until the rain slowly turned to what looked like polystyrene beans, streaming to the ground.

She gritted her teeth, torn with indecision. She'd never find the cat if she wandered the streets, surely. He would have taken refuge somewhere. But what if he hadn't?

Perhaps the cat did have more sense than she did, because she shrugged into her still-damp jacket, gave Arco a treat before locking him in and then headed out into the storm. The wind whipped at her when she made for the car park and the sodden vegetable gardens at the back. She wasn't even sure the cat would hear her over the wind and the hail, but she kept up her calling, checking under cars and behind the bins and in Alex's shed, but Attila was nowhere to be found.

She was about to trudge back to the courtyard and search out on the street, when she heard a distant miaow. Hurrying back in the direction she thought she'd heard it, she couldn't see him, but the sound came again – from behind the wall. Grabbing a rusty drum, she clambered up and peered over to find a rushing creek that she'd never known was there.

It was a kind of rudimentary storm drain – or a creek bed that was used as one. And over the other side of the rushing water was a sodden white cat, all bones and enormous, terrified eyes with his fur plastered to him.

The drum wobbled alarmingly and Jules couldn't reach him from where she was anyway, so she climbed down quickly and rang Alex.

'A-A-Attila!' she said as soon as he connected the call. 'He's stuck – near the water. I'm going to try to get him.'

'Jules, where are you? Wait there. I'm nearly home anyway.'

'He's in danger, Alex. Near the creek at the back of the house.'

'Whatever you do, don't go near the water!'

'I'll meet you on the other side. Come quickly!' she finished urgently as she ran for the courtyard. Pulling up the map on her phone, she located the other side of the creek and set off at a sprint, a smattering of hail bouncing off her shoulders.

There was a car park on the other side, sheltered by trees that weren't providing cover that day. Twigs were scattered already and a layer of hail blanketed the ground like marbles. Wading through thick bushes, Jules made her way to the place where she'd seen Attila and threw herself at the stone wall, leaning over.

Her heart stopped when she realised he was no longer there. Alex would be devastated, losing his connection to Laura. Even more than the old house that had once been hers, Attila was a living thing that his wife had cared for and Jules was devastated for him just imagining the grouchy old cat never coming home.

'Attila!' she called frantically. 'Micio! Pspsps micio!' There was no response. Desperation climbing up her throat, she threw her hands up and cried with inarticulate frustration. Swiping at the moisture on her face, she shook her head to clear it and then threw one leg over the wall, shimmying into the weeds on the other side.

Negotiating the stony bank with one hand on the wall, she stepped carefully, following the direction of the water and combing the banks for any sign of him. There was a flash of something near the bridge where the main road crossed the creek, but she couldn't see properly.

Letting go of the wall, she clutched at the long grass and skidded down towards the rushing water.

'Jules!' came Alex's deep voice from above her. 'What are you doing? Come back up here! It's dangerous!' She was vaguely aware of his voice growing nearer. '*Jules!* I'm serious. Don't go near the water!'

Her heart nearly stopped when she came close enough to see the pale smudge she'd noticed from above. Wedged between two bushes with the water swelling around his little body was Attila. She couldn't tell if he was moving.

'No!' she cried, placing one foot in the water. 'He's here!' she called back. 'He's stuck! I can get him.'

'No, Jules. I'm coming to help. Don't go after him alone, you'll—'

With a splash, she slipped to her waist in the water, and then the drenched ball of fur was within reach and she grasped him with both hands, relieved, but also alarmed when he didn't protest. Tucking his surprisingly frail little body into her arm, she grabbed at the bushes and stumbled back towards Alex, only now realising how strong the current was.

She managed to haul herself back out of the water, but she was grateful for Alex's strong grip to pull her all the way back up the bank.

'What were you—? That was— Putane— *Fuck*, Jules!'

Her mind was now so quiet with purpose that she had the

space to ask herself if she'd ever heard him say that word before. But she let him shepherd her back to the wall and help her over.

'I told you not to go into the water!' he cried, his voice high. 'You could have drowned!'

Finally back in safety, she ignored Alex and peered at the little bundle she'd fished out of the creek. 'Alex, I don't know if he's breathing.'

'What?'

Grasping Alex's arm, she squeezed hard enough to drag him out of the fog of panic glazing his eyes. 'We have to take him to the vet – now.'

She expected him to take Attila, but he didn't. He just looked stricken and half-absent as she clutched his cuff and dragged him after her to the road. When she was sure he was following, she rested her other hand on the little form of the cat, a chill rushing through her when she still couldn't detect any signs of life. She had no idea what kind of first aid people could give to cats. She just made sure she was supporting his body and kept him close.

Arriving back at the courtyard, they ran for the car, Alex with enough presence of mind to fetch a blanket out of the boot before swinging himself into the driver's seat. Jules towelled off the little cat and then shrugged out of her jacket, holding him to her chest in an attempt to keep him warm.

'And?' Alex asked sharply. 'Is he okay?'

'I don't know,' she had to tell him. 'Do you want me to drive?'

Shaking his head vehemently, he steered the car around the tight corners and onto the main road. 'Just tell me if anything— No, don't tell me—'

'Just drive the car, Alex,' she said softly. 'I've got him.'

Alex leaned his head back against the wall in the vet's waiting room and wondered when being only half alive would no longer be enough to keep his organs working. It hurt. So much. The half of his heart that kept stubbornly beating ached.

Jules sat beside him, her expression as blank as he was sure his was. She didn't say a word, even though she must realise he was holding himself together by a thread. He hadn't told her enough for her to understand why, but she was next to him, sparing him questions – or judgement or *anything* that would tip him over into not coping.

The wait for Dr Orsino to hear his doorbell and come to the clinic had been torture with that little lifeless form in her arms. Alex had only taken the briefest glance at Attila before shock had crept up his spine and he knew he couldn't – he just *couldn't*. Giving him questioning looks, Jules had gone with the vet into the treatment room to help, since it was out of hours and the nurse wouldn't be able to get there in the storm.

She'd emerged twenty minutes later with a grave expression

and a shrug. She'd probably struggled to understand the old man.

I should be in there...

He couldn't, not if Attila wasn't going to make it. But if Laura's cat died and he wasn't there, he'd regret that too. The worst possibility... *No.* The dilemma he'd lived with for three years felt fresh again and he couldn't take it – didn't want it. But cats didn't live forever and sooner or later he'd have to—

Dr Orsino came to the door of the waiting room. 'Do you want to come and see him?'

Alex hesitated for long enough that Jules leaned forward to peer at him. Forcing his mouth open, he managed to ask in an alarmingly raspy voice, 'Is he...? Did he...? Dead?'

The veterinarian smiled suddenly and a little indulgently, as though he were the only person in this city who didn't know that Alex was fragile – something Alex usually resented everyone for thinking. 'His name is Attila. Did you think a little drowning would be enough to send him off? No, he's breathing and starting to wake up.'

Alex's body responded before his mind did, tears burning and his face contorting, his spine losing all strength. But his brain lagged a few more seconds in disbelief.

'Alex?' From her tone, he could tell Jules was wondering what was wrong with him. He should have told her – everything, from the beginning, even if that meant she ran screaming in the opposite direction.

He forced himself up, ignoring the spots in his vision. Dragging his feet after the doctor, his emotions swam as he stepped through the door and saw the poor, bedraggled form of Laura's blasted cat, staring at him accusingly from behind the metal grille keeping him in the box.

His muscles turned to mush and his heart started beating

again – even if a little too fast. The memories of the past half-hour raced back as he leaned heavily on the treatment table and eyeballed the furry white cat as though he could make the creature understand what its stupidity had put him through.

Had put *Jules* through. As though watching a film, he relived the moment he'd realised the danger she intended to walk right into – for his cat.

'Ah, he's sitting up. He is a fighter, this one,' Dr Orsino said.

Alex could think of someone else who was a fighter. When he'd been too panicked to comfort the poor animal, she'd done it. That ex-boyfriend of hers that he was supposed to punch in the face hadn't appreciated her tenacity – her generosity. Julia Volpe was a strong woman – like a Furlane, he thought with a twitch of a smile. Berengario would approve of his thoughts.

He pressed his fingertips to the grille. 'Does he have to stay locked in?'

Dr Orsino shook his head. 'There's a heat blanket in there, which will do him good for a little while longer, but if he's awake and alert, then I think we can rule out hypothermia. I saw a little fluid in his lungs on the X-ray, but his vital signs are stable and he doesn't need oxygen. In fact, you can take him home whenever you like. He'll recover better in his familiar surroundings. You'll just need to keep him inside for a few days and monitor his breathing, but animals bounce back from these things more quickly than their owners do.'

Alex glanced at the doctor in dismay. It seemed now even the town vet had worked out that he was an emotional wreck. Glancing at the door, he wondered what Jules was thinking.

'Do you want to hold him?' Dr Orsino asked.

'He's not normally the most affectionate cat,' Alex said, but he did want to stroke the furball, reassure himself Attila was alive and there were no impossible decisions to be made tonight. 'But are you serious, we can just take him home?'

'I'll check his temperature once more, but if he's up and active and you can keep him warm, then he'll do better at home.' The vet opened the box and the damp kitty had the audacity to leap to the floor.

Alex snatched him up, stroking one hand down his back and allowing the tears to prick afresh. They weren't all happy tears, but it would be better to unpack his feelings at home, in the house he'd inherited from Laura – with Jules.

* * *

The storm was over by the time they left the veterinary practice and headed back, but there was hail strewn across the roads and Alex was chastened to realise that he barely remembered the drive there. It was a miracle he hadn't crashed the car and caused more damage – or worse.

Jules held her hand out for the keys and he gave them to her. Only when she parked the car and hauled herself out did he realise she was still soaking wet.

Images from the incident at the creek flashed in his mind and his stomach clenched as though someone had punched him. Let her get inside and warm and dry and all the words would spew out of him and then she'd see more than she bargained for – she'd see who he was under the protective layers.

'I'll just have a shower,' she said after hanging up her sopping jacket and giving the leaping and panting Arco a quelling stroke.

It took some effort to keep his jaw tightly shut and answer only with a grim nod. He found an old electric blanket and set it up in a pile on the windowsill in the kitchen, placing Attila on it to be well out of Arco's reach. He struggled to look at the cat, seeing only scenarios of what could have happened, each more terrible than the last – or the terrible scenario that did happen: Jules wading into a rushing storm drain.

He was just wondering what to prepare for dinner when the doorbell rang and he opened the door to find Siore Cudrig standing behind an enormous saucepan.

'Goulash,' she said instead of a greeting. 'I saw what she did, your... the girl.'

'Jules,' he supplied. 'She saved his life.'

With a nod, his neighbour handed over the pot. 'Goulash,' she said again.

'Graziis.'

She began to turn, then stopped and fixed him with a look from under her curls. 'Jules,' she repeated with a nod. 'She has a nice... dog.'

'Mhm,' he responded.

As she walked away, she tutted under her breath. '...can't see what's right in front of him!'

Closing the door with a lift of his eyebrows at the words she wouldn't say to his face, he breathed in the scent of onions and rosemary and paprika and headed for the kitchen. The bathroom door opened with a burst of steam as he passed and he looked up to see Jules with her head wrapped in a towel.

'Oh my God, what is that divine smell?'

'Goulash,' he said with a twitch of a smile. 'From Siore Cudrig. She said you have a nice dog.'

Jules stared at him, her mouth turned down, and his smile grew. 'You have the weirdest neighbours.'

'I did warn you, that first night.'

'I think you'll find that *I* warned *you* that they were zombies.'

He stared at her, the normality of the moment overwhelming on top of everything already churning inside him. He wanted to kiss her. He wanted to throw her out – of his life. And he wanted to make her stay.

'Are you all right?' she asked, her tone still light.

'No.'

She laughed at first, before something in his expression made her smile fade. 'Are we going to eat that?'

'Hmm?'

'Goulash.'

'Oh, yes. Goulash.'

'And after we've eaten, you can say all that stuff you're holding in.'

She understood Alex had had a shock, but the strange intensity coming off him unnerved her. There was something he hadn't explained about Laura. It might well be none of her business, but when he sat opposite her strongly *vibing* at her and saying little, she thought she had a right to know *something*.

Especially annoying was the fact that his vibes made her want to clasp his face and press her forehead to his and try to explain without using words that he was breaking her heart.

'I didn't understand everything Dr Orsino said,' she began warily, taking a spoonful of thick broth and trying not to groan. How had Siore Cudrig known the overload of iron and vitamin C and the prick of spice were exactly what she needed?

'There is a little liquid in his lungs,' he explained, glancing up to check on Attila again. He was curled up peacefully, his little chest rising and falling – nothing to cause the shadow that crossed Alex's features. 'We should just monitor his breathing.'

'Okay,' she said with a firm nod. Alex studied her for a moment, but then his shoulders relaxed.

Either Alex had taken her seriously about waiting until after they'd eaten to talk or he had no intention of explaining himself, but Jules was itchy from the silence by the time she took her plate to the sink. He came close behind her to slip his in afterwards – very close. Glancing at him, she wondered whether she'd misinterpreted the vibes and he wasn't suffering his usual attack of difficult memories, but was focused on *her*.

Her hair stood on end as she turned to find him... *looming*. There was no other word for the way he stood, dipping his head to look her in the eye, his body taut. His hands landed on either side of the kitchen bench behind her and his face, tight and grim with emotion, was close to hers.

'Is this the talking bit?' she squeaked.

He nodded, then seemed to reconsider and shake his head. 'Some of it.'

Jules gulped, her throat suddenly thick.

Then he said something entirely different from what she'd expected. 'Don't you *ever* do something like that again.'

29

'I saved him,' she pointed out, aiming for pragmatic, but suspecting he'd hear the waver in her voice.

'You disappeared into the water under the bridge. Did you think I'd be happy to witness that?'

'I knew what I was doing,' she insisted.

'You obviously didn't. There is no safe way to walk into dangerous waters. I know Luca didn't appreciate you, but that was his problem. You don't need to prove anything to us.'

'I wasn't trying to prove anything!'

'You don't have to be *useful*. We would be here for you even if you didn't work yourself to the bone and I thought I'd made that clear!'

His expression was hard and when she finally accepted that he wanted a fight, she was ready to give him one. Arco sat up from his blanket by the stove and whined, but she kept her gaze on the man currently hemming her in and thrumming with emotion.

'Alex,' she said, her tone just as hard as his had been. 'I *saved* him. I saved Laura's cat. For you.' She poked him in the chest. 'You should be thanking me.'

'You think I should *thank* you for terrifying me? For thinking I might watch *two* women I— Watch you die too?'

Her heart sank. In those few words were a whole world of meaning – a world of suffering she was only beginning to understand. She stared at him as he took a deep, unsteady breath.

'I only thought— Attila is...'

'I *know* what that cat means to me,' Alex said, his voice softer, but still dark. Lifting his hands slowly to her face, he turned her head so she couldn't escape his gaze. It was an onslaught, all these feelings rushing in her arteries. 'I sat in that waiting room today unable to function, imagining that was the end – or worse, that I'd have to make an impossible decision. I didn't want to lose him, my last living connection to the family I had.'

His expression didn't shift, the line of his mouth as hard as ever and Jules could only watch – and feel her own heart ready to break – as he said what he needed to say.

'I understand the enormity of what you did today.' His voice turned husky. 'For me. I don't know how I feel about that, because it's too much.'

Her hand sneaked to his cheek. *Too much*. That feeling was familiar.

'But Jules, don't *ever* do it again.' His tone was pleading now and he came closer, his breath a gust as he slipped a hand around the back of her neck and kissed her, rough and raw and a little desperate. 'I'm sorry,' he breathed, kissing her again – hard.

Wrapping her arms around his neck, she held tight, shaking her head. 'No, *I'm* sorry. I didn't think.'

He hoisted her onto the kitchen bench, sighing as he wrapped his arms around her, pulling her tight against him. When he said her name, it was with a quality she'd never heard in his deep voice before. And he kissed her again, long and deep, right in front of the kitchen window with its gauzy half-curtains, where anyone could see them. She kissed him back, even though the fleeting thought dashed across her mind that she'd never kissed anyone quite so violently and she might never again.

They stumbled down the hall, pulling each other, the lingering combativeness colouring the experience with breathless fervour. Each touch was a reward and a punishment and a manifestation of the emotions between them that burned brightly. As his mouth seared her skin and her hands fumbled for him, the need to be close rampaged over her lingering reticence.

With his body heavy on hers and his expression harsh, he gripped her tightly and they tumbled over the barriers into somewhere new.

* * *

Jules dozed for a minute – or half an hour, she wasn't sure, since time didn't seem to exist in the melty haze that settled over her. The cold – and then the heat – and then the intense fervour of their lovemaking had drained every solid substance from her body. When her eyelids blinked sluggishly open, she found Alex watching her across the pillow, his expression clouded.

Fumbling a hand to his cheek, she said, 'Hey, you okay?' She wasn't surprised when he shook his head. 'You want to tell me? You don't have to.'

'You're wondering?' he asked softly, propping himself up on an elbow and tucking her hair behind her ear. 'You must be. I know I behaved strangely today and... thank you for letting me be.'

'I've never lost someone like you have,' she said as gently as she could. 'But yeah, sometimes it seems like there's something you haven't said.'

She wasn't happy to be right when he replied with an almost

imperceptible nod. 'Today, I was afraid of having to go through it again, even though I've been so careful since she died.'

She felt it, the way he struggled against himself and his own feelings. 'You can't stop things happening by being careful.' Although Jules wasn't the best person to give advice. She'd never learned to be careful.

'That's not what I mean,' he began, hauling himself up into a sitting position.

Jules followed suit, groping for her discarded shirt and knickers and facing him, cross-legged on the bed.

'He's an animal,' Alex muttered. 'One day he's going to die and I'm probably going to be the one to make it happen.' He took a sudden, heaving breath. 'I don't want to do that again. I can't.'

She watched in dismay as he crumbled in front of her, his head dropping into his hands. She wondered if he'd even bear to be touched right now. In the waiting room today, he'd withdrawn so completely that if she hadn't got to know the grumpy version of him when she first moved in, she might have been alarmed.

But she waited. And trusted that he'd come out when he was ready.

He closed his eyes and his mouth opened slightly to allow an even breath out and then in again. As he calmed down, she could focus on what he'd said, her own heartbeat accelerating when she considered what he might have meant – to make *what* happen? Death?

'Can you tell me? About Laura?'

'I'll try,' he said faintly. 'It's better than you wondering, not understanding why...' Lifting his head, he stared blankly at the wardrobe against the far wall. 'I told you she had a car accident – with a lorry. But that wasn't the day she died – that happened three weeks later.'

Her throat clogged as she pictured him at her bedside for

three weeks in a time lapse, transforming slowly into this sleep-less, sunken-eyed version of himself.

'She was on life support. I mean, maybe she did die that day – inside. That's something I'll never know. But her body... With the machines, she kept breathing for three weeks, long enough for her parents to come to London, for all the endless discussions and appointments and tests and then...' Two tears rolled down his cheeks. 'It was my job, as next of kin, to say it was over.' His gaze dropped. 'I learned so much I wish I could forget. Did you know a brain-dead person still has some reflexes?' His voice broke. 'In recent decades there have been big advances in research into comas and brain activity and lots of people wake up, when they're allowed the chance.'

Jules darted a hand out, clutching his forearm. It was for her own sake, because she couldn't process the shock without reas-suring herself that he was still there – perhaps not quite whole, but still mostly there. He studied her hand but didn't remove it – or cover it with his own. Goosebumps came up on his skin and the light hairs stood on end and Jules couldn't help contem-plating reflexes and souls and what it meant to be alive.

'It was the kind thing to do,' he said flatly, as though reciting from a book. 'Not for her – well, I have to believe she was already gone. But for the others. Her parents...'

It was her turn to feel the tingle of goosebumps as she realised how much he'd sacrificed for Laura's family and the way her parents had repaid him: by breaking ties. But Maddalena and Berengario hadn't and that wedged them a little further down in the crevices of her heart.

'You imagined having to make a decision to put Attila down today,' she said softly. 'And it drew parallels, brought everything back.'

He nodded. 'One day I'll have to make that decision for Attila.

You'll have to for Arco. That dog is easy to love, but one day you'll be telling the vet to end his life – the kind thing to do. I know you probably don't want to think about it.'

'You're right, though.'

He lifted his gaze abruptly to hers. 'This is why I'm careful,' he said, his voice firm. 'Attila... I have no choice. He was Laura's cat – our cat. But otherwise, I can't—' He shook his head.

Jules heard what he was trying to say. *I can't love you.* It was concerning how quickly she understood exactly what he meant, even though he probably wasn't thinking specifically of her and definitely wouldn't have landed on the 'L' word if he'd tried to explain himself more clearly.

But Jules had. She hadn't been careful at all, despite arriving here fresh from the scene of her previous heartbreak. Studying his haggard face, so full of history and character, like this town, her feelings for him seemed inevitable. She had to hope she'd be gone before she fell too far.

She realised with a start that she hadn't even thought about her passports for the past few days. Somewhere deep inside, she'd started to hope they would never come, that she had a curse – or perhaps a blessing – to always remain in Italy.

'Saying you don't want to get another pet isn't quite the same as holding your heart away from other people,' she pointed out tentatively. 'Sometimes you can't help it.' Those words seemed to echo in her mind with more meaning than she'd intended.

'It's self-preservation,' he said with a shrug. 'My life has been self-preservation since the day I had to make that decision.'

'That makes sense,' she had to admit. At least this time she wouldn't make the mistake of deciding to stay here – for him. If Luca had told her upfront he didn't think he could love her, she would have been spared so much heartache.

The only problem was, with Alex, it felt like a choice between heartache now and heartache later.

He swung his legs over the side of the bed and pulled on a pair of underwear. 'I'm going to check on Attila.'

'Sure, I'll... I'd better go to my...' She couldn't find the end of that sentence.

She let him go before half-heartedly searching for her tracksuit bottoms. Her feelings were too raw to head back to her own cold room. She heard the rain pattering in the courtyard, the distant rushing of the creek, and she thought miserably to herself that she'd rather have the heartache later, thank you very much.

Dragging herself out of bed eventually, she was surprised Arco wasn't sprawled in the hallway waiting for her. Padding to the kitchen in her thick socks, she peered in to see Alex sitting in a chair by the stove with Attila in his lap. He looked half asleep, which wasn't a surprise. What she hadn't expected was the woolly figure of Arco next to him, his snout on Alex's knee.

Alex's hand rested on Arco's head and Jules's gaze landed there and stuck. Arco was a young, energetic dog who couldn't always be properly controlled, but he sensed something was wrong. He must be trying to comfort Alex. He'd never felt more *her* dog.

'Alex,' she said gently as she approached. His eyes flicked open. He'd made the most difficult decision a husband could make. It was clear he would rather have died in her place than give the instruction to turn off the machines. But he'd loved Laura enough to do what needed to be done.

When his gaze focused on her, his eyes crinkled and a smile stretched on his lips. 'Jules,' he replied, his voice rasping. 'You didn't go.'

Her knees threatened to give out. 'Are you going to come back to bed?'

'Are you going to stay?'

'I don't particularly want to be alone right now.'

Lifting his hand to her face and around to the back of her neck, he warned her, 'I won't sleep.'

'I know,' she reassured him. 'I'm not expecting to fix you. I just want a cuddle.'

His smile grew broad with a flash of teeth and he leaned up to press a wobbly, affectionate kiss on her mouth. 'A cuddle sounds good.'

After settling Attila on a side table in Alex's room and fetching a blanket for Arco, Jules couldn't help chuckling at the bedroom menagerie. She settled her head on the pillow with a hesitant glance at Alex, who stretched out sleepily beside her.

'Roll over,' he mumbled, nudging her to turn away from him.

She did as he asked, wondering if this was something to help him ignore her and go to sleep, but he shuffled closer and draped an arm over her, holding her against him with her back to his chest. His deep sigh blew her hair onto her forehead, but she didn't care as the weight of his arm over her, the closeness of his body soaked into her skin – beneath her skin.

When he pressed a lingering kiss to her neck and nuzzled her ear, the sensation was so sharp and bright that she thought it *had* to be worth the heartache later. *Much later*, she hoped.

30

She noticed Alex moving around in the night, but only through the haze of brief wakefulness. When her eyes popped open to see the blades of sunlight around the edges of the shutters, she glanced warily across the pillow to find him deeply, solidly asleep, his cheek squashed against the cotton. He snuffled lightly, his breathing as even as the beat of a slow song, his bare shoulders looking impossibly broad when he lay on his side.

He hadn't slept through the night – she knew that and she hadn't expected to solve a deep problem he was wading through himself. But seeing him asleep next to her was its own tiny miracle, no less astounding for its fleeting nature.

Hearing a miaow loud enough to wake him, she slipped out of bed as quickly and quietly as she could and fetched Attila from the table, where he was staring disdainfully down at Arco. The cat didn't seem impressed with the fact that Arco appeared to have adopted him into his pack after the heightened emotions of the night before. Attila was breathing normally and when she set his food bowl in front of him on the windowsill in the kitchen, he ate immediately, which made her smile.

She took Arco out briefly and then she couldn't resist, she opened Alex's bedroom a crack, hoping to catch another glimpse of him gloriously asleep. But he rolled over at the sound of the door opening.

'Come back to bed, Jules,' he mumbled, lifting a hand briefly before it flopped back on to the sheets.

'That's a request I can't refuse,' she said with a chuckle. 'Did you sleep sort of okay? Did I bother you?'

'No,' he said immediately. He cracked one eye open. 'Did I bother you?'

She shook her head, turning back the covers and slipping underneath. 'I slept fine. I really didn't want to go back up to my room. Attila's eaten already, by the way. He seems better.'

'Good,' Alex said, rolling onto his back as though the action took all his strength. He peered at her. 'Thank you,' he said.

'You don't need to—'

'I don't know how else to express it. You just came here and got to work and made everything a little bit better.'

She blinked, refusing the tears that threatened. 'How very Friulian of me, to come here and get to work,' she joked, hoping he was too sleepy to notice her loopy, scrunched expression as she tried not to cry.

'I mean it.' He poked her for emphasis, so she tickled him back, remembering that first night when they'd been different people – or perhaps been more themselves – and created magic. 'Ah, stop! You have evil fingers!' he cried, swatting her hands away and then capturing them in his.

Clasping their hands together between them, he studied her knuckles intently, stroking in circles with his thumb.

'I don't sleep as badly as I used to, you know,' he admitted. 'Sometimes I don't want to see the improvement, but... self-preservation. I have to sleep. I have to relax about sleep. It has got a little better. But last night...'

She held her breath, all her banter deserting her as she waited for the next thing he'd say to break her heart.

'I wanted to be in bed. Even when I wasn't asleep, I didn't want to get up and do something else to stay calm. I just watched you.' He grimaced and glanced over at her. 'Is that creepy?'

'A little,' she replied with a grin. 'But since you protected me from the zombies, I forgive you.'

He gave a huff. 'Why it's not *you* with sleeping problems, I have no idea! Ghosts, zombies...'

'Berengario with a scythe,' she joked.

He grinned, snaking his arms around her waist and hauling her to him with a kiss on her mouth. 'Sleep here, in my room, until you go,' he said softly.

There was only one answer she could give him. Studying him warily, she whispered, 'Okay.'

* * *

Attila recovered quickly and was itching to go out again well before Dr Orsino confirmed he could. The nights had grown chilly, although sunshine during the day still warmed up the clay roofs of Cividale by the afternoon. It was a little too easy for Jules to forget about her passport predicament between the tranquil days with Maddalena, snipping slowly at the vines and preserving green tomato slices in fresh oil and vinegar, and the cosy nights by the stove or curled up in Alex's bed.

Jules was happy to accept a day off on Wednesday to spend with Alex. Leaving Arco home alone, he showed her a few beginners' mountain-biking trails in the forest, stopping to pick a small crop of 'drumstick' mushrooms – another pastime Jules suspected could become addictive if she had time alone in the forest with a harvesting knife.

But without an income now for over a month, she was getting nervous that her card would be declined and knew she would have to ask her mum for an exorbitant sum for a flight home. On the rare occasions that thoughts of Luca intruded on her autumn idyll, it was no longer with hurt and mortification but worry about what could be behind his long silence. She hadn't expected texts about the weather, but she had hoped to hear something about the sale – at the very least that the property had been advertised.

She should care more about her investment, but she was quite happy sticking her head in the sand, even though part of her knew ignoring reality had got her into trouble before. *Just a few more days…*

The few more days turned into the weekend and on Sunday, after their usual ramble in the forest and reheated soup for lunch, there was a knock at the door. Jules was annoyed about the tingles along her hairline – fear that it was Luca, come to intrude on her peace. But she assured herself as she had a handful of times already that he didn't even know where she was.

It wasn't her ex behind the door, it was Siôr Mauri from the other building. After a gruff conversation with Alex, he left again and Jules wondered for a moment if they'd been told off for… she didn't want to know what. But when she peered out of the window to see the elderly neighbour hobbling across the court-yard with a wooden ladder, she gathered he'd stopped by to tell them something.

Jules watched as all of the neighbours – Siore Cudrig, Elena and Berengario, the wizened owner of the tattoo parlour and other familiar faces she hadn't put names to yet – emerged from their buildings with baskets and crates and cardboard boxes and they all stood around the persimmon tree.

At first, they only talked – and laughed and measured unscientifically with hands and one eye closed. Then came the arguments that appeared more habitual and obligatory than truly rancorous. And then Siôr Mauri held the ladder and up Berengario climbed.

Alex returned to the kitchen, slipping his arms around her waist and leaning his chin on her shoulder. For someone who'd told her in no uncertain terms that he was too damaged to fall in love, he did a good job of convincing her that's what they had. In combination with her willingness to ignore warnings – and reality – her rational mind knew she was setting herself up for a rather potent explosion of grief when she left.

But she wasn't leaving today. It appeared that today was the persimmon harvest. Turning to catch Alex's eye, she asked, 'Are we going to help?'

'It's your day off,' he pointed out, pressing a kiss to the side of her neck, but there was a sudden knock on the window and then Berengario's pinched face appeared, his hand raised to block out the light as he peered in.

Jules expected Alex to jerk away from her, but he just sighed and rested his forehead against her as he chuckled. It made her happy to have her height when he rested on her shoulders. She rather liked being the strong woman who helped Maddalena run a farm and held up Alessandro Mattelig when he was weak.

'I think that's our summons,' she said, extricating herself gently. Grasping his hand, she dragged him into the hallway to fetch their shoes. The day was mild for November and she knew how warm she got when she worked, so she pulled on only her thick, rainbow cardigan with her boots before heading into the courtyard, Arco at her heels.

'So, what do we do?' she asked Berengario, studying the tree. She was struck by the memory of when she'd first arrived and the pale fruit had been sheltered by leaves. Now the tree was bare and the fruit a vivid orange. A few short weeks had made such drastic changes in its appearance.

When Berengario opened his mouth, she smiled and wondered if she should fetch a chair from inside for the duration of the monologue to come. 'Ah, the cachi is a very fragile fruit, especially now we allowed it to ripen on the tree. The first frost is over, so the sweetness has developed, but we need to take care when harvesting or they will bruise and spoil before they are really sweet to eat. Here, take the scissors,' he said, handing her a pair of pruning shears, a tool she was now intimately acquainted with from her work at Due Pini. 'Hold the fruit gently and cut all of the calice, the flower part here, and then place the fruit in the box in a single layer. They shouldn't touch. This way they keep for the rest of winter until we bring them into the warmth to ripen fully. Do not let the fruit touch!' he repeated.

'All right. I got it,' she reassured him indulgently.

He waved his shears for emphasis and said, 'If I thought you would still be here to eat them yourself, you would have more motivation to store them well.'

Jules froze, her fears clogging in her throat again. Berengario approached the tree and studied it, either unaware of how his words had affected her or allowing time for the barb to sink into her flesh. He couldn't expect that she would stay – could he? Her bank balance was crashing and, as hard as she'd tried to be useful, she was still dependent on the goodwill of these friends and neighbours – and whatever Alex was to her.

Despite all the devastating affection and new-found intimacy with him, nothing had changed from that first night: he'd only opened up to her because she was leaving. He didn't want to let go of Laura and she would never ask him to.

She almost forgot to add that she would have to be a foolish nitwit to choose to stay in Italy for love *twice*. Even if she did love him...

Ouch. Shaking herself as she approached the tree and gripped a smooth, plump persimmon, Jules struggled to tear her thoughts away from the dawning of truth creeping over her skin like sunshine from behind a cloud. She didn't love him. She'd only known him a few weeks – a shorter time than she'd known Luca before she'd torn up her life for him, and look where that had got her.

The swell of rebellion inside her, however, ripped off the Band-Aid. It was too late. She did love him. It was a different kind of love from what she'd felt for Luca: quieter, softer – hotter. Deeper. *Oh dear...*

She stole a glance at Alex and it all flashed through her. He was speaking companionably to Siore Cudrig as he snipped the fruit, a faint smile on his lips. She loved how he still mourned his wife, even though it hurt – even though it meant she couldn't stay here for him.

She couldn't stay – but she wanted to.

Her desire to escape had never been about leaving Italy. She'd been running from her mistakes. Staying with Luca had no longer been possible, but here... She glanced around the courtyard, blinking wildly against the prick of tears.

Feeling a pinch at her back, she turned to find Alex peering at her, his hand settling at her waist. 'Are you okay?' He dipped his head to study her.

She was now. 'Yeah,' she said, giving him a quick, hard kiss on the lips.

'Enough of that now, lovers!'

Jules flinched away at the sound of Berengario's voice from behind her and turned to find all of the neighbours taking surreptitious glances at them.

'If you can't stop touching each other, how about you two work with the ladder?' Berengario suggested gruffly. 'You're both tall enough. Up you go. Alex, hold it steady.'

Jules followed his instructions with a wry smile, brushing past Alex as she climbed the rungs. She passed the fruit down to him, meeting his gaze occasionally at the graze of his fingertips over hers.

'*Romeo e Giulietta*, eh?' Siôr Mauri joked to Berengario.

'The unlucky lovers?' Berengario replied, giving Jules a sidelong look.

'Star-crossed lovers,' Alex corrected him tightly. 'That's the expression, isn't it?' He glanced at Jules for confirmation.

'The original story was based in Udine, not Verona,' Berengario added, as though the change of setting personally offended him. 'But there are no "star-crossed" lovers today – only stupid ones.' He slapped Alex on the back, making the ladder wobble.

Jules lost her footing, arms flailing for a sturdy branch as her balance shifted precariously, but Alex's hand closing in the waistband of her jeans steadied her again and she heard him grumble something in Berengario's direction.

He didn't move his hand for long enough to heat her skin and she glanced down, expecting to find him giving her a cheeky smile, but he stood frozen, his gaze fixed on the entrance to the courtyard. The neighbours had all gone quiet too and only Arco's barking – suddenly agitated – sounded in the courtyard.

She dipped her head. 'What's going on?'

Cold slid down her spine when she heard a response from the direction of Alex's gaze in a voice she knew too well. 'I could ask you the same thing, Jules.'

31

Alex had never truly experienced the urge to punch someone. Perhaps that was why the force of his resentment took him by surprise when he finally accepted that the man walking into the courtyard with one hand in his pocket like he owned the place was Luca, the turd who'd hurt Jules, stolen her confidence and destroyed her livelihood.

His grip on her jeans tightened, dragging his concentration out of the haze of anger, disappointment – fear.

'Alex,' she hissed. 'Let me down.'

He resisted, keeping his fist tight in her waistband. He wanted to hold her up, safely away from the fool who'd put the shadows in her eyes. If he just kept his grip on her, maybe Luca's hold would fade, maybe he'd just go away again and leave her alone – leave her here.

As much as he was angry on her behalf, it wasn't anger that turned his stomach – it was the fear. Luca spelled the end. The intrusion was a wake-up call: Jules didn't belong here and as soon as she had her passport, she'd be gone.

Maybe the man had finally realised what he'd lost and come

to take her back. She wouldn't go. He was *sure* she wouldn't go. He knew how much Luca had hurt her. But he also knew she'd loved him and love... Love was never entirely rational.

'Alex!' she called, more loudly. Arco continued to bark from where she'd tied him up to the bike stand a few metres away.

'Jules?' Luca repeated, coming nearer. He peered through the branches to where she was perched at the top of the ladder.

He was well dressed: a casual jacket over dark wash jeans and loafers. He was good-looking and smooth and so totally *wrong* for Jules that rebellion rose in Alex's chest. Then Luca's gaze fixed on Alex's hand, clenched in her waistband with casual intimacy. The cloud that passed over the man's expression was ugly.

'I did not expect to find you up a tree with a stranger's hand on your arse. And what on earth are you wearing? Did someone drop the sheep into a vat of dye?'

'Alex, let me down.'

This time he responded to her dark tone, extricating his hand and steadying her around the waist as she descended. He wanted to keep a hand on her, remind her that he was there and he wouldn't leave her alone, but her rigid body language made him keep his distance – for now. It was probably for the best, given the churn of outrage swimming inside him.

Berengario stepped up to them before Jules could say anything. 'Do you know this person, Jules?'

'Of course she—'

'Not really,' she interrupted Luca weakly, walking away to place a quelling hand on Arco's back, shushing him gently. Unhitching his lead from the stand, she allowed the dog to drag her back to Luca. Arco leaped and turned in wild circles and Alex was reminded that Luca was the one who'd once been in the dog's pack. Alex had never wanted to be – except that was plainly untrue as he watched Arco greet his former master with joy.

Alex was jealous – because of a dog's affections and loyalty.

His stomach sank as he admitted to himself that he was jealous for a few more reasons. His hand closed into a fist as he remembered Jules talking in a defeated tone about feeling useless – the way this man had made her feel. He would never hit Luca, but he had a few choice words brewing, if he could get them out around the lump in his throat.

But did he have any right to say them?

Luca fended off Arco with a huff. 'Still no manners,' he mumbled. 'Jules, what is going on? Who are all these people and what were you doing up a tree?'

'I was picking persimmons – exactly what it looked like,' she snapped. 'How did you know where to find me?'

'Picking...' He glanced at the tree as though the bright orange fruit confused him. 'Can we talk somewhere?'

Berengario approached, his expression hard. 'Yes, why don't we go inside?' By the time Alex could see through the haze of feelings he didn't want, Berengario had invited Jules's ex into Alex's kitchen and the rest of the neighbours had piled in after them, all narrow looks and threatening demeanour – especially threatening since everyone was holding harvesting shears.

Luca paused at the door to Alex's flat, inspecting the fresh label by the doorbell that read 'Volpe', just above his own faded 'Mattelig'. Julia's ex studying the simple evidence of their cohabitation made Alex squirm.

The man looked nervously from face to face, but took a seat when Berengario gestured for him to do so, sitting down opposite.

'Caffè?'

'Ehm, sì grazie.'

Berengario looked up at Alex as though the kitchen were a bar, but if Luca was on the back foot, then he'd play along. As

Alex set to work making coffee, Elena and Siore Cudrig and Stefano the tattoo artist took the other seats around the table.

Jules came alongside him and took the moka pot. 'You don't have to make him coffee,' she mumbled.

'*You* don't have to talk to him.'

'Unfortunately, I do.' She pressed the button on the coffee grinder with a little too much force and the loud buzz filled the kitchen.

'Aren't I supposed to punch him for you?'

'I know you wouldn't.'

'No,' he agreed with a shrug. 'But Berengario is prepared to get rid of him for you.'

She glanced at the tense little gathering, full of too many menacing looks and not enough small talk. Leaning close to speak into his ear, she said, 'Would he bury Luca in the kitchen garden? I'm not sure the tomatoes would benefit.'

The joke pricked him again with affection, but her eyes were grave. Grasping her forearm, he turned her to him. 'Are you all right with this?'

'No,' she answered faintly, sending spikes of that impotent fury through him again. He wanted to protect her, but it was more than that. He wanted to erase Luca from her past – a realisation that made him panic. If he felt this way about Luca, how did Jules feel about Laura?

* * *

When Jules forced herself to turn away from Alex's comforting presence, what she saw made her pause. Siore Cudrig had on her best pinched expression. The tattoo artist leaned an arm casually on the windowsill, but his eyes were sharp, as though hinting at concealed weapons. And Berengario... His bushy brow had never looked so grim as he studied her ex without flinching.

Jules wanted to laugh – she wanted to cry. These neighbours had watched and gossiped and judged, been gruff and stand-offish at times, but they had their pitchforks lined up now – for *her*. She almost wished Berengario had brought his scythe.

The sheen of sweat on Luca's smooth brow suggested he had picked up on the hostility. Just hearing his voice again had made her want to run. Seeing his face made her taste her own failure again, the twinge of memories she'd tried to save but now wanted to erase.

Her thoughts were consumed with possible reasons for his sudden appearance. He hadn't called. Her feelings swerved from joy at the possibility that they'd sold the B & B easily and her troubles were over, to misgiving about the conversations they needed to have about their relationship. He wouldn't have come all this way just to say goodbye.

The brief thought that he could want her back flitted across her panicked brain, but she dismissed it. She'd never been more certain that everything between them was over and he'd known it before she had.

The lively, intense man who'd captured her attention so fully when they'd met in London wasn't who Luca really was – at least not with her any more. Looking at him now, without a scrap of lingering attraction, only hurt, she had to admit she'd been deluded during their relationship – irrational. Maybe she was being irrational now, imagining herself in love with Alex.

Making decisions for *love* was a laughable approach. For commitment, maybe, but nobody committed after knowing someone a matter of weeks – and Alex had always been clear that he couldn't commit.

More than irrational, Jules had been utterly foolish to ignore reality and allow her feelings to develop, but something still squeezed around her heart and insisted Alex was *different*.

Luca glanced from one intimidating face to another and then beseechingly at Jules. 'Who are all these people?'

'Neighbours,' Berengario said. 'Jules is our neighbour.'

'And *you*, I'm assuming—' Luca turned to Alex, his eyes narrow '—are Signor Mattelig? Her new...'

'Housemate,' he said flatly.

Jules's stomach sank. Yep, she'd walked right into another mess, when she'd been determined to pull herself out of her old one. Her skin crawled; not with the revulsion she felt when she looked at Luca, but with the first sparks of loss. She would lose Alex. Her stupid, irrational heart had forgotten that she had to go – and his heart already belonged to someone else.

His hand landed at her back, fisting in her shirt. How many times had he gripped her like that, as though he couldn't let her go? How difficult it was to believe what he said and not what he did.

'Jules,' Alex said softly, 'you don't owe him anything – not your feelings.'

She swallowed, trying to get her racing heart under control. Alex thought she was upset about Luca? It was almost funny.

'Are you going to talk to me now I've come all this way?' Luca asked with a huff.

'I didn't tell you where I was. You could have called instead.'

'Well, when a letter arrived confirming your postal redirection, I was confused myself. I'd never heard of this place and I have no idea how you found it.'

'That was the idea,' she said weakly.

'But you obviously didn't realise that the redirection doesn't work for couriers and I couldn't exactly give you your passports over the phone, could I?'

'What?'

He rummaged in his leather shoulder-bag, coming away with two fat envelopes, one of which bore the seal of the Australian High Commission in Milan. No wonder she'd been waiting a little longer than expected for her passports. She took the envelopes automatically, her mind stalling. The letters in her hand were supposed to be the open door to a brighter future, but they felt heavy in her feeble fingers.

Luca continued, 'You should thank me, really. I came out to this place in the middle of nowhere to give them to you.'

Berengario and the others bristled and Luca eyed them warily.

'It's not the middle of nowhere for the people who live here,' Jules said firmly. 'Friûl is the crossroads of Europe.' She kept her gaze trained on Luca's stifled sneer. She didn't dare try to work out what Alex was feeling.

'"Crossroads of Europe" or "arse of Italy", I see you've settled in well here with these people. Do you even need your passports, now you've found your next "passion"?'

She flinched and before she'd had time to react, Alex was pushing forward, nudging her behind him. 'Don't blame her for what *you* did wrong!' He continued in Italian, but Jules understood enough to know he was accusing Luca of exploiting her and the slap of his palm onto the table was clear.

'Ehi, stai calmo, amico.'

'I'm not your friend,' Alex snapped in reply, switching back to English with a glance at Jules. 'I'm *her* friend.'

'With certain benefits, I can see.' Luca flashed his eyes from one to the other. 'I knew you wouldn't be able to support yourself, but I didn't expect you'd solve that problem... *this* way.'

The passports fell from her hand as the words landed like punches. She hadn't made herself dependent on the men in her life, had she? That wasn't how it had been with Luca and definitely not with Alex, but she *had* accepted help – more than she could repay. She'd let Alex feed her and Maddalena and Berengario take care of her and give her purpose. She'd relied on Luca for too long and perhaps she hadn't broken that cycle.

'Get out of here!' Alex's raised voice startled Jules out of her panic, especially when he added a foul Italian insult she'd learned from television. But he continued in English for her benefit. 'Now! She doesn't have to listen to that *shit*.' His clenched fist came into focus in her field of vision. He was breathing hard. Even Berengario and the others had frozen, watching the discussion in alarm. Siore Cudrig couldn't understand a word of English, but her eyes were still huge.

Luca rose to his feet. 'I still have business—'

'Not in my kitchen, you don't. Take your lies and your delusions and get out!'

'I think "delusions" might be more apt for your situation, hmm?' He reached once more into his bag and turned to Jules. She recoiled, but forced herself to face him. 'We've had a few viewings of the B & B. If we get an offer, I'll need your procura – so I can act on your behalf. Unless you're not leaving the country after all?'

'My what?' she asked, her thoughts a haze.

'Power of attorney,' Alex translated. 'Leave the paperwork here,' he instructed Luca gruffly. 'She won't sign right now.'

Why not? If they could sell the B & B, then she wouldn't need help from anyone ever again – she wouldn't need to rely on Alex.

'I can sign,' she insisted.

Alex's grip on her sleeve grew tighter. 'Do you trust him?' he asked through his teeth, his body taut.

Squeezing her eyes shut, Jules shook her head. 'No,' she admitted. 'But what else can I do?'

'We'll work something out.'

We... There was no 'we' unless she counted Arco, and the poor pup was just as wild and abandoned as she was.

'Leave the paperwork,' she forced herself to say to Luca. 'You have my number and I have yours.'

'You'd better not try to obstruct the sale.'

'Why would I?' she asked.

'I know you were too attached to the place – your Italian dream,' he said with an ugly chuckle. 'It would have been kinder to let you down earlier.'

'*Out!* Now!'

Jules had never heard such a wild edge to Alex's voice.

'Is he going to hit me?' Luca asked, his voice high, but his tone still sneering. 'Where did you find this caveman, Jules? You'll have simply enormous children.'

She didn't know if he understood how much his cutting joke hurt, but there was little else he could have said that could catch her straight in the heart. She'd been stupid enough to picture a family with Luca once – in the very distant future, they'd agreed – but with Alex – oh God, the picture was too real and so entirely impossible.

Arco gave a bark as Luca headed for the kitchen door. With a heavy sigh, he turned to the animal and gave him a perfunctory pat on the head. 'Yes, goodbye, stupid dog.' Alex gave a sharp gesture to hurry him along, following him into the hallway where the squeak of his loafers faded and then the door clicked firmly shut behind him.

Berengario was on his feet in an instant, grasping Jules's upper arms and peering into her eyes. 'Jules,' he said firmly. When she couldn't bring herself to look him in the eye, he enfolded her in an embrace and she was mortified to feel the heat of tears on her face.

In a flurry of neighbours, Jules found herself pushed down into a chair, her shoulders squeezed and her back rubbed and a steaming espresso and a biscuit placed in front of her. Siore Cudrig tut-tutted and Jules heard muttered imprecations and a quiet conversation between Berengario and Alex in the garbled language that had become nearly as familiar as standard Italian to her sluggish ear.

Then the kitchen was quiet. Only Alex was left, leaning heavily on the door-frame, his legs and arms crossed in front of him as he stared at the floor with a troubled expression. His hair fell over his forehead and just looking at him brought on the smarting tears again.

There wasn't anywhere to go from here – except away from him.

32

_____

Blood rushed loudly in Alex's ears, filling in the silence when everyone had left. He wanted to take Jules by the shoulders and shake her and tell her that everything her ex had said reflected on Luca and not her.

But he could see how deeply the words had affected her – how she panicked at the prospect of being dependent on anyone else.

His gaze snagged on the envelopes on the floor and he forced himself forward to retrieve them and place them on the table with more gentleness than he'd thought he could muster. Lowering himself heavily into the chair opposite her, he lifted his gaze to hers.

'Are you going to open them?'

She picked one up, but just held it in her limp hand. 'I'm sorry,' she whispered.

'None of that was your fault.'

Her grimace was eloquent. 'I can't believe I moved to Italy for *him*.'

He swallowed, his fingertips brushing the other envelope. 'You can go home now, though.'

When her gaze flew to his, it was unexpectedly haunted. 'Yeah. I won't have to scrounge off you any longer.'

'Jules,' he began sharply, 'Luca was aiming to hurt you. You earned your way – both with him and with us.'

'With you?' she asked quietly.

Smothered in indignation and frustration, the right words refused to come and he opened his mouth stupidly. What could he say? Yes, she'd more than earned her keep – but not the way Luca had sneeringly suggested. Or no, she hadn't earned anything. She didn't need to earn anything. It was a minefield he didn't have the focus to cross. There was too much adrenaline still pumping in his veins.

'I *wish* I'd punched him!' he blurted out, resting his forehead on the heel of his hand when he couldn't seem to hold himself up any more. 'Damn it, Jules! I *hate* that he hurt you! I hate that you listen to him!'

She dropped the envelope to clutch his forearm with both of her hands. 'I'm glad you didn't hit him. He's not worth getting upset about. I'm trying not to let his words sink in.'

He turned his arm over and grasped hers tightly. 'Try harder.' If Luca hadn't destroyed her confidence, maybe she would have had some bravery left to stay – here, with him.

She opened her mouth, hesitating and licking her lips before she said softly, tentatively, 'I'd rather listen to you.'

And I'm asking you not to go...

His breath was tight, words he wasn't ready to say pulling at their restraints. He almost asked her. He almost told her he didn't know what he'd do without her. But that wouldn't be fair. He couldn't manipulate her into loving him when he didn't know if he could ever love her back the way he'd loved Laura.

She'd lost so much because she'd been brave and tried to love someone. He couldn't ask her to do it again.

Letting his eyes drift shut, he released a long breath and leaned over the table to be closer to her. She met him in the middle, her cheek against his forehead.

'I wish your passports had got lost in the post,' he murmured – true, but far too shallow for what was inside him. Her fingers drifted into his hair and he finally allowed himself to be soothed, even though part of him didn't want to be.

'You know the post doesn't come on the weekend.' He felt her smile against his skin.

'It doesn't. Nothing ever arrives on a Sunday.'

Her hand slipped to the back of his neck. 'The post will arrive tomorrow. Nothing came today. Sundays are for other things entirely.'

He turned his head and grazed his lips against her jaw. 'Kissing – yes. Never post.'

'Definitely for kissing.' Her words were more breath than voice and he grasped at the chance to show her how much he felt, even though it could never be enough.

When he came closer the pull between them was different, as though she understood his turmoil – or were experiencing her own. She sucked in one last breath before their mouths met, a little desperate.

'I hope you're not thinking about him,' he said gruffly as he hauled her to her feet, wrapping an arm around her as they stumbled into the hallway in the direction of his room.

'I'm not,' she reassured him between kisses. 'You're a much better mistake than he ever was.'

Her words tugged at him even as he tumbled onto the bed with her and soaked up her fragrant skin and soft body.

'You're not a mistake to me,' he said firmly. 'You're a page in my book – one I want to bookmark and return to over and over again.'

She peeled his shirt off, her hands and her lips eager and busy as always. 'Just stay on the page with me for a minute, Alex. We don't have to turn it yet.'

* * *

Although Jules tried her hardest to ignore the envelopes, her gaze seemed to fall on them every five minutes as she stirred the polenta for dinner. It disturbed her how much she wanted to sneak them into the bin, but a small, panicky part of her also insisted she needed to take control of her life again. Alex was not Luca, but she had fallen into a familiar pattern of relying on him.

'How about you open them.'

She glanced up to find him studying her gravely. 'I suppose I should.'

'Is it difficult to book flights to Australia? The farthest I've ever been is Turkey.'

Do you want to visit Australia?

'It's a really long flight, isn't it?' he prompted.

'It's awful,' she agreed distractedly as she slipped her finger under the seal and pulled out her red Italian passport, stroking her thumb over the gold embossed star and wreath.

'All official now,' Alex said, pressing a kiss to her cheek. She caught his quick smile that might have been half-hearted. 'Julia Volpe of the Calabrian Volpes.'

'After all of Berengario's comments, I kind of feel like a Furlan Volpe.'

'You can visit, you know.' That comment was definitely half-hearted and she didn't want to ask herself why.

'Maybe I will. That's part of the reason I wanted to make sure

I had the passport – so nothing would stop me coming back.' *Or you could ask me to stay...*

After checking over her passports, she grasped the power of attorney forms – although 'grasped' was the wrong word for the flood of Italian legalese she had no hope of understanding. Her hair stood on end when she remembered how close she'd come to signing it without thought.

'I can help you with that,' Alex offered from his position at the stove.

'You already did,' she said weakly. 'You asked me if I trust him and the answer is no. Maybe I'll have to take out a loan and fly back for the sale. Unless...' She glanced up at him and quickly back down. No, she couldn't ask him that.

'Hmm?'

'I'll find a way,' she said with a sigh.

After dinner, she opened up her laptop and started looking at flights while Alex sat across the table with a book he didn't seem to be paying much attention to. But he'd taken out his contacts and he always looked hot in his glasses.

The quoted amount for last-minute flights was far more than she'd feared – twice the credit limit on her card – and she chewed on her lip as she imagined coaching her parents through an international transfer and then finding a way to pay them back. Then she clicked through the information about transportation of pets, panic rising the more she researched.

'Oh, shit!' she said under her breath.

Alex wrenched his gaze up. 'What?'

'I can't go. Oh, God, I'm an idiot.' She was even more of an idiot for the shot of hope that rushed through her at the prospect of more time here – with Alex.

'You can't go?'

She froze, her heart squeezing. The longer she stayed, the

longer she was a burden on Alex and the others. 'I thought transporting Arco would be expensive,' she began, her voice high, 'but I didn't realise it required blood tests and vet certificates and all kinds of stuff! Australia has really strict requirements for animals entering the country.'

'Okay, what does he need? Immunisation?'

She tried to tell herself that Alex was just being helpful and not a little too keen for her to leave, but the idea took root anyway.

'The whole process takes six months. I'm *such* an idiot. What am I supposed to do?' Her heart sank, torn between the idea of staying for another six months, but horrified by the thought of making her own way for another half a year here.

'Shh,' Alex said, snatching her waving hand and placing it gently back on to the table. 'You've had a lot on your mind. It's not your fault and it's something we can find a solution to.'

'I can't just stay with you for six months, Alex.'

He gave an odd grimace and half a shrug that confirmed her suspicion. 'Perhaps not, but Arco can.'

'What? Leave him here?'

'Dr Orsino will know what to do with the tests and immunisations and I can pack him up and get him on a plane to you when the time comes.'

She shook her head. 'Alex, I can't ask—'

'You're not asking. I'm offering. Arco is already settled here. He knows me and to be honest, I won't mind the reminder of you to hang on to a little longer.'

His words were a punch to the gut. Still reeling from seeing Luca, from being forced to confront her future and all the secret desires those things had uncovered – and now the enormous oversight of forgetting to prepare to get Arco out of the country with her – she couldn't contain all the hurt she could already feel when she thought about Alex letting her go.

'You'd rather have Arco as a reminder than me here right now,' she accused, hating the bitterness in her voice. His brow furrowed in confusion and she realised she hadn't explained herself very well. 'That's what you do, isn't it?'

The bitterness dissolved slowly into bleak acceptance.

'You hang on to things that have gone,' she continued. 'If I weren't leaving, you wouldn't know what to do about *this* between us – you wouldn't know how to let yourself be happy! I'm not blaming you,' she said in a rush when he opened his mouth to defend himself – although he looked wobbly and his chest heaved. 'You've lived through a real trauma and I think you're dealing with it however you can. But you don't know how to do anything else.'

'I tried to explain—'

She nodded slowly. 'I see that now. We were only ever together because I'm leaving and it didn't count as moving on – because you can't let yourself move on. *You're* the ghost in this house.'

His sigh was long and shaky. 'Maybe I am.'

'I understand,' she mumbled. 'You'd rather be a ghost than let her go.'

He shook his head. 'If I let her go, I don't know what I'll find. I'm a ghost anyway.'

She wanted to argue, but she knew there wasn't any point. 'You've been pretty real to me.'

Tugging off his glasses, he peered at her from beneath his brows. 'Leave Arco with me.'

'Another woman who leaves you with her pet?' She laughed darkly.

'I'll enjoy having him. I'll take him into the forest every day.

It'll do both of us good.' He paused before adding, 'The way *you* did me good.'

Her eyes fell shut, a sting starting up behind her eyelids. 'Alex,' she began, her voice threatening to break, 'if I leave him with you, it won't be hanging on – not for me.'

'Hmm?'

'It would be an excuse to stay in touch – into the future, not hanging on to the past. I might start hoping.'

As she expected, he looked stricken at the prospect of allowing her to develop false hope – or keeping in touch. She wasn't sure which, but her thoughts wound back to that first night when they'd agreed not to exchange numbers. So much had changed and yet nothing had.

'Maybe Maddalena could look after him – or Berengario,' she muttered.

He swallowed thickly. 'I'll look after him, Jules. I want to.'

'He'll miss you afterwards,' she said, suspecting he saw through her statement to the truth: *I'll miss you – so badly.*

'I think that damage is already done.'

33

Julia's last week in Cividale seemed to progress at double speed. Her mum managed to transfer enough money for a flight the following Monday. It didn't feel right, leaving without Arco, but nothing felt right anyway. Dr Orsino assured her he understood the procedure and would make sure the blood samples and immunisations were sent to the right place at the right time. At least the six-month delay in transporting the dog would give her time to save up for the quarantine and flight costs so she wouldn't have to borrow anything more from her parents.

After a boisterous discussion over lunch at Due Pini, where Berengario had so thoroughly bad-mouthed Luca that Jules had been tempted to laugh, he'd offered to take on the power of attorney for her and travel to Parma for the sale on her behalf. When she'd hinted that she might ask Alex, the old man had been surprisingly firm, suggesting Alex might not be able to take on the responsibility if the sale took too long.

She was uneasy for a moment, but Berengario smiled and joked that he could see the future – at least as he wanted it to be – and made a throwaway comment about the possibility of Alex going back to his real profession as a draughtsman that made little sense to Jules and even less to Alex, when she told him. But after an appointment with a notary, she was one step closer to tying up all her Italian loose ends.

Aside from practicalities, Jules and Alex avoided speaking about her departure, although she'd come to recognise the sheen in his eye when he was thinking about it. She didn't want to go over the heartache again and again, but having the important topic completely off limits was a first taste of the complete withdrawal she'd experience when she left.

She wondered if he'd prefer sleeping in separate beds again, but every time she was about to offer, he grabbed her and held on.

The weekend was the Fiera di San Martino, the Saint Martin's Day fair. All of the local farms and businesses set up stalls in the town during the day and the vineyards were open to visitors into the evening. Jules and Davide ran Maddalena's stall, selling wine and olive oil and jars of preserves.

Arco was with Alex at the bike shop to get used to his new routine and Jules missed him already, although she had Fritz to contend with. The big black dog was tied up behind the stall, occasionally pulling at his lead and startling customers.

'You're really going home then?' Davide asked during a lull on Saturday morning. 'Nonno was convinced you were the one to drag Alex back to life.'

'Not everything Berengario sees actually comes to pass,' she answered carefully.

Davide's smile slipped and she waited for him to say whatever was on the tip of his tongue. 'Is he okay? Alex?'

'Yes,' she replied immediately. 'You don't need to worry – none of you do. He doesn't need to be dragged. He's muddling through himself. Maybe all he needs is a friend.'

'I haven't always been the greatest friend to him. Laura was the favoured cousin – always so successful, married and settled young with a person everyone loved. Sometimes I think he's a better son to Mamma than I am – and Laura was a better daughter.'

Jules couldn't help it. She knew it was insensitive, but she laughed at him, pressing the backs of her fingers to her mouth in a vain attempt to stifle it. 'I'm sorry, Davide, but that's not how family works – especially not your family. Alex just needs them more than you do.'

He gave her a perplexed look, but Jules turned away, her own observation echoing in her mind.

'You know Berengario and Maddalena would do anything for you,' she continued. 'Even Alex's gruff neighbours who never even asked my name have offered help when needed.'

Davide smiled. 'And watched your every move, frowning and judging, no?'

'That too.' At least she was leaving Italy with a better understanding of the trade-offs of community. It had taken the lowest moment of her life to discover that she'd never be alone if she had work to do.

On Saturday night, the restaurant at Due Pini was packed with locals and visitors for the open vineyard event. Jules waited tables with Alina, getting by with her broken Italian and the goodwill of the customers.

A fire roared and Alex sat squashed in a far corner playing the shiny red Fantini accordion which he'd managed to fix – moving the bellows gently, so the diners could still hear each other speak. As the evening wore on, a small group of guests gathered around him to sing old songs in tipsy voices.

When the last guests finally trudged off in the early hours of the morning, Jules pulled up a chair with the others around the fogolâr and accepted the little glass of grappa that Maddalena poured for her.

'I believe congratulations are in order,' Maddalena said quietly, once they were all seated by the fire: Maddalena and Berengario, Alex, Elena, Davide and the two dogs.

Jules glanced up in confusion. 'Congratulations?' On leaving? Or on cracking open Alex's shell a little for a few weeks?

'It's past midnight. Happy birthday!'

'Ohhhh, thanks,' she said, accepting kisses on the cheek. 'How did you know?'

'Alex told us,' she explained.

Jules looked across the fire to see Alex's eyes on her, but he glanced away after giving her a brief smile.

'Here.' Maddalena handed over a small parcel wrapped in butcher's paper. 'I hope you can fit it in your luggage.'

Inside, she found a ceramic vase painted with swirling flowers in yellows, reds and purples. The words 'Un salût dal Friûl' were painted below the neck in sharp lettering. *Greetings from Friuli.* It was a kind gift, but tears pricked her eyes. All she'd have when she went home was this souvenir vase.

'Jules, dear!' Maddalena said in alarm.

'Sorry, I—' She waved at her face to stem the tears. 'Thank you. It's so thoughtful.'

As the conversation moved on around them, Maddalena drew closer and clutched her hand. All the quiet hours Jules had spent with this woman seemed suddenly precious. There was no effusive emotion, only steady friendship.

'I'm going to miss this place,' she said – entirely inadequately.

'This place will miss you,' Maddalena replied. 'I'm only sorry – about Alex.'

Jules shook her head. 'You don't have to be sorry about Alex.'

Maddalena's eyes clouded in an expression Jules now recognised. 'I have no regrets.'

'But *he* will – one day.'

Jules choked. 'Well that's *his*— I can't—'

Maddalena sighed. 'I know. As much as I'd like to, I can't lock you both in a room until you find a way to be together.'

Jules tried not to let those words soak through her skin: *find a way to be together.* 'Or force him to share his house with me, push us together during the harvest and then strand us in an isolated village,' she joked, laughing to cover the fresh urge to cry. 'Berengario did his best and it wasn't enough. I can't change Alex's mind and if I could, it wouldn't be right. I respect him too much.'

Silence stretched between them for so long that Jules glanced warily at her host.

'But if he did change his mind?'

Jules shook her head vehemently. 'Maddalena,' she warned, 'it's no good even thinking about that, no matter what I feel—' She cut herself off before she said too much, although the look in her friend's eye suggested it was too late.

'What you feel,' Maddalena repeated softly.

Jules squeezed her eyes shut. 'It'll pass,' she insisted. It had to.

As soon as Alex led Jules into the bar by the old Roman baths on Sunday night, he knew it had been a bad idea. If the curious looks from Salvino from the first night had made him uncomfortable, he discovered how much worse it was to have Berengario's friend watching him with wary disapproval, as though it were his fault that she was leaving.

'How was your birthday?' he asked after they'd ordered their drinks – beer for him and a glass of lightly sparkling Ribolla

Gialla for Jules, accompanied by a tight smile at the bittersweet reminder.

'Busy,' she said, smoothing her hair back self-consciously. 'But that's good. I wouldn't have wanted to be lying around moping at h—' She swallowed. 'At your place,' she finished, her expression wobbly. 'I still have to pack.'

He felt the usual twinge at the return of their conversation to superficial topics, like turning back the clock to the time he'd fought this intimacy with everything inside him. Perplexed, he realised that in this case, he didn't want to turn back the clock – stop it, perhaps, but not turn it back.

'We don't have to stay long. I just wanted to take you out for your birthday.'

'I appreciate it.'

He couldn't think of a thing to say. His chest was too heavy for banter and his mind was suffering under the weight of so many things he couldn't express.

'I still can't believe your nearest major airport is Munich, not Rome,' she said stiltedly. 'Although, you know, I came here because it was as far from Italy as I could get without leaving Italy.' Her laugh was strained. 'But it is beautiful here. I'm glad I'm not leaving just with memories of Luca and how everything went wrong.'

'You found your own way through and it worked out well for us, anyway – Berengario and Maddalena and... me.' When he met her gaze, her eyes were dark and wary and he had to look away again. He felt, rather than understood, that he was on the very edge of hurting her and he wasn't sure how to stop himself going over. She wasn't supposed to get hurt.

But as the stiff conversation progressed, he became increasingly panicked that there was still time for their relationship to go wrong, even as his thoughts scrambled trying to avoid it.

'I, ehm, I got you a birthday present, but it's not much – sorry. I tried to think of something you'd like. And don't take it as a suggestion that you can't cook, it's just something that reminded me of all the time we spent in the kitchen together and maybe you...' He realised he was babbling.

'If it's a cookbook, I'll love it,' she said softly. 'For the reminder, and not because I'll ever manage to cook any of the dishes properly. You never really taught me anything...'

'I enjoyed cooking for you.'

He could only say the wrong thing, it seemed, as her eyes were shining and she frowned deeply. 'Are you going to give it to me?'

'Ah.' He rummaged belatedly in his rucksack and handed her the poorly wrapped book, feeling the inadequacy keenly.

She ripped the paper off to reveal the beautifully bound hard-back from the antiques market, smoothing her palm over the jacket with its dated photos of gubana and sweet gnocchi stuffed with plums.

'It's great.'

He could tell it wasn't – or that something was wrong, anyway.

'Alex,' she began, her expression pained, 'can we go? I don't think I want an... audience tonight.'

'Of course.' He shot to his feet, hastily thrusting some money at Salvino on their way out.

She was silent as they walked the narrow lanes under the wooden eaves of the old town. His thoughts returned to the first night they'd walked like this together. After the five weeks that had passed and everything they'd shared, he felt as though they were back at the beginning.

But this was supposed to be the end.

Passing under a wrought-iron street lamp attached to the crooked wall of a house, he noticed her cheeks sparkling with tears and panic shot through him again. When they passed the persimmon tree – now completely bare – and finally closed the door behind them, she sank into him, bowing her head and pressing her face into his chest.

Wrapping his arms around her, he kissed her hair, her forehead, her cheek – and then, when she lifted her head, her mouth. This much still made sense.

It took him a long time to fall asleep that night, startling awake again every time he began to drop off, his hand fumbling for her, as though she'd just dissolve without saying goodbye. He heard his own heartbeat loudly in his ears and the old panic seized him.

He felt adrift – again – examining his choices obsessively and cursing that life didn't come with an instruction book. For a moment, he was gripped with fear that he'd spiral, he might find himself back in the dark places he'd been. But as he waited, forcing himself to breathe – in and out, as slowly as he could – there was no pull down into despair. Jules snuffled softly next to him, the faint scent of her herbal shampoo reaching his nostrils.

She was very much alive. She was just leaving. His heart rate sped up suddenly and he grew restless. Trying not to disturb her, he held himself rigid on his side of the bed, but he couldn't keep his eyes off the blurry silhouette an arm's length away and she stirred enough that he worried she could sense his gaze.

After a frustrated hour of shifting under the covers as gently as he could, he sighed, staring wide-eyed at the ceiling as he accepted what he was going to do. He rolled over and slung an arm heavily over her, tucking himself tightly against her. He shouldn't use her as a teddy bear, but she could catch up on sleep another night.

He swept her hair aside so it wasn't in his face and nuzzled her gently, pressing a kiss beneath her ear. She sucked in a sleepy breath and stretched, tipping her head forward as though inviting another kiss. He couldn't resist giving it to her and she snuggled back against him.

Then she opened her mouth and, in a tone that was all drowsiness, more asleep than awake, she murmured words that most definitely sounded like 'Love you.'

He froze, his blood rushing as he waited for her to roll over and look at him, expecting a reaction – waited to see what his reaction would be. But with a soft exhale, her breathing returned to normal and she slept on. Alex slowly relaxed his body, his heart still beating an absurd rhythm.

Was that what she really felt? Was that even possible, when he was half a ghost and she was so alive it hurt? But it would hurt just as much – more – when she was gone, even though she wouldn't be as gone as Laura was. Resting his forehead against the back of her head, he held on tight, confused but knowing he had to let her go and make her own life instead of trapping her in his.

Even if this was love, she wouldn't stay for him and he couldn't let her.

34

Jules felt like a ghost early Monday morning as she dumped her backpack into the boot of Alex's tiny Fiat and fell on Arco for teary, doggy hugs. Her eyes were puffy and her heart was sore and this wasn't how she was supposed to feel, to be finally on her way home.

She wouldn't even have Arco to be lonely with at the other end of this flight. 'I'll see you soon, pup,' she whispered, stroking his curly head heavily and letting him lick her hand.

When she'd closed him inside Alex's apartment and headed for the car on shaky legs, his voice cut into her hazy thoughts: 'I'll look after him.'

'I know you will,' she muttered. 'I'm just going to miss him.'

Alex had offered to drive her to Udine for an early train north, but now her stomach churned with nerves and she wondered if it would have been better to take that funny diesel train with the retro upholstery instead, even if it meant leaving at the crack of dawn. How was she supposed to say goodbye? All she could think about was the first time she'd kissed him goodbye and they'd ended up in bed together instead.

Actually, that didn't sound like a bad idea.

'Is there any way we could cross the Ponte del Diavolo? One last time?'

'Sure,' he replied in a clipped tone. 'We've got time.' Time was one thing they'd never had enough of.

Jules pressed her nose to the window as they clattered across the cobbled bridge for her final glimpse of the gorge and the Natisone river. The forest paths had been a haven for her, as they had been for generations of Furlans. It was strange to remember the twenty-seven-year-old who'd arrived in Cividale full of bitterness and obsessed with her own failure.

She'd stood on that bridge, clinging to her bitterness, while the river and the mountains stubbornly stole her breath. That woman had had no idea what she would find here. The middle of nowhere had become somewhere special and a week or two to lick her wounds had become five weeks to rebuild her life.

She hated how quiet they were on the twenty-minute drive to Udine, but her vocabulary seemed to have shrunk until it only included dangerous words like 'love' and 'stay'. She wondered briefly what she would have done if Luca had gently told her she shouldn't make a life-changing decision for him. She probably would have been embarrassed and walked away. She couldn't imagine she would have been fighting the urge to shake him and make him change his mind.

God, she'd never cried this much over Luca. She had to face up to the truth: now she could finally leave the country, she wanted to stay, even if that made her a reckless fool, repeating her own mistakes.

He pulled into the drop-off zone outside the station in plenty of time for her train north for her final departure from Italy, first through Austria, Germany and then on an Airbus A380 to Singapore.

'Are you coming in?' she mumbled.

'I wasn't going to.'

She swallowed. 'Okay.' Her voice came out on a sniff and she gulped back a sob.

'Jules.' His voice was low and gravelly. 'It'll be all right.'

She tried to laugh, but it came out as a choke. '*You're* telling me it'll be all right?' Throwing open the car door, she stalked around to the back and wrenched open the boot, swinging her heavy backpack onto her back and tugging out her smaller day bag.

Slamming the boot wasn't as satisfying as she'd hoped and she turned for the station mixed-up and lost. Why was she going again?

'Are you going to say goodbye?' The indignation in Alex's tone made her whirl around.

'I don't want to!' She watched him trying to make sense of her words, his brow twisting and his mouth opening to speak words that wouldn't come. 'I don't want to say goodbye at all.'

'I thought you didn't like being dependent on me.'

'I didn't like being dependent on Luca.' Her vision narrowed. Planting her feet in front of him, she licked her lips and allowed the words to tumble out. 'Ask me to stay.'

He drew up straight, his expression going blank in surprise. 'What?'

Her jaw wobbled as she repeated herself. 'Ask me to stay.' Cold seeped along her skin as she began to suspect that she'd made a difficult situation worse by pushing him. But if she'd already made it worse, she might as well continue. 'Ask me!' she said again. 'I'll say yes. Just ask me!'

Her vision blurred with tears as the shock creeping over his face made her confront the truth. He wasn't going to ask her. He was content to keep her in the pages of a book where she couldn't hurt him.

'Your flight is tonight!'

Her eyes slammed shut, and in her mind his voice twisted until it sounded like Luca. *Be reasonable, Jules.* 'You're right. It was a stupid idea.' She headed for the station, only daring to open her eyes when he was safely behind her.

'Jules, wait!'

His footsteps behind her triggered a twinge of panic and she hurried for the station. Missing the train was one complication she didn't need on top of confusion and rejection and failure – at least that was the excuse her pride came up with.

'I *want* to ask you!'

She paused, the automatic doors swishing open as though encouraging her to take the next steps and leave him behind. 'But?' she prompted, stupidly hoping there wouldn't be a 'but'.

'But what if it doesn't work? It's not fair to ask so much of you. I can't be responsible for you—'

'It was stupid of me to suggest it,' she called over her shoulder. She wanted to hit something. Why did she keep hanging around too long instead of making the necessary break?

'No, it was brave—'

'I know you're not ready. I never meant to get my hopes up, and I *especially* didn't mean to push you.' Forgetting she was supposed to be protecting herself, she turned back and caught sight of him, this gorgeous man who put old accordions back together but couldn't do himself the same service. The flash of his blue eyes reminded her of the day they'd met, when she'd had no clue of what he would come to mean to her, but she'd sensed the magic already. 'You don't have to feel guilty. No expectations, remember?'

'I'm struggling with that.'

Before she could process what he could mean, he gripped her cardigan and tugged her closer, reminding her of the many other occasions he'd done the same. Her gaze dipped to his mouth, her breath catching.

But instead of pressing close for one more mind-blowing kiss that she wouldn't have trusted herself to stop, his shoulders drooped – and her heart wilted.

'I'll miss you,' he whispered.

That was safe – and it was true, even though 'missing him' didn't begin to cover the breadth of her regret. 'I'll miss you too.'

With a pained expression, he pulled away, his fist still clamped around her cardigan. 'Text me when you land. I'll be worried.'

'I will,' she promised. 'Send me pictures of Arco – and Attila.'

The way his expression softened when she mentioned her dog only made her want to protest her departure more loudly. 'Okay.'

For a long moment, he just looked at her and a hopeless smile stretched on her lips.

Lifting a hand to his face, she brushed his cheek and ran her hand over his mouth one last time. 'Goodbye, Alessandro Mattelig.' *I love you.*

The sudden hiss of a train startled her and she stumbled as she tried to shake herself back into the present.

'I should—'

He gave a single nod. She headed into the station forecourt in a daze, struggling to focus on the departures information. She glanced back to see him still standing there, frowning, his hands limp at his sides. She gave him a wave, which he half-heartedly returned, and then she gave a concerted effort to pull herself together, studying the board until she found her platform.

When she took one last look out of the glass doors, he was gone.

35

Alex forced air into his lungs, watched the lines on the road flit by and carefully observed the oncoming traffic as he puttered back from Udine. Only when he pulled up in his parking space out by the creek did his focus begin to crack.

This is not like Laura...

He tried to reason with himself while part of him screamed that she was *gone*, just like Laura, and another part of him was outraged at the comparison. He'd known Jules a matter of weeks, not the years he'd been with his wife.

The most uncomfortable thought was that she wasn't even gone, not really. She was alive somewhere – else. Perhaps her departure was a lucky escape. She could discover her bright future, while he sat in his car, leaning on the steering wheel and staring at the creek where he'd nearly had a heart attack watching her wade in to rescue his cat.

He'd never be able to cross the Ponte del Diavolo again without thinking of her stopping and staring – or of the first time he'd seen her, when she'd impulsively asked him out to dinner and held her stubborn chin high when she'd thought he would reject her.

Rubbing his swollen eyes with a sigh and resting his forehead on his hands, he was vaguely annoyed to acknowledge that time would make everything better. He'd lived the truth of that. Even when he hadn't wanted his life to get better, it had.

He'd held on to Laura with everything in him and he'd still accidentally fallen in love with Jules.

Jerking his head up, he blinked out of the windscreen with a shiver of panic. Had that word really just crept into his thoughts? Perhaps just because she'd said it – in her sleep last night, which didn't really count.

There are no star-crossed lovers here – only stupid ones.

He was even more irritated that Berengario's words came back to him right then. He was still picturing Jules standing under the arches at the station, telling him she'd stay if he asked. After everything she'd been through with Luca, she'd still been brave enough to stay.

Oh, God, should he have asked her? Should he have let her take the risk? But he hated the idea of her giving up her chances – giving up her *home* for his. Her relationship with Luca hadn't even been an outlier in the statistics of couples from different countries and he'd known her such a short time to ask so much – he had so little to offer.

He heaved himself out of the car and slammed the door. There were no right answers. He should have accepted that by now, but he was back at the beginning of this new journey to acceptance and... he was a long way off acceptance.

He'd made the wrong decision.

Turning back to the car in agitation, his fingers were on the handle of the door before he stopped himself. As much as he could already feel the words on his lips – *I love you. Please stay –*

he was terrified. What if she ended up resenting her life here? And what did he think he'd do: race the train to Austria and pluck her off the station platform? Call her and ask her to get off? He'd given her no reason to trust him.

With a growl of frustration, he turned back in the direction of the courtyard. At the door to his apartment, he remembered Arco waiting for him with a twinge of regret. In the bleakness after Laura had died, Attila had been both a painful reminder and a source of comfort, but he found little comfort in the thought of sharing his regret with Jules's dog. He'd been foolish to think Arco would help him come to terms with her departure.

Opening the door with too much force, he was surprised when it took the little curly furball several long seconds to appear at the kitchen door and tear down the hall to him. He crouched to give the dog a thorough rub on his back and tummy, smarting from the feeling that his pack was incomplete.

Then he heard voices and froze. A cackle from Berengario. A soft admonishment from Elena. When he rounded the kitchen door, he even found Maddalena brewing tea by his stove, Stefano the tattoo artist doodling on a piece of paper and Davide sitting off to the side.

They all looked up and immediately fell silent when he walked in. He watched them warily. Nobody appeared to even breathe as they shot glances behind him at the empty doorway.

'Is this some kind of commiseration committee? I'm not really in the mood.'

Maddalena broke the silence. 'She *left*?'

'Of course she left. I took her to the train station! What did you think would happen? There was no alien abduction.'

'Gesù, Maria e i santi, have you no respect for your elders, boy?' Berengario looked ready to hit him over the head.

'What?' He stalked to the stove and rattled with the moka pot as loudly as he could. Now was no time for Maddalena's sage and mauve infusion.

'Nonno, after everything he's done for you,' Davide said, rolling his eyes. Now Davide was defending him? Alex was even more deeply confused.

'You were supposed to ask her to stay!' Berengario snapped.

'No one told me that!'

Between the growl in the back of his throat and the gnashing of his teeth, Berengario was the wild animal in the room, not Arco. 'You should have worked that out for yourself. Imagine how you would have reacted if we'd told you she was the best part of your future!'

'I'm discovering how I would have reacted right now,' Alex snapped. 'How am I the one to promise her a future? She's better off without me and you should understand that.'

'You empty-headed fool!' He added several more muttered insults in Furlan, most of them about how badly he smelled. 'You're just lucky your family is looking out for you.' He took a deep breath and released it on a huff, before looking from Elena to Maddalena to Stefano with a sharp nod. 'It's time for plan B.'

Alex groaned. 'Is this some kind of intervention? Can I have a coffee first, or is coffee not allowed in the war room?'

'Sit and be quiet while we fix your life.'

'The last time you tried to fix my life I got stranded overnight in the hills!'

Berengario straightened. 'And look how well that turned out! If it weren't for us, you'd still be here spending more time with accordions than people, thinking your life was over! Just imagine if she'd never come to stay here, hmm? Or if she'd moved back to the farm when I fixed the wiring?'

'You fixed the wiring? When? Why didn't you tell me – or her?'

'Three weeks ago! You were already half in love with her and torturing yourself with guilt – and behaving extremely rudely, I might add. We had to take action.'

'She could have been staying with Maddalena all this time? You made her think she was a burden on me!'

'*You* made her think that as some twisted excuse for your own feelings.'

Alex's chest seized up and his mouth snapped shut. His hair stood on end remembering the day Berengario had turned up with the woman who'd lit his feelings on fire in what should have been a one-night stand, how he'd lashed out and felt terrible about it. He *hated* it when Berengario was right.

'But *you're* Laura's grandfather!' he said, raising his voice. 'Jules was on the farm Laura loved, in Laura's jacket, sleeping in *my bed*. Shouldn't you have been worried she'd take Laura's place? That I'd forget her – or at least forget some small detail of her, with Jules right in front of me?' His voice rasped at the end, losing strength.

Berengario gripped his forearm tightly. '*No one* will ever take Laura's place,' he said, his voice low and hard. 'It's not even possible. Do you think I loved her so little that I could replace her?'

'That's what you think of me!' Alex accused, his mind racing.

This time he did get a slap to the back of his head. 'Stupido!' Then another one for good measure. No wonder he'd been tempted to deck Luca, if his own grandfather-in-law cuffed him over the head. 'You can't replace her either. Do you think Elena is a replacement for Maddalena's mother? Of course not! She is Elena. Laura is even more deeply etched into you than that stupid tattoo on your arm. Falling in love again doesn't change that.'

'But if that's true, I belonged to someone else first; if Laura truly is so deeply etched in me, why would Jules want to stay with me?'

'Sometimes I ask myself that,' Berengario mumbled. 'Did she say it was a problem that you were married before? We don't come as naked babies into our relationships. We come with scars – sometimes we come as grizzly old men into new relationships.'

'You're not a grizzly old man,' he assured Berengario.

'Of course not! I've reclaimed my youth. I was talking about *you*. I *know* it hurts. I know you don't think you're ready. But you can't pretend it didn't happen anyway.'

'You pushed us,' he protested weakly.

'Would you have preferred it if I helped her pack her things and move down to the farm? Left you in peace? If given the chance, maybe she would have preferred Davide! *He's* certainly never been in love before.'

'Nonno,' Laura's cousin grumbled. 'If Alex was half in love after two weeks, then so was she. You can quit using me to make him jealous.'

'That worked last time too,' the old man pointed out. 'But we're not here to go over the past. We have to make a plan for the future – foolproof, this time. Stefano, thank you for bringing your designs.'

The long-haired old man shuffled a few papers in front of him. 'Yes, since we've got the bay leaves, I thought something else botanical would be nice and I've brought a few ideas.' Selecting a picture of what looked like an olive tree, Stefano held it up next to Alex's arm with a thoughtful hum.

'Yes, there'll be time for that later,' Berengario said. 'Do you have those forms, Elena?'

She adjusted her reading glasses. 'I checked again to be sure and technical draughtsman is definitely on the list of occupations allowing visas. He'll need a translated copy of his diploma and an English test result. You have that already, yes?'

Alex managed to nod, his mouth hanging open. 'I took the IELTS exam in England.'

'We'll need police clearance certificates from Italy and England, too, but I think we can fill in the form expressing interest while we wait for those. Apparently the process can take three to five months.'

'*Three* months,' Berengario said firmly. 'If I have to travel there myself and give those immigration officials a shake!'

'Immigration?'

Maddalena peered over Elena's shoulder at the sheaf of print-outs from the Internet neatly stapled together. 'The visa costs *how much?*'

'Money isn't a problem, after the payout from Laura's life insurance,' Berengario said dismissively. 'He can't have spent it all during that first year in shock. Most importantly, I've contacted the Fogolâr Furlan in Brisbane—' The way he mangled the pronunciation of Jules's home city almost made Alex laugh.

'There's a Fogolâr Furlan in Brisbane?' he repeated, his thoughts pleasantly diverted by the idea of Jules joining the cultural association of Friulian émigrés. She was a Furlan Volpe after all.

'Yes, and they were very keen to help you settle in.'

'Hang on a minute!' Alex said, giving himself a shake. 'What exactly is going on?'

'We're shipping you off to Australia, boy.'

The utter disbelief that descended on him with that statement put pressure on his lungs until he was wheezing – either with laughter or incredulity or a mixture of both.

Australia... Half the world away from his friends and family –

the support network that had held him together through his darkest time.

'Did you think I'd just turn up at her door with all my possessions on my back and ask to move in?'

'It worked for Jules,' Berengario pointed out.

'That's because Jules is brave. And tough.' And beautiful. His throat thickened.

'Don't you think it's your turn to be brave?'

His vision tunnelled as those words burrowed into his consciousness. He couldn't go. His well-being depended on frico and tocai and Bianchera olive oil – to say nothing of his meddling family. There was an invisible barrier that would make him disintegrate if he stepped out of Friuli. He felt it. Laura had died when they'd left Friuli.

When he reached the last item on that list, he recognised it was irrational. He was afraid. But he'd enjoyed living in London before the accident had changed his life. It wouldn't have been fair to ask Jules to stay for him, but could he be brave enough to go to her?

With a cough, he stretched his hand out to Elena. 'Give me the papers.' When she didn't immediately respond, he clicked his fingers urgently until she placed them warily in his hand. 'You too, Stefano.'

Gathering up the forms and lists and the intricate tattoo designs, he made a neat pile, tapping them on the table. 'Thank you for your input,' he said tightly. 'I admit, I've been a few steps behind my own feelings since I met Jules.' He paused, allowing those words to settle over him. 'You're also right,' he continued softly with a self-deprecating smile, 'I fell in love with her and I didn't deal with it well.'

He ignored the gasps and gleeful noises of his family.

'But if anyone is doing something to fix this, it's got to be me.'

Looking up slowly, he met Berengario's calculating gaze, holding it until the old man gave him a small nod and his combative posture softened. 'You know we'll help you with anything you need.'

'I know.'

36

Reverse culture shock was real.

Back in the glaring sunshine the day after she landed, under the shade cloth and the spreading jacarandas clinging to the last of their purple blooms, Jules was dreaming of stone pines in the mist and persimmons and the silver leaves of squat, gnarled olive trees.

The city was sweltering and full of people, but just as lazy in the summer heat as she remembered. Brisbane was a different planet from the foggy Friulian plain and Jules was an alien – one of those extraterrestrials who could make themselves look exactly like a human to blend in.

The way her family treated her, she was one hundred per cent Julia Volpe on the outside, the exact woman who'd left Australia for an extended backpacking trip and was now home again, her thighs sticking to a plastic chair placed on the tough buffalo grass of her brother's lawn. It was another plane of existence and she felt out of focus inside.

The little sting that assailed her every time a photo from Friuli arrived on her phone didn't help her attempts to adjust.

Alex had even managed to engineer a photo of both Arco and Attila, although Attila was only in the top corner, peering superciliously at the dog from the windowsill outside Alex's bedroom.

She'd have Arco back in a few months and that would help, although it still wouldn't be the pack back together.

Feeling the twinge again, she picked up her phone to text Alex:

> I still feel guilty for making you bond with Arco for six months.

Seeing her father Tony approaching, beer in hand, she quickly stuffed her phone back into her pocket as he collapsed into the chair next to her.

'Back from the old country, ay?'

'Yep.' Her phone vibrated, adding to her distraction.

'But without the bloke.'

Jules wished she had her own beer in hand – or anything to distract her from the ache of absence. Her dad hadn't meant to upset her. In fact, she hadn't realised he knew about Alex.

'Yep,' she repeated, trying to muster a fake smile.

'Mum said the dog will come over later.'

Another twist in her stomach. Missing Arco was almost physical, like quitting caffeine. She missed him in her hands – like she missed Alex in her skin.

'Aw, Jube,' Tony said, slinging an arm over her shoulders. While she appreciated the gesture and settled her head on his shoulder for a moment, the hug was in sad contrast to the cosy fireside touches she wished for. 'If he wouldn't come after you, then he doesn't deserve you – and he doesn't know what he's missing out on.'

'Thanks, Dad,' she mumbled, even as she disagreed vehemently inside. Alex deserved everything and she'd never have asked or expected him to leave his carefully constructed support network, not after everything he'd been through.

'You don't believe me? You never know. Maybe he'll turn up at our doorstep one day begging for you to take him back.'

'Tony!' her mother called from where she was emerging through the screen door from the kitchen with a bowl of salad. 'Even if he did, Jules would tell him where he could put his apology. Right, honey? After everything he put you through, he's not welcome here.'

'But it wasn't Alex's fault—' She cut herself off when both parents gave her an identical frown.

'Who's Alex?'

Goosebumps rushing to her hairline, Jules stared at her sandals to cover her faux pas. 'Oh, a... friend.'

'I know you'll think I'm speaking with hindsight, but I never liked Luca. He wasn't the type to bend, you know? Life's full of disruptions and you don't want someone who can't deal with them.'

Jules stood and gave her mum a squeeze around her middle. 'You're right, Mum,' she said softly. 'Life is about learning to bend and not break.'

The words reminded her of grumpy Alex, who'd taken her in despite his reservations. He'd thought he was broken, but he'd bent for her and she treasured that. Luca hadn't even tolerated the inconvenience of the dog, while Alex had bonded with Arco, despite the fact that it would bruise him again when he said goodbye.

Unable to resist any longer, she glanced at her phone to see Alex's reply:

Maybe bonding isn't as bad as I thought it was.

She stared at the screen, trying to convince herself he didn't secretly mean bonding with *her*. His profile photo on the messaging app was him wearing his rumpled felt Alpino hat with the top of his black accordion in the corner and a wry smile on his face. Then her gaze snagged on the time and she frowned.

> You're not asleep?

> I wouldn't be texting you if I were asleep.

His little joke was all it took to transport her right back to Cividale, to the familiar courtyard with the persimmon tree and Alex's bedroom.

> Your insomnia is kind of practical for this time difference.

She wished she could judge his reaction to her joke, but she'd mostly stopped walking on eggshells around his grief.

> But Arco is asleep. I suppose I could take a dark video of him snoring for you.

It wasn't only Arco she wanted to see.

> How's your family? I bet they're happy to have you home.

With a sigh, she looked out at her brother's big yard with its chain link fence. Her two nieces jumped on the trampoline while her little nephew raced around squealing. It was precious being back with all three generations of her family, but she stubbornly thought it wasn't *everyone*.

She didn't know how long she would feel that Alex was missing. But their families were separated by oceans and continents and cultures and if she could be rational, she'd tell herself they hadn't known each other long enough to get so attached. She wrote back:

> I hope it'll feel like home again soon. Send me a picture in the morning.

* * *

As Jules recovered from her jet lag and reluctantly adjusted to the high temperatures, it was easier than she would have liked to settle into her life from before she'd left for Europe. She arranged to start back at her old office job temporarily after Christmas. Her parents were taking an extended holiday after schools went back and she was doing them a favour by living at home for a while longer.

Her family treated her as though she'd never left and if they occasionally asked why she was staring out the window with her brow drawn tight, she told them she was wondering about the sale of the B & B.

She texted Alex every day, still keeping to the pretext of missing the dog, but living for the glimpses of his hands on Arco's furry back or holding the lead. Then one day he sent her a selfie, poking his head into the shot while he crouched next to Arco at the top of a hill, the Friulian plain and the dark silhouette of the mountains behind him. The way her heart banged against her ribs was almost painful.

In her room late at night, she searched job listings in Italy, not even willing to admit to herself what she was doing. She missed Berengario and Maddalena and all the others as well. But the kind of job she'd walked into here, she had no hope of obtaining in Friuli with her limited Italian. Alex had already encouraged her to go home. Holding on made no sense, but she struggled to stop.

What if one day she heard about Alex and a new girlfriend, the way she'd discovered Luca's relationship with Claudia the estate agent?

No, the only option was to get over him. The problem was, she didn't want to. She wanted to hang on to the past the way he did. As much as it hurt, there was something good in the way she felt.

Berengario sent her the occasional wonky picture of the sunrise or a plate of frico, which made her laugh. She searched for Friulian restaurants in Brisbane but drew a blank, and her parents' well-meaning attempt to cheer her up with dinner at an Italian restaurant backfired when it turned out to be a Sardinian fish restaurant. The food was delicious, but it wasn't the comforting fare she'd hoped to find – although she carefully kept her disappointment off her face and allowed her parents their indulgent smiles.

She hadn't told them much about Friuli, beyond that picking olives had been fun – and even that had felt like a half-truth because when she thought about picking olives, she thought about Alex's tall frame up a ladder.

At the beginning of December, Berengario sent her a text that made her wonder if he could read minds. There was no explanation, just the website for the Fogolâr Furlan – the Friulian Club – in Brisbane. When she clicked on the link and scrolled through the photos of past events, the sudden nostalgia was powerful.

Children in folk costumes with black vests and little ties posed for photos with older men in bright blue T-shirts with the alpine eagle and the word 'Friûl' in yellow lettering. There were felt Alpino hats and posts remembering the earthquake of 1976 and greetings in English, Italian and Furlan.

But it wasn't only the memories of Friuli that struck her. All of the events took place in the bright Queensland sunshine. The war memorial stood in front of an enormous eucalypt and the members of the association smiled and ate their barbecue lunch off paper plates and drank Kirk's soft drinks straight from an Australian supermarket.

The combination made her throat thick.

When she found a poster for the upcoming picnic and AGM in the middle of December, the temptation was too strong. It was downright weird to get such a zing of excitement about the annual general meeting of a little association she wasn't part of. She imagined driving out to the property at the edge of the city and turning up with an awkward smile and just the prospect was mortifying.

But none of that stopped her.

On the Saturday morning of the AGM, she mumbled an excuse about going shopping and jumped into her mum's car before anyone could question her. Crossing the city took time and patience and by the time she arrived at the iron gates, the leafy property surrounded by bushland was already full of people.

A banner reading 'Benvignus Fogolâr Furlan Brisbane' hung limply on the fence in the still sunshine and a grin spread on Jules's face as she parked the car and crossed the street.

She wouldn't find Alex here, but maybe she could keep some of her new-found roots and it wouldn't hurt so much to be separated. As the thrum of an accordion reached her ears, the sound expanded in her chest like the bellows.

Wow, the feelings hadn't faded in the weeks since she'd left Italy. If anything, she was realising just how much Alex had meant to her – how many emotions she'd refused to acknowledge.

Taking a deep breath, she snapped a photo and sent it to Berengario along with a smiley-face emoji. He'd sent her a picture of Arco eyeing Maddalena's goat earlier that morning – yesterday in Italian time – which had only made her picture Alex out at Due Pini.

It was the middle of the night in Italy, but a reply from Berengario dropped in almost immediately.

> I'm glad you're there! Mandi dal Friûl – say hello to Alice from me.

Alice? Was this another weird Friulian situation where everyone knew everyone – even the ones who'd emigrated years ago? With a perplexed frown, Jules stowed her phone and crossed through the gate to join the picnic.

Although there were no chickens and no goats eating the tablecloths, and none of the old men were wielding chainsaws, the trepidation in her steps reminded her of walking up the drive to the farmhouse at Due Pini. She would never have guessed that she was meeting dear friends that first day and her skin prickled at the thought that she was back at the beginning.

A woman in a smart patterned dress carrying a bowl of radicchio salad slowed her steps to study Jules.

'Uh, mandi,' Jules mumbled, hitching her bag higher up her shoulder.

A smile broke out on the woman's face as though the Friulian greeting were a magic word. Jules hated to think what would have happened if she'd said 'Ciao' instead.

'Mandi,' the woman said warmly, juggling her salad to hold a hand out. 'Are you... joining the picnic?'

'Is that okay? I'm not a member. But I just got back from a few years in Italy. I was in Cividale...' That made it sound as though she'd spent longer in Cividale, but she had no desire to change the misconception. 'And I have Italian heritage. My surname is

Volpe. I'm Julia – Jules. Spelled the English way. And I'm supposed to pass on greetings to Alice.'

'Ahh, Alice,' the woman said, correcting Jules's pronunciation to the Italian *A-li-chey*. 'Come with me.' Jules followed her to the tables set up under a large open patio and beckoned to an energetic woman in her forties.

After Jules repeated her spiel, the other woman drew back and gave her a calculating smile. 'A Furlan Volpe?'

Jules snapped her gaze up in surprise. 'Unofficially.'

'It's good you're here,' she said. When she clapped her hands for attention and the buzz of conversation quietened, alarm sizzled down Jules's spine.

Alice grasped her arm gently and began in the three languages of the association. 'Allora, ducj cuancj! Tutti quanti! Everyone!'

She paused for long enough for Jules to hear the blood rushing in her ears. A hundred smiling faces stared up at her from their folding-chairs and plates of sausages and polenta.

'This is Jules. She's just arrived back from Friuli.' What she said next nearly made Jules's knees give out. 'She's *Alex's* girlfriend!'

37

All the rational thoughts in the world couldn't stop Jules from frantically combing the guests for a familiar head of wavy brown hair. Her gaze swerved to the accordion-player, her heart in her throat, but he was a reedy older man with a shiny, black Hohner accordion, not Alex's Victoria or the old Fantini he'd restored.

Of course he wasn't there. He was looking after Arco – and hopefully himself. Getting in touch with the Fogolâr Furlan was just a way for Jules to stay connected, which she'd been looking forward to anyway before she'd briefly got it into her head that he might be there.

'Did Berengario put you up to this?' Jules asked Alice as the woman steered her to a table. Conversation had resumed, but Jules could still feel curious looks and twinkling eyes on her.

'Berengario? Yes, he sent us an email saying we should expect you.'

Jules glanced at the sky with a huff. 'Still interfering from thousands of miles away.' She only wondered how he'd known she would come today, or perhaps he'd just hoped – but for what?

That she'd find her new Friulian family? 'What you said about Alex... Does everyone know him?'

'Not yet,' was all she said. 'Here, have a sausage.'

'I've been dying for frico, actually. And please tell me you have gubana.'

'Elisabetta over there makes the best frico. She sells it at the markets. And yes, there will be gubana. Here, come and sit with Antonella. She's from Udine.'

Jules was pleasantly overwhelmed as the late morning wore into the afternoon with music from the indefatigable accordion-player and conversations in a wild mix of languages. The grey-haired members were keen for every detail she could pass on from the patrie, the old country, and her voice gave out after a couple of hours, leading Alice to place a schnapps glass of something strong and peach-flavoured into her hand that she knew she had to be careful with since she was driving.

At some point, the official business of the AGM commenced and in the heat, with a full stomach, Jules pleasantly zoned out. She was glad at least that no one had thought it even slightly strange that this Calabrian Volpe who couldn't speak Italian well wanted to join in with their festivities – and that she'd had so much to tell them about the forest and gnot dai muarts and the olive harvest. She hadn't told her family this much about Luca and the B & B and she'd spent years working for that.

If only Cividale really were her home, she could have stayed and given Alex more time. Maybe one day he would have—

'Mandi, sorry I'm late. There was a delay.'

Jules froze at the sound of a deep voice, speaking between heavy breaths. If she was dreaming, she wanted to stay asleep for long enough to catch a glimpse. He was saying something in Furlan now, in a low voice, so she had no hope of understanding anyway.

She sensed a ripple of interest through the people sitting at her table and warily opened her eyes to find them watching her. Her hair stood on end as she wondered whether Berengario had planned some kind of stunt with a video call. Would she turn and find a cardboard cut-out of the person she loved and an apology for letting her go?

That would be nice. She had to stop her heart from jumping erratically in her chest as though he were actually standing behind her in real life.

She heard a muffled thump and a sigh and then the president of the association cleared his throat and continued. 'Just a brief interruption to our proceedings to welcome our newest member, who has just arrived from Friûl – by which I truly mean *just arrived*.' He chuckled and goosebumps raced over Jules's skin at the sound. 'I told you all about him earlier. He was a member of the coro alpino and brings his accordion and I'm looking forward to the musical enrichment of our meetings. He's moved to Australia for the best reason imaginable – for love. Welcome to Brisbane, Alessandro Mattelig!'

Jules still sat unmoving, although her vision swam in the heavy Queensland sunshine. After weeks of dampening every hope, of telling herself she was hanging on to nothing and trying to be rational, the big idiot had been making the most foolish decision of all.

Turning slowly, her breath shallow and fitful, she saw him, really standing there, in jeans and short sleeves, his hair mussed and his shirt rumpled and an enormous backpack at his feet, along with the accordion case she recognised from the day they'd met.

His eyes were trained on her, soft and bright and wary with hope – for the future, *their* future. He had some explaining to do, but she was looking forward to hearing him out. Finally she was truly at home.

* * *

She was more tanned than the last time he'd seen her. Her messy ponytail was the same, but he'd never seen her in shorts and a T-shirt before. He was impatient to see Jules in every type of weather, annoyed that he'd missed the past month, excited for her to show him where she'd grown up – just as soon as she accepted that he'd solved their problem in this unexpected way, the only way he'd been satisfied would be fair to her.

Her disbelief lingered longer than he'd anticipated. He was taking a big risk on the basis of two words she'd spoken while half asleep.

As she rose out of her seat, he was torn between admiring her long limbs in summer clothes and succumbing to the worry that this wouldn't work. It would feel sudden to her, his transformation from stubborn, grieving widower to Friulian émigré in Australia.

'Jules,' he murmured as she stumbled in his direction.

Coming to a stop in front of him, she lifted her chin and looked him square in the face and he couldn't believe he'd ever doubted how much she meant to him. Then she gave him a shove with both hands, hard enough to make him stagger.

'All this time I've been trying to get over you!'

'I hope your efforts were as unsuccessful as me trying not to fall in love with you in the first place.'

'What about everything you've left behind? You can't just *move* here!'

Taking a risk, he grazed his thumb along her forearm and

gripped it lightly. 'It turns out Australia needs draughtsmen. I've got an invitation to apply for a working visa and I can stay temporarily for now. Berengario is looking after Attila and Arco, but we can pick up both of them in a few months. I think they're kind of attached to each other – although Attila pretends they aren't.'

Her lips wobbled. 'You don't know anything about Australia.'

'I know *you're* here.'

'But Laura isn't.'

The caution in her tone both broke his heart and melted it. 'Yes, she is,' he contradicted her gently. 'I carry her around with me, it seems. She doesn't have to haunt our old home town – and neither do I. It turns out I'm not dead, not even a little bit.' The frantic beat of his heart was proof of that.

She gripped his shirt in her fist, staring at it. 'Aren't you afraid? What if something happens to one of us?' Her brow twisted and every little thing she did reminded him of why he loved her.

Taking her face in his hands, he said softly, 'I'm sorry I held back from you for so long – and I'm so sorry I convinced you I was done with love after Laura.' He paused, holding her gaze until the familiar sparks zipped along his skin. 'I'm not done with love. The way I feel about you is proof, no matter how much I pretended it wasn't happening. Yes, I'm afraid. But I want to be with you long enough that something *does* happen to one of us.'

Her eyes crashed shut and her forehead fell to his shoulder and he marvelled at how stupid he'd been to deny that this was his future – their future – to think he could stop himself falling in love with her.

'I want *life* with you,' he said softly. 'And if that means death parts us, then… that's just the way things are.'

'God, damn it, Alex. You keep breaking my heart,' she said with a choke.

'I don't mean to— I don't *want* to.'

'Aw, enough with the psychoanalysis and get onto the good bit! Some of us got up in the middle of the night for this!'

Alex snapped his head up in surprise. They found Alice holding out a phone.

'Berengario?'

Jules snorted a laugh. 'It seems everyone knows everyone – even outside of Friuli.'

The little image on the screen showed Berengario squinting back at them from Alex's kitchen, Elena and Maddalena in the background and a silhouette of Attila on the windowsill. A bark sounded, an enthusiastic exclamation mark from Arco at hearing the voices of his pack.

'I can't get away from my nosy neighbours, even when I come to Australia,' he said wryly.

'A good thing too!' Berengario called back. 'If it had been up to you, you'd be moping around here with only a cat for company, being grumpy to your guests!'

'Excuse me, I'm the one who decided not to wait for the visa and come immediately.'

'You're just impatient,' Berengario quipped. 'What do you know about romance? You can't even tell a woman you love her! Young people these days think they don't need any advice from their elders, when—'

Jules rolled her eyes and then her hands came up to Alex's cheeks, turning him firmly to face her. She hopped up on her toes and kissed him. Sharp and hot, the relief in the kiss – the comfort, the intimacy – flooded him. He held her tight and the world around him faded, his focus narrowed to this woman in his arms, this love. He was dimly aware of cheering and applause from the AGM of the Fogolâr Furlan, but he drew out the kiss a little longer.

When they reluctantly broke apart, hesitating for a few

mingled breaths to decide if they could get away with doing that again – at least that was how he interpreted the twinkle in her eyes – the words flowed out of their own accord: 'I love you, Jules.' Another cheer, drowning out Berengario's dry comment over the video call. 'Ti voglio bene,' Alex repeated in Italian with a growing smile. 'Ti vuei ben,' he continued, to more applause from the strangers watching their reunion. 'That's Furlan,' he explained.

'I got it,' she said with her own wobbly smile. 'What was it? Ti vuei ben?' she repeated slowly.

He nodded, watching her, waiting, enjoying the suspense because he could already see the truth in her damp eyes.

Then she poked him. 'Ti vuei ben, Alessandro Mattelig. History and all.' The poke became a shove. 'I love you – way more than is sensible. Wherever we are, I don't want to be without you ever again.'

As the first tear fell with a hiccough, he gathered her up and soaked up her words. 'You won't be without me. I'm here. If you'll let me be where you are, I'll stay.'

'I'll look after you – I promise,' she said earnestly, drawing back to look at him. 'When we're in Australia, with my family, when we have tough decisions – everything. You won't be alone.'

'I know,' was all he needed to say in reply. 'Even before we were together, you didn't leave me alone.'

Her nose scrunched up and he grinned in anticipation of whatever she was going to say with that adorable expression. 'If you get your visa rejected, we could get married.'

'That's always an option,' he said with a straight face.

'I kind of like the idea of rushing a wedding for immigration purposes.' She glanced at him warily. 'Of course if you're not ready I shouldn't assume... Even if you never want to get married again, it's okay.'

With a chuckle, he pressed a kiss to her forehead. 'Maybe we should hope my visa gets rejected then.' But if the visa really took five months to process, he might jump the gun, the way the future was suddenly stretching out so brightly before him.

'I do have one condition,' she said, her cheeky expression creeping back over her features. He lifted his eyebrows to prompt her. 'Can you get a chestnut tattoo? In honour of my eyes?' She snorted a laugh.

He flashed her a mysterious smile and pulled away. 'That was the first order of business when I decided I was coming after you.' With exaggerated flourish, he lifted the sleeve of his T-shirt to show her Stefano's artwork: a frilly chestnut leaf with two shaded nuts nestled in their spiky case, inked alongside the two bay leaves, as though the picture had always been meant to look that way. 'I had to get it done early so it could heal for a few weeks.'

'Oh, my God! I was kind of joking!'

'Kind of? Or actually joking?' He cocked his head. 'I know it's a bit much. I'm happy with it anyway.'

'It's gorgeous – but then you know you're gorgeous. I just hope it didn't hurt too much.'

'It was my idea!' Berengario shouted through the speakers of the phone.

'Oh, I had the idea long before you did!' Alex called back, not looking away from the gleam in Jules's eyes.

'We can think about going back to Italy. I wouldn't want you to live without chestnuts.'

'It doesn't matter where we are,' he reassured her. 'I'm ready to be here. Home will always be home and Furlans have a history of emigrating,' he said with a quick glance at the beaming faces of the members of the association. 'Wherever we are, we'll be there for love.'

EPILOGUE

'Berengario! You brought Attila to the airport?' Alex called incredulously when they emerged through the doors into the arrivals lounge.

'I couldn't leave him at home – not at a time like this!' Berengario replied, juggling Arco's lead and a plastic travel crate containing a very unimpressed Persian.

Abandoning her suitcase, Jules crouched to wrap her arms around her dog, who wriggled and alternated excited hops on his back legs and swipes of his tongue over whatever skin he could reach. 'Hey, boy. We missed you so much.'

'I'm not even sure Attila cares,' Alex said with a wry smile as he peered into the crate. The cat merely flicked his fluffy tail.

'Arco cares enough for both of them,' Jules said.

'I suppose that's why we're a family,' Alex quipped, sending another shiver of anticipation through Jules. They weren't quite officially a family yet, but in a week, they would be – no matter what country they lived in.

'All right, all right. If you're going to start the honeymoon early, you'll have to put up with a lot more gloating from your wise elders who knew you were perfect for each other the moment we saw you together,' Berengario grumbled.

Jules beamed up at her future husband. 'Berengario's pretty quick on the uptake. Only a few hours after I knew.'

But it had been Alex who'd rushed into the next step. His work visa had been approved, but the idea had apparently long taken root in his mind and only four months after they met, Jules had found a small blue topaz ring on her left hand – chosen together for the colour of the Natisone river.

Maybe it was reckless – it was definitely very fast – but after her experience with Luca, she at least felt she'd learned to discern real love from an imitation and she couldn't doubt a commitment that had grown and thrived in the most meagre circumstances last autumn.

In the car on the way back from the small airport near Trieste where their connecting flight had arrived, Berengario piled on the work immediately. 'We're thinning the leaves on the vines and you know we always need to prune those wild olive trees. They grow faster than your kids will,' he said with a wink.

'Berengario,' Alex grumbled. They'd talked about the possibility of kids – coming to no conclusion other than that they weren't ready, but one day, maybe.

When they arrived back at Alex's building, Jules took a second to inhale the scent of spring in the air and appreciate the neon green of the leaves on the persimmon tree.

'Thank you, Laura,' she whispered to herself. She'd long since accepted that there was no right or wrong way to honour Alex's first love – only authentically. Arriving at the building Laura had inherited and passed on to Alex, Jules wondered whether one day they'd reopen the B & B – perhaps when she'd finished the hospitality management diploma she was thoroughly enjoying.

Since Alex had got back into mountain biking in the hinterland around Brisbane, Jules kept wondering whether they might be able to make a living offering tours and accommodation around Cividale. She would start small, offering the rooms to budget travellers until they'd saved enough to renovate a few of them.

But first, they had more important things to attend to.

On a sunny May afternoon, in Saint Martin's church by the Ponte del Diavolo – both in honour of the day they met on the square outside and of Jules's birthday, the day after the festa di San Martino – they pledged their futures to each other, in sickness and in health, for as long as they would live.

ACKNOWLEDGEMENTS

This was one of those times where I have a mountain of research for things that never made it into the book. In my short time in Cividale, so many places and people contributed tiny pieces of the story, most of them without even realising it.

From Francesca at my B & B, to the team at Olio Ducale and Terre Petrussa, to the ladies at the tourist office and the Monastero di Santa Maria in Valle, everyone helped to create the snapshot of the city that I fictionalised. If you travel to Cividale one day, you might find that some of the little places in the book really do exist, although you won't find the characters there!

For the original inspiration for the story, thanks go to my sister for discovering Cividale and telling me I needed to go. The other building block of the story came from my own time volunteering as part of WWOOF (Willing Workers On Organic Farms) – a time where I met many wonderful people I have never forgotten.

As a very quick note on the Fogolâr Furlan in Brisbane, I purposefully used their previous premises in this book as a tribute, even though the old place is now being redeveloped. Time unfortunately passes and Brisbane is not as I remember it.

We've now reached book nine together and it's been a joy as always working with my editor Sarah and the team at Boldwood. Special thanks also to Tatiana, for falling in love with Alex before anyone else got to meet him. Also to my agent Saskia for adding her input even after I messed up my dates and in general, holding up the difficult bits of my career while I focus on my characters! I'm immensely thankful for the team we're growing.

As always, big, grateful hugs to my family, my husband in particular for all his cheerleading for me (and always doing the washing).

A big thank you this time also to my regular readers. Hearing from you guys is the stuff of dreams and I hope you've loved Jules and Alex's story as much as I loved writing it.

ABOUT THE AUTHOR

Leonie Mack is a bestselling romantic novelist. Having lived in London for many years her home is now in Germany with her husband and three children. Leonie loves train travel, medieval towns, hiking and happy endings!

Sign up to Leonie Mack's mailing list here for an exclusive bonus chapter to A Wedding in the Sun!

Visit Leonie's website: 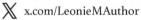https://leoniemack.com/

Follow Leonie on social media:

ALSO BY LEONIE MACK

LOVE NOTES

LOVE IN EVERY CHAPTER

WHERE ALL YOUR ROMANCE
DREAMS COME TRUE!

THE HOME OF BESTSELLING
ROMANCE AND WOMEN'S
FICTION

 WARNING:
MAY CONTAIN SPICE

SIGN UP TO OUR
NEWSLETTER

https://bit.ly/Lovenotesnews

Boldwood

Boldwood Books is an award-winning fiction publishing company seeking out the best stories from around the world.

Find out more at www.boldwoodbooks.com

Join our reader community for brilliant books, competitions and offers!

Follow us
@BoldwoodBooks
@TheBoldBookClub

Sign up to our weekly deals newsletter

https://bit.ly/BoldwoodBNewsletter

Printed in Great Britain
by Amazon